THE
PANACEA
PROJECT

A Novel

CATHERINE
DEVORE JOHNSON

GREENLEAF
BOOK GROUP PRESS

Published by Greenleaf Book Group Press
Austin, Texas
www.gbgpress.com

Distributed by Greenleaf Book Group

For ordering information or special discounts for bulk purchases, please contact Greenleaf Book Group at PO Box 91869, Austin, TX 78709, 512.891.6100.

Design and composition by Greenleaf Book Group
Cover design by Greenleaf Book Group
Cover Images from rawpixel.com

Publisher's Cataloging-in-Publication data is available.

Print ISBN: 979-8-88645-015-6

eBook ISBN: 979-8-88645-016-3

To offset the number of trees consumed in the printing of our books, Greenleaf donates a portion of the proceeds from each printing to the Arbor Day Foundation. Greenleaf Book Group has replaced over 50,000 trees since 2007.

Printed in the United States of America on acid-free paper

23 24 25 26 27 28   10 9 8 7 6 5 4 3 2 1

First Edition

To Matthew, for his love and unwavering support

ONE

CALLA FLIPPED THROUGH THE BOOK she was supposed to be putting away. She had always been fascinated by what other people checked out of the library. Her co-workers dreaded shelving duty, but she loved the time alone—organizing, straightening, reading to her heart's content. No one bothered her when she was in the stacks.

Calla blinked a few times as the words on the page slipped out of focus. The blurriness was getting more frequent. She might need to go back to the doctor. God, she was sick of doctors. She pushed the thought from her mind and returned to her book—an introductory text on astrophysics. She was just getting into an early chapter on the birth of stars when she was interrupted by a rustling sound on the other side of the bookcase.

"Come here." The voice was quiet, full of need.

A giggle. "Someone will see us!"

"No, they won't. No one's here."

Calla peeked through thin slices of empty space at a man and a woman standing in the next row. She watched as their bodies—hands, hips, mouths—slowly merged.

A sigh. A soft moan.

Calla spun away, ashamed of herself for spying. She set her book down on the shelving cart and started to leave, but she couldn't help stealing one last glance at the intimacy unfolding only three feet away. What was it like to be that close to another person without having them recoil from your touch?

Distracted, Calla didn't hear the other two men approaching.

"Check it out," one hissed, elbowing his companion. "Get a room, you two!"

The couple broke apart, and before Calla could react, the men walked past her row.

"Enjoying the show?" one of them sneered.

Calla whipped her head around and saw them laughing at her.

She stumbled backward to rush away, but her head suddenly exploded with pain.

Totally disoriented, Calla lurched to the side and slammed into the heavy shelving cart. The impact sent her slender frame crashing backward. Her head hit the floor with a sickening thud, and the world momentarily went black.

As light and sound began filtering back into Calla's consciousness, she sensed movement around her and heard murmurings, but everything was jumbled. Her head throbbed, and a strange ringing filled her ears. She tried to shift to a more comfortable position, but nothing happened. She opened her mouth to call for help, but her tongue was thick and heavy. The only sound she could produce was a harsh grunt. With a thrill of horror, Calla realized she was paralyzed.

Help me! She screamed silently, hoping her eyes were capable of conveying her terror. Someone leaned close to her face. It was one of the men who had laughed at her. His voice cut through the ringing.

"Dude!" he shot a look over his shoulder. "What should we do?"

His breath reeked of pizza and cigarettes, and he seemed more worried about getting in trouble than helping Calla.

"I don't know," the second man said. "Why's she shaking like that?"

Shaking? The only thing Calla felt was a sudden warmth spreading across her thighs.

"What's that smell?" The man leaning over her wrinkled his nose. "Fuck. I think she's pissing herself!"

What the hell is happening to me?

A strange numbness crept over her, dulling her panic, her fear, even her embarrassment. The men's voices receded into the background. Calla felt as though her body was being wrapped in a warm blanket. She was being lifted up like an infant into arms that offered nothing but comfort and rest. She was just relaxing into the feeling when her head erupted in pain again, and she was sucked out of her temporary cocoon, back into the present moment. All around her, sounds and colors and sensations snapped to full power. Vomit burned in her throat.

"What's wrong with her?"

"She's having a seizure." A new person leaned into Calla's field of vision long enough for her to recognize the man she had been watching through the stacks.

"Turn her head to the side," a woman's voice ordered.

"Are you sure you should touch her?" The guy with pizza breath was talking again. "Her skin—"

"Her skin has nothing to do with this," the woman cut him off. "Back up. We're med students. If you want to help, call 9-1-1."

TWO

CALLA WOKE TO THE SOUND of strangers talking about her.

"I've never seen such an extensive case."

"Me neither."

"I saw one on my derm rotation, but it was nothing like this."

"Can you imagine living like that?"

Calla's eyes popped open indignantly. She blinked as a harsh overhead light assaulted her retinas. It took her a moment to recognize that she was lying on a stretcher in a cramped hospital room. As her vision cleared, she looked around and saw three people in white coats huddled just outside the doorway. She glared in their direction, but something in the hallway had drawn their attention away, and they didn't see her.

Two new voices entered the mix. When Calla heard the first one, she relaxed a bit, assured that her defense was in good hands.

"Excuse me." A woman's voice, full of cold rebuke. "I wasn't aware that they'd stopped teaching manners in med school."

Her statement was met with a resounding silence.

"What's going on here?" A man's voice, harried, with a hint of exhaustion. "Why are all of you blocking this doorway?"

The woman's voice again. "I just overheard these young people saying some rather negative things about this patient's appearance." A pause. Calla took satisfaction in imagining the look of disdain being delivered to the young people in question. The woman continued. "Calla encounters enough prejudice out in the world. Surely it's not asking too much to expect a little more sensitivity in a professional medical setting."

"But the patient is still unconscious." A panicked plea from one of the offending doctors. "We didn't think she could hear—"

"That's enough," the man interrupted. "You didn't think. That's obvious. The three of you are dismissed from this patient's care. Check in with Dr. Thomas for a different assignment. We'll discuss this further at the end of your shift."

"Dr. Mott, we're really sorry."

"I'd be concerned if you weren't. Now go."

The trio of doctors scurried away, giving Calla her first clear view of the two people left standing there. It was a woman in her early fifties, effortlessly stylish in jeans, a white button-down shirt, and a navy blazer. She was standing with a lanky, balding man who looked like a plant that hadn't seen the sun in a while.

The man shook his head apologetically. "I'll address this incident with them later." He glanced at the chart in his hand. "But, it's probably better that we have some privacy to discuss Calla's condition." He held out his hand. "I'm Jordan Mott."

"Rae Wiley."

They shook hands.

"You're Calla's mother?"

Rae paused. "No, but I'm the closest thing she's got to one."

"What exactly is your relationship to her?"

"I am—I was her social worker."

"Was?"

"Until she aged out of the system. Now I keep an eye on her. Kind of like an aunt, if you want to put a label on it."

"She doesn't have any parents? No family at all?"

Rae shook her head. "Her mother died of an overdose when she was four. We were never able to track down her father. There's no one else. I'm probably one of the only contacts in her phone. Someone from this hospital called me from it."

"Well, if you're not family or a legal guardian, I can't talk to you until I get Calla's permission."

At this, Calla finally spoke up. "You can talk to her," she croaked.

Both Rae and Dr. Mott jumped at the sound of her voice.

"Calla!" Rae rushed into the room and placed a gentle hand on Calla's cheek. "How are you feeling, honey?"

"Like I got hit by a bus." Calla winced. It was an enormous relief to discover that she could talk again, but the effort had triggered a pounding headache.

"Calla, I'm Dr. Mott." The doctor walked around to the other side of the bed. "Do you remember how you hit your head?"

"I—I think I ran into something and fell." Calla tried to piece together the memories. The couple kissing. The two oafs in the stacks making fun of her. The terrifying realization she was paralyzed.

"You banged it pretty hard. You may have a concussion."

"Is that why I couldn't move or talk? And why I—" Calla's voice dropped to a whisper. "Why I wet myself?"

Dr. Mott shook his head. "I don't think so. But we need to run a few more tests to confirm exactly what's going on."

"You've already run some?" Rae asked.

"We have," Dr. Mott said gently. "Calla, I must emphasize that we need more information before coming to any conclusions, but the CT scan we ran when you were admitted to the ER revealed a significant growth in your brain."

"A growth?" Calla asked. "Are you saying that I have a—a brain tumor?"

"Yes."

For a moment, Calla's world stopped. No sound, no movement. Just that one terrifying word—tumor—expanding to fill her entire consciousness. She was dimly aware of Rae pressing her hands to her mouth in shock and Dr. Mott inclining his head in a consoling manner. But she felt separated from them, as though an invisible barrier had slammed down around her, sealing her in, claustrophobic. She struggled to breathe.

When she snapped back to attention, Dr. Mott was describing the CT scan results.

Calla cut him off. "Is it cancer?"

Dr. Mott shook his head. "I know this isn't easy to hear, but we just don't have enough information to answer that question yet. What I can tell you is that based on the tumor's location, it probably caused your seizure and may have contributed to your fall." He pulled a rolling stool over to her bedside and sat down. "Have you experienced any changes in your health lately?"

"Changes in my health?" she asked numbly. She thought about the string of random illnesses that had sidelined her over the last year. But none of those had had anything to do with her head. At least, not until recently.

"I'm wondering about headaches, dizziness, unexplained nausea, problems with balance or walking, changes in your vision or speech."

"Well, yeah actually. I've had headaches and blurry vision for a few months now. Nausea, too. But when I went to the doctor, she said she couldn't find anything wrong. That it was all in my head."

"When did you see this doctor?"

"Last week."

"Oh."

"Guess she was right." Calla struggled to keep the bitterness out of her voice as another surge of fear washed over her. "The problem really *is* in my head."

Dr. Mott cleared his throat. "Well, uh, these things can be difficult to diagnose at the early stages. The symptoms are often very vague. The important thing is that we've caught it now and can start treatment."

"What kind of treatment?"

"It's hard to say until we know for sure what we're dealing with." Dr. Mott spun around on his stool to face a nearby computer terminal, his tone suddenly more businesslike. "Dr. Pearce is the neurologist on call today," he said as he tapped on the keyboard. "He's great. I've already called him in for a consult here in the ER. He'll order more tests and start putting together a team for your care." He turned back around and locked eyes with Calla. "I'm not going to sugarcoat this. You'll probably need to make some important decisions about treatment in the very near future. In the meantime, I'm admitting you to the hospital at least overnight to make sure we've got you stabilized."

He placed a hand on Calla's shoulder. "I know this is a lot to take in all at once. Take your time, and don't lose hope. We see people with brain tumors like yours every day who respond remarkably well to treatment."

Calla noted that he didn't say anything about *curing* people with brain tumors like hers.

Dr. Mott stood up and looked from Calla to Rae. "Do either of you have any questions before I go?"

Rae shook her head.

Calla looked up at him. "Am I going to die?"

Dr. Mott waited a second too long before answering. "Not today."

THREE

EIGHT DAYS LATER, Calla opened the door to her apartment and found Rae standing inches from the threshold, bearing a paper bag and a huge to-go cup filled with something green.

"I've been doing research," Rae announced as she marched inside. "You need to start eating healthier. You can't live on pumpkin bread alone." She set her purse and the paper bag down on the counter that separated the tiny kitchenette from the rest of Calla's efficiency.

"But I like pumpkin bread."

"And yours is the best I've ever had, but still." Rae pressed the cup into Calla's hands. "Drink this."

Calla took a tentative sip. "What is it?"

"Something good for you. It has kale in it."

Calla made a face. "What else did you bring?" she asked, trying to divert Rae's attention while she hid the drink behind a stack of cookbooks.

Rae started unpacking the paper bag. "A quart of bone broth, some watermelon, and a kale salad."

"Lots of kale," Calla observed drily.

"Did you know that watermelon has anti-inflammatory properties?" Rae asked, ignoring the comment.

"I did not."

"Anti-inflammatory foods are really important to fighting cancer. I'm reading this book . . ."

Calla zoned out as Rae chattered on. She wandered into the kitchen, her gaze settling on her reflection in the microwave door—on the blotches of bright white skin around her eyes and mouth. She stretched out her arms and examined the familiar streaks and patches of un-pigmented skin that covered her from head to toe. And made her feel so set apart from the rest of the world.

Calla's vitiligo had presented early. There were no pictures of her as an infant, so she didn't know if she'd been born with the condition, but she was painfully aware that the white patches had begun their progressive march across her body at a young age. She had never known a time when she didn't look different from other people.

Calla had never met her father, and memories of her mother were dominated by visions of hiding in the shadowy corners of cheap motel rooms, avoiding the gaze of strung-out addicts who taunted her and threw things at her for sport. Calla remembered no love, no tender moments. She'd been only a burden and embarrassment to a junkie mother who lived (and eventually died) for her next fix.

After her mother's fatal overdose, Calla was placed into the Texas foster care system. Too old to be of interest to adoptive parents (no one wanted a four-year-old with a progressive skin condition), she spent her childhood and adolescence being shuffled between individual foster family homes, group homes, and residential facilities. Every day was a struggle. The years of neglect she had experienced at her mother's hands had left her with serious developmental delays. She didn't speak until she was six years old and suffered from severe anxiety that rendered her practically mute in new social situations. Woefully uninformed about vitiligo, people avoided touching her—afraid they might "catch" what she had. Over and over again, no matter the real reason, Calla felt rejected by foster parents, foster siblings—even social workers.

Rae was the only bright spot in Calla's life during those endless years.

Rae Wiley had been Calla's fourth social worker and the first person to ever show her affection. They met the day after Calla's seventh birthday. Calla was sitting on a plastic chair in the dingy hallway of the Child Protective Services building in downtown Houston, swinging her little legs back and forth, examining a new white spot that had recently appeared above her left knee. Another social worker was leaving her (nothing new to Calla), and she was waiting for her new lady, Miss Rae. The name struck her as unusual and called to mind a picture of a sun with orange and yellow rays emanating from a smiling face, something she'd seen once in a book.

"Calla?"

Calla studied the woman standing in front of her. "You don't look like the sun."

The woman laughed. Then she knelt in front of Calla. This was unexpected. All of the grownups she knew preferred to look down on her when speaking, not straight into her eyes.

"My name is Rae." She held out her hand. "It's nice to meet you."

Overcome by shyness, Calla dropped her eyes to her lap and did not respond.

"I've heard a lot about you, Calla." Rae gently touched Calla's knee. The one with the new white mark. This made Calla look up. Hardly anyone touched her. Ever. She examined Rae for any sign of disgust or discomfort but found none.

"From what I've heard, you're a very brave girl. A tough girl. I'm a tough girl, too. Do you think we can be friends?"

Calla shrugged. "I guess."

"I'd like that. Us tough girls need to stick together."

Rae held out her hand again. This time, Calla took it. Rae gave her a little squeeze.

"You know what, Calla?" she asked.

Calla shook her head.

Rae smiled. "I think today is my lucky day. You're a very special person. I can tell."

Calla was never convinced about the special part. And she never knew that the only thing stopping Rae from adopting Calla herself in those early years were the ethical rules of the agency where she worked. But Calla did know—and never doubted—that Rae was a woman who kept her word. She stuck by Calla and made sure she got what she needed—speech therapy, decent healthcare, an education, and love (tough and otherwise, in equal measures).

Rae was a mother to Calla in every way possible.

Now, fifteen years later, Rae was still by Calla's side, bringing her kale smoothies and watermelon and unconditional support.

"How are you feeling today?" Rae asked, concern in her voice.

"I'm okay," Calla said as she placed the containers of food in the refrigerator. "Not having as many headaches." In fact, she hadn't had a headache at all in the past two days. And the rest of her symptoms—the blurry vision, the dizziness, the nausea—were subsiding. She could almost pretend there wasn't something deadly growing in her brain.

"Well, that seems like a good thing, doesn't it?" Rae said in an overly bright voice. "Your body is gearing up to fight this thing!"

"Or it's throwing in the towel and giving me a break from feeling like crap before I kick the bucket."

"Don't talk like that!" Rae scolded.

"Why not?" Calla crossed the room and threw herself down on the futon that doubled as her bed. "You heard what the oncologist said the other day. I've probably got a glioblastoma. I looked it up. It's the worst kind of brain tumor. Even with surgery and chemo, it's gonna come back eventually. All I can do is delay the inevitable. So, why bother?"

"You can't give up," Rae said fiercely as she sat down next to Calla. "You've been a fighter your entire life. And that's not everything the doctor said. The tumor is smaller than they originally thought and in an operable place. The surgery could be effective."

"For a while," Calla reminded her. "He said the surgery could be effective for a while."

"Well, a while is better than nothing."

Calla gave a snort.

"I'm not letting you give up." Rae's mouth was a grim line. "You're meant for something special, Calla. I know it."

Calla sighed. "You've been saying that since the day we met. It's not going to come true."

"Then do it for me," Rae said. "Do it because I've spent the last fifteen years trying to keep you alive." Her voice broke a little. "Trying to keep you safe."

Calla slipped her arm around Rae's shoulders.

"Please, Calla," Rae whispered. "Have the surgery."

Calla gave Rae a squeeze. "You know they're gonna shave my head."

"I'll knit you a hat."

"You don't know how to knit."

Rae kissed her cheek. "You're going to beat this. I know it."

Calla didn't say anything. She was much less optimistic about her prognosis, but if having the surgery gave Rae some hope, however futile, she figured it couldn't hurt.

At this point, hope—even borrowed hope—was pretty much the only thing she had left.

FOUR

ON THE MORNING OF THE SURGERY, Calla was strangely calm for a person about to let someone open up her skull and rummage around inside. Rae was far less serene. She sat in a chair next to Calla's stretcher in the pre-op holding area, her foot tap-tapping as she flipped through a magazine.

It was 7:45 a.m. They had arrived at the hospital two hours earlier. After a series of stops at various administrative desks, Calla was presented with a plastic wristband, a locker key, and two surgical gowns. She changed out of her clothes and stowed her belongings, then followed a nurse to her assigned bay in the holding area. The nurse got Calla settled on the stretcher before hooking her up to a series of machines to track her vital signs and starting an IV.

"I'll be back in a little while," she said as she closed the curtain surrounding Calla's bed.

"A little while" turned into thirty minutes, but Calla didn't mind the delay. She was content lying still, trying to appreciate the feeling of being whole and relatively healthy. More than relatively healthy, actually. Calla felt better this morning than she had in a while.

Rae closed her magazine and looked at her watch. "What on earth is taking so long? Your surgery was scheduled for eight."

"Maybe they forgot about me." Calla lowered her voice. "Come on, Rae, unhook me from this stuff. Let's make a break for it."

Rae narrowed her eyes. "Fat chance, young lady." She jumped a little when the curtain next to her suddenly whipped open to reveal a cluster of doctors and nurses.

The youngest member of the group—a man with an athletic build and trendy black glasses—stepped forward with a smile.

"Good morning, Calla!"

"Good morning, Dr. Cho." Calla shook his outstretched hand and marveled at his soft skin and manicured nails. She supposed it made sense for a surgeon, a brain surgeon, no less, to take good care of his hands.

Dr. Cho turned to greet Rae. "It's nice to see you again, Ms. Wiley."

"You too, Doctor."

"So," Dr. Cho clapped his hands together, "how are you feeling?"

"Good. The headaches are completely gone, and I haven't had any more seizures. So, how about canceling this whole brain surgery thing?"

Dr. Cho laughed. "I'm afraid you still need the surgery. But I'm glad to hear the steroids and anticonvulsants are working."

"Doesn't hurt to ask."

Dr. Cho flipped open a metal chart and glanced at it before continuing. "Okay, as we discussed last week, I will be performing a craniotomy this morning. I'll make a small opening in your skull close to the area where the tumor is located."

"Sounds groovy."

"Calla!" Rae hissed. "Behave!"

Dr. Cho smiled. "Once I'm inside, I will attempt to remove as much of the tumor as possible. My primary goal is to avoid major damage to surrounding brain tissue, so I may not be able to get all of it. At a minimum, I'll take enough for a biopsy so we know exactly what we're dealing with. After that, we'll close you up and get you to recovery. You'll have to spend a day in intensive care so we can monitor you for complications, then at least a day or two in the neurosurgery ward. A lot will depend on how you react to the surgery. Once we have results from the biopsy, your oncologist will put together a plan for further treatment."

"I'll definitely need more treatment after the surgery?"

Dr. Cho hesitated before answering. "Honestly, Calla, every patient is different, so I can't say for sure, but there will likely be some form of additional treatment in your future."

"Like chemo or radiation."

Dr. Cho nodded.

"Or more surgery."

"Potentially. As I said, every patient is unique. We won't know exactly what you'll need until pathology gets a closer look at your tumor. Any other questions?"

"How much of my hair are you going to shave off?"

Dr. Cho looked relieved to be back on safe, surgical ground. "I only need to remove a quarter-inch strip where I make the incision. We do our best to take as little as possible."

With that, he turned around and beckoned to a blond woman in pink scrubs. "Debra, why don't you come meet Calla?"

The woman smiled. "Sure!"

Dr. Cho turned back to Calla. "This is Debra, your nurse anesthetist."

"Or bartender, if you prefer," Debra quipped.

Calla smiled.

Dr. Cho patted her leg. "You're in good hands, Calla. I promise." He glanced at Rae. "Will you be staying at the hospital during the surgery?"

"Yes, indeed."

"Then I'll talk to you afterward. Just make sure you give the folks at the registration desk your cell phone number so they can call you with updates."

"Already done."

Dr. Cho looked from Rae to Calla. "If there's nothing else, ladies, I'll take my leave."

For the first time that morning, Calla felt a surge of apprehension that she couldn't cover up with bravado. *This is really happening.* "Just, uh, thank you. In advance. For taking such good care of me." Her eyes filled with unexpected tears.

"You're welcome, Calla. I'll see you later today in the ICU, okay?"

"Okay," she sniffled.

Debra handed Calla a tissue. "How does a margarita sound right about now?"

Calla blew her nose and tried to compose herself. "Sounds great."

"Coming right up!"

As Debra turned to gather supplies from the table at the foot of Calla's bed, Rae grabbed Calla's hand.

"You're going to do great. I know it."

"Thanks for being here."

Rae gave her an incredulous look. "That tumor really has addled your brain. Where else would I be?"

Debra inserted a needle into Calla's IV tubing. "Alright, Calla. Bottoms up!" She exchanged a look with Rae. "This should help settle your nerves."

"How long does it—oh."

Both Rae and Debra laughed.

"Wha's so fun-nee?" She could hardly push the words past her suddenly sluggish tongue.

"Nothing at all, sweetheart." Rae gave Calla's hand another gentle squeeze. "You look very relaxed."

Calla felt her eyelids droop as she was drawn into the blackness of drug-induced sleep.

"Close your eyes, baby. I'll be here when you wake up."

FIVE

THIRST.

That was the first sensation Calla registered when she woke up . . . seconds, minutes, hours later? She swallowed, trying to ease the dry, scratchy feeling in her throat, and was immediately acquainted with a second sensation—pain. Why the hell did her throat hurt so much?

The pain caused her to cough, which set off an ache in her head and caught the attention of a passing nurse.

"Ma'am?" Calla rasped.

The nurse just stared, her eyes and mouth forming little circles.

Crap. How bad do I look?

Calla tried again. "Can I—" She stopped there. It simply hurt too much to talk. She tried to gesture toward her throat, which amounted to little more than a feeble flapping motion, her arms still heavy from the effects of anesthesia.

The nurse gave a little squeak and scampered away.

What the actual hell?

Suddenly worried, Calla summoned all of her energy and raised her hand—slowly, awkwardly—to feel her head. It was a relief to find that most of her hair was still there. It was matted and coated liberally in some sort of gel-like goo, but still there. Part of her head was covered by a bulky bandage. Otherwise, it seemed that Dr. Cho had kept his word and confined his shaving to the area just around the incision.

She wondered how much of the tumor he'd been able to remove.

The mousy nurse reappeared with a much larger colleague in tow. She pointed in Calla's direction, and the two women exchanged heated whispers for several seconds.

You know I can see you, right? She wanted to speak but settled for the go-ahead-and-stare-motherfuckers scowl she'd perfected after a lifetime of being on the receiving end of unabashed rubbernecking.

Finally, the larger nurse (Calla dubbed her Nurse Spratt) approached her bed.

"How are you feeling?"

"Thir-sty." Calla lifted her hand again and hoped she was pointing at her throat. "Hurts."

"That's normal. You had a breathing tube during the surgery."

"How . . . did . . . it . . . go?" Calla managed to ask.

Nurse Spratt didn't answer her. Instead, she pulled a penlight out of her pocket and shined it into Calla's eyes. "What is your name?"

"Cal-la. Did—"

"Do you know where you are?"

"Hospital. Where is—"

"What month is it?"

"August, but—"

Nurse Spratt clicked off the penlight. Without another word, she stepped over to a nearby computer terminal and began typing.

Dr. Cho had warned her that she might find it hard to concentrate and stay awake immediately after the surgery, but Calla didn't feel loopy or distracted or sleepy. As a matter of fact, other than a raging headache made worse by Spratt's piercing penlight, she felt increasingly alert.

Calla glanced over at the ID badge clipped to the pocket of Nurse Spratt's scrubs. Her real name was Sharon. Maybe a personal approach would have more success.

"Sharon?" It was getting easier to talk, despite the intense pain.

The nurse turned around and eyed Calla warily. "Yes?"

"What happened?"

"What do you mean?"

"In my surgery. Did something . . . go wrong?"

"I can't—" Sharon shook her head and started again. "You need to wait for the doctor."

Calla's stomach dropped. "Where is my friend?" she asked, switching subjects before Sharon could end the conversation (which she seemed quite eager to do).

"Your friend?"

"Rae. She was with me before." Rae would know what was going on and wouldn't hesitate to tell her.

Sharon frowned. "Dr. Kraft ordered no visitors until he's talked to you. I need to let him know you're awake."

"Dr. Kraft? Don't you mean Dr. Cho?"

"You need to wait for the doctor."

"But—"

"That's all I'm allowed to say."

Calla was stunned into silence. Something horrible had happened.

Sharon's voice softened. "I'm sorry. About all of this." She glanced furtively over her shoulder and then gave Calla's leg a quick, nervous pat before hustling away. "I'll bring some ice chips for your throat, okay?"

And that's when Calla realized: Sharon wasn't being bitchy. She was completely freaked out.

SIX

CALLA HAD BEEN AWAKE NOW for roughly two hours and seven minutes. There was a clock on the wall opposite her bed and not much else to do in the recovery room but mark the passage of time. She was also extremely agitated. Since their initial conversation, Sharon had continued to politely stonewall her, offering no answers, no visitors—and worst of all—no pain meds. Just ice chips. It all struck Calla as highly suspicious. She was clearly being treated differently than the other patients, whom she knew were allowed one visitor, sometimes two. (It turned out Sharon was a softie underneath the gruff exterior.) And none of them seemed to be lacking pharmaceuticals.

Her head hurt like hell.

Calla was sucking on a particularly large ice chip when Dr. Carson Kraft appeared at her bedside. "Calla Hammond?"

Finally. "That's me."

The man standing before her was tall and stately looking, with broad shoulders, a chiseled jaw, and hair streaked liberally with gray.

"I'm Dr. Kraft."

"I'd say it's nice to meet you, but I'm pretty sure you're the reason no one in this place will give me anything to take the edge off this headache." Doctor or not, Calla wasn't about to give this guy a pass.

"Blame the lawyers," Dr. Kraft said without a hint of apology. He began flipping through some papers attached to the clipboard he was holding.

"The lawyers?"

"They've been meeting with the hospital administrators ever since Dr. Cho reported a wrong patient surgery." He rolled his eyes. "It took a while. Lawyers tend to do that. No sense of urgency."

"Back up a minute. *What* kind of surgery?"

"A wrong patient surgery." Dr. Kraft enunciated each word slowly, as though Calla should understand what he was talking about. When it became clear she didn't, he widened his eyes for emphasis. "You know, when a doctor operates on the wrong patient?"

"I understand what the words mean," Calla said coldly. "But not how they apply here. I wasn't the wrong patient."

"Exactly."

Her headache surged. "What are you talking about?"

Dr. Kraft glanced around and spotted a rolling stool nearby. He pulled it next to Calla's bed and sat down. "When Dr. Cho opened you up to remove your tumor this morning, it wasn't there."

"What?"

Dr. Kraft nodded. "He couldn't find a trace of it. So, of course, he thought someone had made a mistake. That *he* had made a mistake," he amended with a chuckle. "From what I've heard, all hell broke loose in the operating room. Dr. Cho is very concerned about losing his job at this hospital." Dr. Kraft didn't even try to disguise the satisfaction in his voice.

"But—are you sure? The tumor just wasn't there?"

"Correct. It was gone. Completely gone."

"What does that mean?" Calla tried to make sense of what she was hearing. "Did someone make a mistake?"

"No." Dr. Kraft shook his head firmly. "I've looked at your scans. You *had* a tumor. And don't forget, you were experiencing symptoms. Headaches, nausea, and a pretty significant seizure."

"Well, yes, but how is this even possible?"

Dr. Kraft eyed Calla like a particularly juicy steak. "That's precisely what I would like to find out." He held up his clipboard. "Sign these consent forms. Let me look through your medical records and test results. Give me the opportunity to study you, and I will explain how this happened."

Calla took the clipboard and glanced at the top sheet. *Consent to Participate in Research and Authorization to Use and Disclose Medical Information*. A terse description under a section marked "Purpose of Study" referenced gathering data about immune responses to different types of cancer.

"What exactly is this?"

"A research study."

"What would I have to do?"

Dr. Kraft waved a dismissive hand. "A few additional tests. Maybe an hour here and there at the hospital for follow-up appointments." He leaned closer and looked straight into her eyes. "My team is doing cutting-edge research on harnessing the power of the immune system to prevent and fight cancer. If I'm right about what happened today, we may have proof that your body fought your cancer without any outside intervention. And won." He paused to let the enormity of his statement sink in. "You may be the key to answering some very important—"

"Excuse me," Dr. Cho interrupted from the foot of Calla's bed.

Dr. Kraft ignored him. "What I'm proposing can't possibly hurt you and could potentially help millions of people."

Calla shifted her gaze to Dr. Cho. "Do you know anything about this study?"

"What I know is that you should let me examine you before making any major decisions." He aimed a look at Dr. Kraft. "She's in no condition to be signing consent forms."

"I disagree. She hasn't been given any narcotics since her surgery and is clearly alert and coherent."

"What?" Dr. Cho barked. He turned and called over his shoulder, "Sharon, could you come here, please? Now!"

Sharon bustled over. "Yes, Dr. Cho?"

"Has this patient received any post-surgery pain management?"

Sharon looked uncomfortable. "Well, no, Sir. Dr. Kraft insisted on meeting with her first, and with all of the commotion after the surgery, I thought he was taking over her care."

Dr. Cho bristled. "Calla is still my patient. Regardless of the outcome, she underwent a craniotomy today, and I am sure is in a significant amount of pain." He pointed a finger at Dr. Kraft. "It was irresponsible of you to withhold pain medication. Not to mention unethical and inhumane."

Dr. Kraft brushed off the criticism. "I couldn't risk rendering her incapable of making a decision. This is a time-sensitive matter—"

"That's enough! Nothing, not even your precious research study, is that time sensitive. I have half a mind to report you to the ethics committee." Dr. Cho jabbed a finger toward the exit. "You need to leave. You can get your consent later. *If* Calla decides she wants to give it. Right now, she needs rest." He glanced back at Sharon. "And some pain meds."

"Right away, Doctor." Sharon scurried away, clearly glad to extricate herself from the exchange.

Dr. Kraft looked at Calla. "It's your decision. Not his."

"I guess I'd like some time to think about it," she said.

"Fine," Dr. Kraft snapped, abandoning his charm offensive with head-spinning ease. He stood up abruptly and pointed at the clipboard in Calla's hands. "Read through those documents tonight," he ordered. "I'll send my nurse to bring you by my office in the morning."

Without waiting for an answer, he turned on his heel and stomped out of the recovery room.

"That guy is like a dog with a bone," Dr. Cho muttered.

"What do you mean?"

He coughed softly. "I'm sorry. That was unprofessional of me. Dr. Kraft is an exemplary researcher. Brilliant, actually."

"But?" Calla pressed.

Dr. Cho seemed reluctant to continue. "It's just that he's married to this grand unified theory about cancer that he won't ever be able to prove."

"Grand unified theory?" Calla repeated. "Like, one single explanation for how cancer works?"

Dr. Cho looked impressed. Calla hated that look—the one that made it clear her intellect had once again been underestimated. "Pretty much, yes. He's convinced that he can find *the* cure for cancer in the human immune system." He shook his head. "But it's a pipe dream. Cancer isn't one disease. There's no one cure for it. It's a group of diseases that we lump together under a single umbrella term for efficiency." He paused, then added grudgingly, "Don't misunderstand me. Immunotherapy is a critical field of study in cancer treatment, and Dr. Kraft is doing important work to expand its efficacy. But it's just one tool among many that we use to fight these diseases. Not the only one."

"So, what do *you* think happened to my tumor?" Calla asked.

"I don't know," Dr. Cho admitted. He sat down on the stool that Dr. Kraft had recently vacated. "Listen, Calla. I can't deny that what happened this morning was unusual. But it's unlikely that your body cured itself. There is probably a much more rational explanation." His mouth tightened. "Potentially a diagnostic error of some sort."

Calla could tell it was painful for Dr. Cho to entertain the thought that he had been party to a mistake of that magnitude.

"Do you really think that's possible?" she asked. "I mean, more than one scan showed that I had a tumor."

Dr. Cho adjusted his glasses. "There's a chance that your records got swapped with another patient's. It's happened before with people who have similar names or dates of birth. One data entry error at the beginning of the process can link all test results to the wrong patient."

Calla was skeptical. "You think my records got switched with another patient who just happened to have multiple brain scans done on or around the same days as mine, who also happens to have a tumor that perfectly explains my seizure and other symptoms?"

"It's possible, yes." Dr. Cho's voice took on a defensive edge. "Also, your initial visit to the ER was precipitated by a blow to your head, correct?"

"Which the ER doctor said was probably caused by a seizure."

"But what if he got the order of events wrong?" Dr. Cho spoke slowly, as though he was working through a tricky logic problem. "What if the blow to your head caused the seizure? And a concussion? A concussion explains all of the symptoms you experienced. It also accounts for why you started feeling better so quickly. You really *were* getting better."

"Then what caused me to fall in the first place?"

"Bad luck? A wrong step?"

"And what about my symptoms before the fall? The headaches and the blurry vision and the nausea?"

"Those are symptoms of many common health problems, not just brain tumors." Dr. Cho said. "Don't get caught in a confirmation bias trap, Calla. And remember, it's good news that you don't have a brain tumor. Not so good for the surgeon who operated on you." He grimaced. "But great for you."

Calla couldn't deny that. "You really think this was all a mix-up?"

"It's a lot more likely than a tumor disappearing on its own."

"Is that really so impossible? A tumor disappearing on its own?"

"Not . . . impossible." Dr. Cho hesitated. "There have been documented cases of spontaneous regression of malignant tumors. But they aren't well documented or understood. And they're often reported in connection with patients who received at least some form of treatment, which clearly isn't the case in your situation."

"Uh-huh." Calla mulled over this new piece of information.

"It's been a long day." Dr. Cho sounded as tired as he looked. "A confusing day. For all of us. I don't blame you for having questions. And I suppose Dr. Kraft is right. It can't hurt to let him take a look at your case. But just . . . be careful, okay? He can get aggressive when he thinks he's onto something."

"Okay. Thanks."

"Who's ready for some morphine?" Sharon materialized like some nurse version of a fairy godmother.

Calla raised a finger. "That would be me."

"You got it." Sharon turned to Dr. Cho. "Doctor, Ms. Wiley just called again. She's getting rather testy, and I'm running out of excuses to keep her from coming back here."

Calla laughed. "Testy?"

"She's worried about you." Sharon frowned at Dr. Cho.

"Wait." Calla looked from nurse to doctor. "Has anyone talked to her yet?"

Dr. Cho's shoulders slumped. "No. I only just got out of a meeting with the legal team and wanted to check on you first. I'll go talk with her now." He stood up. "I'm not supposed to say this, Calla, but I'm sorry for what happened today."

"You mean about the surgery?"

"Yes."

"I don't blame you. Though I do wish I hadn't been kept in the dark for so long. And you can be damn sure Rae isn't happy about the delay."

Dr. Cho gave her a tight smile. "I understand. Is there anything else I can do for you right now?"

"Not as long as I get some of Sharon's good stuff."

"I'll check in on you later, then." He glanced at Sharon, who inserted a needle into the injection port on Calla's IV bag. "Take care of her."

"Of course, Doctor."

Dr. Cho strode away, and Sharon finished administering Calla's morphine. "There you go. You should start to feel that in a minute or two, okay?"

"Thanks, Sharon."

"And Calla?"

"Yes?"

Sharon's hands twisted nervously. "I'm sorry I couldn't tell you anything earlier. I wanted to, but Dr. Kraft sent word that anyone who talked to you would be risking their job."

"It's okay. Now that I've met him, I understand why you were worried." When Sharon didn't look reassured, Calla added, "Really."

Sharon gave her a grateful look. "Call if you need anything, okay?"

"I will."

Calla laid her head back on her pillow and closed her eyes.

As she waited for the pain medication to kick in, she tried to make sense of everything that had unfolded over the last fifteen minutes.

Her tumor was gone. Everyone seemed to agree on that point. Or maybe she'd never had one? That's what Dr. Cho seemed to think. And that couldn't be an easy thing for him to admit. But his explanation didn't sit quite right with her. Even if (a fairly big if) she accepted his theory about a medical records mix-up and a concussion (which, she had to concede, made a lot of sense), that still left the fact that she'd been feeling lousy for several months before she hit her head at the library.

And Dr. Cho didn't know—he couldn't know because she hadn't told him—about the other episodes from the last year. Like the weird lumps she'd found from time to time in her armpits and the sides of her neck that seemed to come and go at random. Or the bouts of unexplained fatigue and weight loss. Or the week she'd suffered from such awful, bloody diarrhea and pain in her abdomen that she couldn't leave her apartment. By the time she'd gotten an appointment with a gastroenterologist (a minor miracle given the limitations of her health insurance plan), she was feeling significantly better but couldn't shake the conviction that something was horribly wrong with her. The doctor chalked it up to a bad case of food poisoning and told her to stay off the Internet.

"Don't underestimate the power of your mind to blow things out of proportion," he'd said when she'd confided her nagging worries to him. He'd been so condescending that she'd vowed never to mention her suspicions to another medical professional.

Calla liked to think she was a rational person. A person who didn't blow things out of proportion. A person who could accept that a simple data entry error might have led to conducting a craniotomy on the wrong patient. But she also knew her body. And her body seemed to be telling her that something unusual was going on.

Maybe, with Dr. Kraft's help, it was time to do something about it.

SEVEN

"GOOD MORNING, SUNSHINE!"

A cheerful voice woke Calla from a deep sleep. She opened her eyes and saw a man in purple scrubs beaming down at her, his hair swept up in a pristine pompadour.

He whistled appreciatively. "Girl, those eyes are stunning! But"—he made an apologetic gesture—"don't take this the wrong way; your hair's kind of a mess."

Calla yawned. "Gee, I can't imagine why." She waited a second, then gave the man a crooked smile. It was hard to feel offended after waking up to such a nice compliment. No one had ever referred to any part of her as "stunning" before.

"I can," Rae grumbled as she stretched and began to extricate herself from the uncomfortable-looking nest she had constructed the previous evening from armchairs and thin pillows. Despite Calla's protests, she had insisted on spending the night at the hospital. "Nothing like a little unnecessary brain surgery to cramp a girl's style." She looked over at Calla. "How are you feeling?"

Calla took a quick inventory of her body. "Head definitely still hurts a bit. But other than that, I think I'm okay."

"Okay enough to take a ride with me to see Dr. Kraft?" the man asked.

Calla noticed he had brought a wheelchair into the room. "He wasn't kidding about wanting an answer this morning, was he? What time is it?"

The man laughed. "A little past eight. He wanted me to pick you up a couple of hours ago, but I talked him out of it." He helped Calla sit up and swing her legs over the side of the bed. "I'm Reuben Sanchez, by the way. Nurse practitioner and assistant extraordinaire to Dr. Carson Kraft." He took a little bow.

"Nice to meet you. I'm Calla, and this is my friend Rae."

Rae gave him a wave.

"A pleasure to meet you both," Reuben said. "Are you ready to stand up, or do you need a minute?"

"I think I need a minute." The incision in Calla's head was starting to scream at her.

"No problem. Take your time."

She took a couple of deep breaths. "So, what's it like working with Dr. Kraft? He seems like he might be . . ." She didn't know how to finish.

"Challenging?" Reuben suggested with a sly smile. "Obnoxious? Slightly dictatorial?"

"Something like that."

"Dr. Kraft is one of those stereotypical brilliant types with absolutely no people skills. A big part of my job involves smoothing the feathers he tends to ruffle all over the hospital."

"He was definitely ruffling Dr. Cho's feathers yesterday."

"No surprise there," Reuben said disapprovingly. "Those two have never gotten along."

"Sounds like a real charmer," Rae said as she began rummaging through her overnight bag. "Are you sure this can't wait? I've got a home visit in half an hour that's already been rescheduled twice." She looked up at Reuben. "I'll be back by noon."

Reuben looked torn. "Well—" His cell phone buzzed. He rolled his eyes as he looked at the screen. "That's Dr. K. He wants to know where the—uh, where we are."

Calla pushed herself to a standing position. "Don't worry about me, Rae. You already helped with the hard part. Let's not get Reuben here in any deeper shit."

She and Rae had pored over the consent forms for the research study the night before. Well, it had been mostly Rae, in deference to Calla's still-sore head. From what they could tell, it seemed relatively innocuous.

"It's just some blood and tissue samples, right?" Calla asked Reuben as he helped her pivot and sit down in the wheelchair.

"Yup. Maybe a CT scan, but that's about it. We've never needed much more than that from participants."

"See, Rae?" Calla said. "No big deal."

Reuben released the brakes on the wheelchair. "You okay if we hit the road? I'm afraid there's no time for hair and makeup."

"Darn. And here I was hoping to impress the good doctor with this fetching hospital gown."

Reuben let out a laugh. "Honey, I don't think he'd notice if you were in an evening gown and heels."

"Oh. Is he . . . ?"

"Playing for the same team as *moi*?" Reuben pressed his hand to his chest, then shook his head. "No. My best guess is that the man doesn't play for any team. His one and only passion is his work."

Rae shook her head in wonder as she handed the bundle of consent forms to Calla. "Call me as soon as you're done. I want a full report."

EIGHT

IT TOOK A WHILE to get to Dr. Kraft's office, which was located in a far corner of the hospital's lower level.

"Isn't this cozy?" Calla remarked as Reuben steered her down an isolated hallway.

"Ruffled feathers," he replied. "Lots of ruffled feathers."

They stopped in front of an unmarked door. Reuben knocked a few times.

"Dr. Kraft?" he called through the faux wood. "It's Reuben. I have Ms. Hammond with me."

They waited several seconds but heard no response.

Reuben knocked again. "Dr. Kraft?"

Finally, a grunt. "Come."

Reuben opened the door and maneuvered the wheelchair into a cramped office. Dr. Kraft was seated behind a battered metal desk, surrounded by stacks of paper, journals, empty take-out containers, and dirty coffee mugs.

Calla spotted her name scrawled on the edge of a folder sitting open in front of him.

"Shut the door on your way out, Reuben." Dr. Kraft did not look up from the papers he was studying.

"Yes, Sir." Reuben gave Calla a friendly pat on the shoulder, then left the room.

Calla waited for the doctor to acknowledge her presence, but he remained silent, reading through the file and occasionally jotting down a note.

"When did you first menstruate?" he asked a minute later.

"Excuse me?"

"When did you get your first period?"

"Uh," Calla faltered. "I don't—I don't understand what that has to do with my brain tumor."

"You don't have a brain tumor anymore."

"Right."

They stared at each other.

"So," Dr. Kraft continued, "when did you get your first period?"

"Last year." She gave him a grim look. "Obviously, I was a late bloomer."

"Mm-hmm." Dr. Kraft jotted something down on the paper in front of him. He did not appear unduly surprised by this information. In fact, he seemed pleased.

"And your vitiligo?" he asked.

"What about it?"

"When did it present?"

"I don't know. I've had it as long as I can remember."

"Surely your parents can tell you."

"That would be difficult. I have no idea who my father is. I don't even know if he's aware that I exist. And my mother died of a drug overdose eighteen years ago."

Dr. Kraft tapped his pen a few times. "Let's move on. Have you ever been diagnosed with cancer before?"

"You mean before the brain tumor?"

Dr. Kraft nodded.

"No."

"Any unexplained illnesses?"

"Yeah." This was it. Her chance to talk to someone knowledgeable who didn't treat her like a crazy person. "There've been a few."

Dr. Kraft perked up. "And they happened since you started menstruating?"

"Uh, yes?" Calla shifted in her seat. What was the deal with this guy and her period?

"Tell me about them," he demanded.

So, she did. He pressed her for the minutest details. When the interrogation was over, Calla felt like she was waiting for a final verdict. As Dr. Kraft's pen scratched against the paper, she rubbed the back of her upper arm idly.

The movement caught his attention. "Why do you keep touching your arm?"

"What?"

"Your upper right arm. Why do you keep touching it?"

"Because it's itchy?"

"Let me take a look."

Calla lifted the sleeve of her hospital gown.

Dr. Kraft grunted.

"What is it?" she asked.

"I'm not a dermatologist, but I think you might have a nice little melanoma growing there."

Calla twisted her arm so she could take a closer look. "A melanoma?"

"Indeed." Dr. Kraft sounded way too happy about this objectively bad news. "I'd like to get a biopsy of that as soon as possible. Just a small one. We need to leave the majority of the lesion intact."

"What? Why?"

"Because if it's cancerous, I'd like to see if it takes care of itself without any treatment."

"Are you insane?"

"Quite the opposite."

Calla was tempted to reach across the desk and slap the smug look off his face. Instead, she crossed her arms. "Listen, I don't know if you noticed, but I'm a human being, not some science experiment. I think it's time for you to explain your thinking to me."

Dr. Kraft's lips twitched in annoyance. "Fine." He set his pen down with a snap. "Why do some people smoke for years, an activity that is considered the top risk factor for developing lung cancer, but never develop the disease?"

"Uh—"

"And why do other people," he continued, "people who arguably live the healthiest lifestyles in terms of diet, exercise, and avoidance of environmental toxins, develop cancer?"

This time, he seemed to want Calla to give him an answer.

"I assume you're going to tell me it has something to do with the immune system?"

"Yes!" Dr. Kraft smacked his palm on his desk. "I think it has everything to do with the immune system."

He stood up and began to pace in the narrow space behind his desk.

"Medical history is replete with reports about the spontaneous regression of cancerous tumors and remission of diseases. Over a century ago, doctors discovered that certain bacterial infections triggered immune responses in cancer patients that attacked and sometimes completely cured their tumors. This discovery gave birth to the field of oncological immunotherapy. But other patients have reportedly recovered with no intervention at all. Why is that?" He stopped pacing. "I believe it is because some people are naturally immune to cancer, in all its forms. I'm interested in those people. The problem is finding them."

"And why is that?"

"Any number of reasons. Most probably never get sick enough to seek medical attention. Others may be told they were misdiagnosed and discontinue treatment before their cases can be documented. Physicians might be reluctant to publish data about such patients due to concerns about authenticity and replicability." He sat back down in his chair and tapped his finger on the folder bearing Calla's name. "That's why you are so special. If my theory about you is correct, Calla, you are the needle in the haystack I've been searching for."

"You think I'm immune to cancer?" Calla struggled to hide her skepticism. If she was immune, why did she get a brain tumor?

Dr. Kraft fixed her with an intense look. "I think you might be more than that."

"More?"

"You're aware that vitiligo is an autoimmune disorder?"

"So I've been told."

"Then you know that your immune system mistakenly attacks the pigment cells in your skin, causing widespread depigmentation."

"No shit, is that how it works?"

Dr. Kraft ignored her sarcasm. "I think your vitiligo, combined with the delayed onset of puberty you experienced last year, triggered a unique set of circumstances in your body. For some reason, the introduction of hormonal changes at such a late stage in your development is causing you to develop cancer. And your immune system, which was originally programmed to attack healthy cells, has responded to this fundamental shift by attacking those cancers. Your body is at war with itself. And your immune system appears to be winning."

"You think I'm getting cancer over and over again?"

"Yes."

"And that my immune system is curing it?"

"Yes."

"What makes you so sure? Every doctor I've seen in the last year had reasonable explanations for my symptoms. Food poisoning. A virus. A bad night's sleep." She ticked them off on her fingers. "And Dr. Cho seems pretty sure I never had a brain tumor. He said this was all probably a mistake caused by a data entry error."

Dr. Kraft snorted. "Dr. Cho has no imagination. Of course he would blame this on a data entry error. But I have proof."

"Proof?"

"Well, not definitive proof," Dr. Kraft waffled. "But close enough. I ordered a blood draw yesterday after I heard about your non-surgery surgery. Reuben oversaw the process and personally escorted the tubes to the lab. There is no question that it was your blood."

Calla bristled at Dr. Kraft's audacity. "You took my blood? Without my permission?"

"Yes." No hint of compunction.

"You realize you could get in a lot of trouble for doing that, right?"

"There wasn't time to ask for your permission," Dr. Kraft said coldly.

"Anyway, do you want to know the results? Or would you prefer to continue your lecture on medical ethics?"

Calla stared. This guy was unbelievable. "Tell me the results."

"They showed an elevated level of GFAP. That's the tumor marker for a glioblastoma."

"You're saying the fact that this tumor marker was still showing up in my blood after the surgery proves that I had cancer at some point."

"At some point very recently, yes. It can take tumor marker levels a little time to go down after a tumor is removed from the body. If we discard the medical error theory and add those results to your previous scans, blood draws, and the symptoms you experienced, we have a strong case for the presence of cancer. A very strong case."

They sat in silence for a few moments.

Finally, Dr. Kraft said, "You are the next step in the evolutionary journey that humans are on, Calla."

"Oh, come on." This was all getting to be a bit much. All she wanted was for someone to look at her labs, maybe figure out if she had a random food allergy that had been missed.

"I mean it. Imagine a world where people diagnosed with cancer didn't have to endure surgery, chemotherapy, or radiation therapy. Those treatments may be effective at keeping cancer at bay and prolonging life, but they aren't very good at curing the disease. As a matter of fact, they often cause more problems than they solve. Chemo and radiation suppress the immune system. They damage healthy tissue and cells along with the cancerous ones. Not to mention the secondary cancers they cause down the line." Dr. Kraft shook his head. "And surgery? So crude! Surgeons can talk all day about improved precision in their techniques, but anytime they cut into or around a tumor, they run the risk of spreading the very cells they seek to remove to other parts of the body. That's why surgery is so often coupled with chemo and radiation. To mop up the mess."

He pointed at her. "Your body may hold the key to making all of that go away. If I can prove that your immune system can fight cancer, and if I can figure out how it does it, we may be able to teach everyone else's to do the same thing. Potentially with something as simple as a pill." He fixed her with an earnest look. "Millions of people all over the world are fighting cancer every day. If there's even a chance you could help them, don't you want to do that?"

"When you put it that way, who wouldn't?" Calla wrinkled her brow. "But it all just sounds so . . . implausible."

"You're not the first person to say that," he admitted. "But consider this. If I'm wrong, what's the harm? You're out some time and a little bit of blood." He paused. "Even if you're not getting cancer, the tests we're running might tell us what's causing the strange episodes you've been experiencing. But if I'm right . . ." He let the unspoken end of his statement hang in the air for a moment and then pointed to the documents in her lap. "Sign those, Calla. Sign them, and let's see if we can cure cancer. Together."

He seemed so sure of himself. It was hard not to get caught up in his enthusiasm. And he made a good point. What was the harm in a few tests?

"Well then." Calla picked up a pen from the desk and signed the forms.

"Great." Dr. Kraft took the papers and placed them in her file. Then, he pulled his cell phone out of his pocket and tapped on the screen. "Let's get started."

"Right now?"

"Right now." Dr. Kraft looked up from his phone. "Reuben!"

Reuben opened the door and popped his head into the office. "You rang?"

"We're going up to meet Juhi and Ralph." Without another word, he stood and marched out of the office.

Reuben raised his eyebrows at Calla. "Guess you passed the test."

"Guess so," she replied, listening to Dr. Kraft's footsteps echo down the hallway.

He was a strange man with some really radical ideas, but at least he didn't treat her like a raging hypochondriac. For that, she could tolerate his eccentricities. For now.

Reuben took up his position behind her wheelchair. "Welcome to the team."

NINE

DR. KRAFT WAS TAPPING HIS FOOT when Reuben and Calla arrived at the second-floor research lab.

"What'd you do, take the freight elevator?" Dr. Kraft pointed to a skinny, twenty-something guy who was munching on a bag of Cool Ranch Doritos. "This is Ralph Grimes, my lab tech. He also handles a lot of our IT needs. Ralph, this is Calla Hammond."

Ralph's face was studded with acne, and he sported a t-shirt that declared: *I'm an engineer. Let's save time and assume I'm never wrong.*

"Nice to meet you," he said. "I'd shake your hand, but . . ." He held up a hand covered in chip residue.

"That's gross, Ralph." The last occupant of the room, a woman who looked to be in her early thirties, narrowed her eyes in his direction.

"Whatever, Juhi."

"That's Dr. Pemmaraju to you." The woman dismissed the lab tech with a shake of her head. She turned toward Calla and offered a mercifully clean hand for her to shake. "It's a pleasure to meet you. You may call me Juhi or Dr. Pemmaraju, whichever you prefer."

In addition to having zero problems standing up for herself, Dr. Juhi Pemmaraju was almost intimidatingly gorgeous, with huge, expressive eyes and a lustrous mane of black hair. But she also exuded a warm, friendly vibe that immediately set Calla at ease.

"Nice to meet you, too," she replied, feeling strangely certain that Dr. Pemmaraju was someone who would always have her back.

"Dr. Pemmaraju is a hematologist–oncologist," Dr. Kraft explained. "She handles the blood and lymph side of the research. I'm the lead on solid tumors." He clapped his hands together. "Okay. We need to get started right away while there's still a chance of documenting the regression of Calla's tumor and any immunological connection. I want a complete work-up. Labs, full-body scan, and whole-genome sequencing. Oh, and we need to biopsy a spot on her arm. Take the smallest sample possible. Leave the majority of the lesion intact." He pointed to Dr. Pemmaraju. "Do that today."

She furrowed her brow. "That's not how we usually handle skin lesions."

"It's how we'll handle this one."

"Where will we get the money to cover all of this?" Dr. Pemmaraju asked. "We can barely keep ink in the printer on our current budget."

"I'll cover the funding." Dr. Kraft's response was curt. "Just order the tests."

Dr. Pemmaraju looked like she wanted to discuss the issue further, but she backed down when Dr. Kraft glared at her. With a slight shrug, she said, "Consider it done."

"This could be big, people." Dr. Kraft turned to address the entire group. "I expect you to work hard and keep quiet. I want discussions outside of this room kept to a bare minimum. If for some reason you find it necessary to talk about your work outside of the lab, please refer to this project as the PP."

"The PP?" Ralph snickered. "Are we gonna need some TP for it?"

"Oh, grow up, Ralph." Dr. Pemmaraju rolled her eyes.

"It's a dumb name." Ralph turned back to Dr. Kraft. "What the hell does it stand for anyway?"

"The Panacea Project."

Ralph smirked as he popped another chip into his mouth. "Isn't that a bit presumptuous? No offense, Calla. I'm sure your immune system is great and all, but aren't we jumping the gun a little? We don't even know if she's the real thing yet." He crumpled the chip bag with a flourish. "You've been wrong before, you know."

"You can leave now if you're not fully committed to this research, Mr. Grimes." Dr. Kraft's voice was ice cold. "Despite what you think, you are replaceable."

Ralph pursed his lips.

"Any more editorial comments?" Dr. Kraft looked around the room, daring someone else to speak up. "No? Good. Let's get to work."

TEN

THUS BEGAN CALLA'S TENURE as a glorified lab rat.

Dr. Kraft took full advantage of the two days Dr. Cho kept her in the hospital for observation before clearing her to go home after her not-surgery, cramming the forty-eight hours with as many tests and procedures as possible. A full-body PET scan. A biopsy of the lesion on her arm. And blood draws. Lots and lots of blood draws.

Calla had never been more poked and prodded and nipped. It was quite a bit more than she had been led to expect when she'd signed on to the study.

"Back again?" she asked when Reuben wheeled his cart into her room for the fourth time on the final day of her hospital stay.

"Last one for today, I promise." He flashed her a scout's honor sign.

As he began the now-familiar routine of drawing her blood—applying the tourniquet, finding a vein, swabbing her arm with alcohol—Calla asked, "How many more of these is he going to want? He knows I'm going home tomorrow, right?"

"He knows," Reuben replied as he slid the needle into her arm. "He wanted to track the changes in your tumor marker levels as closely as possible until they were back to normal. You were almost there after my last poke, so he'll probably just order one more test before you take off in the morning."

"I'm surprised he didn't just hook me up to some machine so he could get a constant stream of information," Calla said, only half joking.

"He probably would if he could," Reuben replied, his tone dead serious. "But Dr. Pemmaraju won't let that happen. Gotta maintain a good life-slash-lab-rat balance for you, right?" He gave her a wink.

They laughed and then fell into a comfortable silence as they watched Calla's blood fill up a series of collection tubes.

"It's official," Calla declared as Reuben bandaged her arm afterward. "You're a magician. I barely felt that one." She'd been praising Reuben's phlebotomy skills ever since he'd taken over her blood draws.

"Just doing my job."

"Well, you're damn good at it." She watched as he double-checked labels and organized tubes. "When did you decide you wanted to be a nurse?"

Reuben winced a little.

"Sorry," Calla said. "That's a personal question. You don't have to tell me."

"You're fine," he assured her. "It's just . . . complicated."

"We don't have to talk about it."

"No, I want to. I actually think you'll understand better than most people. May I?" He patted a spot at the foot of Calla's bed. She nodded her assent, and he sat down.

Reuben took a second or two to collect his thoughts and then launched into his story.

"My great-aunt Linda was a nurse back in the eighties, at the beginning of the AIDS epidemic. Her baby brother, Emilio, was closeted at the time, but then he got sick. When the family found out, they abandoned him. Linda was the only one who would take care of him. After he passed away, she kept working full-time with AIDS patients. The men she cared for—mostly men back then got sick—were like brothers to her. One by one, she watched them die. Alone. Rejected by their families. Like Emilio." His voice grew thick with emotion. "I came out to my parents when I was sixteen. They told me I was going to hell and kicked me out. I was on the streets for five days before Linda found me. She took me in and gave me a home. Told me she loved me no matter what I did or who I did it with. She made sure I finished high school and paid for me to take classes at the community college." He looked down at his hands. "I'm not sure it ever occurred to me that I *wouldn't* become a nurse and follow in her footsteps."

"She sounds like an incredible woman."

"She was."

"Was?"

He took a shuddering breath. "She died two months ago. Heart attack in her sleep." He brushed a hand across his eyes. "By the time I found her the next morning, it was too late."

Calla leaned forward and placed a comforting hand on his shoulder.

"My parents came to the funeral, and I—I hoped that maybe things would be different. I hadn't seen them in ten years. But they took one look at me holding hands with my boyfriend, Michael, and acted like we weren't there. The rest of the family went along with it. No one said a word to us or even looked in our direction the entire time." His voice dropped to a whisper. "It was like I was invisible. Like *I* was the dead person."

The thought of his humiliation from that day pierced Calla like the blade of a hot knife, slicing into her gut and twisting painfully. She knew this anguish. She knew rejection and abandonment and disloyalty. And she grieved for the beautiful person hunched at the foot of her bed, who had lost his anchor—his version of Rae—without whom she knew she'd be bereft.

Reuben was right. Calla did understand better than most people. And she was deeply touched that he had sensed this about her and trusted her with his story.

She hesitated for a second before she scooted down the bed and wrapped her arms around his neck.

"I see you," she said softly, half afraid he would push her away.

An undiscovered door in her heart opened when Reuben leaned his head against her shoulder. He exhaled slowly and said, "I see you, too."

. . .

The next morning, Calla waved goodbye to the day shift nurses she had gotten to know over the past few days as Reuben pushed her toward the elevator in a wheelchair. Calla had protested (she could walk perfectly fine, thank you), but apparently, it was hospital policy.

Dr. Pemmaraju kept pace beside them. "Dr. Kraft is sorry he can't be here to say goodbye."

"Sure he is," Calla said.

She'd only seen Dr. Kraft once since their initial meeting—a quick check-in before a PET scan. Since then, she'd interacted primarily with Reuben and Dr. Pemmaraju. Occasionally, Ralph would unglue his eyes from his computer screens and grunt a greeting as they'd passed through the lab.

When they reached the front doors of the hospital, Calla turned and patted Reuben's hand. "Thanks for the ride."

"My pleasure, as always." He leaned down and gave her a quick hug. "Text me tomorrow, and we'll set up dinner. Michael wants to meet you."

"Sounds good." Calla turned to shake hands with Dr. Pemmaraju and was surprised when the doctor held out her arms for a hug as well.

"You're a real trooper, Calla," Dr. Pemmaraju said. "Thanks for being so patient with us this week. The next time you're here, I'll try to schedule things so that you're only here for about an hour, okay?"

"Next Thursday, right?" Calla asked.

"Yes, unless something comes up in the meantime." Dr. Pemmaraju leaned forward and said softly in Calla's ear, "I'll make sure it doesn't. I know you need a break."

"I appreciate that." Calla hefted the plastic drawstring bag the hospital had given her to carry her personal belongings.

Reuben peered at the line of waiting cars. "Is Rae picking you up?"

"She had to be in court this morning, so I'm taking the bus."

"The bus?" Dr. Pemmaraju glanced sideways at Reuben.

"Is there something wrong with that?" Calla asked.

"Is it safe?"

Calla stifled a laugh. Their concern was endearing. "As safe as any other mode of public transportation in this city."

"Well, please be careful," Dr. Pemmaraju said. "And remember, don't talk to anyone about the PP."

They all laughed, and Calla mimed zipping her mouth shut. Behind her, the hiss of air brakes signaled the arrival of a Metro bus. She turned and hustled down the sidewalk as quickly as her still-tender head would allow.

"Mornin' Ma'am," the driver greeted her.

"Good morning," Calla replied as she swiped her fare card.

"Name's Charlie. Haven't seen you on this route before."

Calla wasn't used to bus drivers being so chatty, but Charlie seemed friendly enough. He was an older man, maybe mid-sixties—a little stout, wearing a sweater vest, a newsboy cap, and a sincere smile. "This is my first time from this stop. I'm Calla."

Charlie touched his fingers to the brim of his hat. "A pleasure to meet you, Calla. Welcome aboard."

"Thanks."

Calla made her way through a handful of passengers to an open seat near the middle of the bus. One woman stared openly, but Calla ignored her. It was a beautiful day, and she was tumor-free. More importantly, she was heading home, where there would be no procedures, no scans, and no needle sticks for the next six days. Just Calla, completely and blissfully alone.

. . .

Her third-floor apartment was just as she had left it a week earlier— small and slightly shabby but still home. She was glad to be back. Her stomach rumbled as she tossed her hospital bag in a corner. A quick peek in the refrigerator reminded her that she hadn't gone shopping in a while. The nearest grocery store was a twenty-minute walk, which she would gladly have taken if not for the gathering storm clouds she'd spied on the way home, and an Uber was out of the question with her dwindling finances. She'd have to make do with what remained in the freezer and pantry.

Calla's phone started to buzz. She smiled. Rae had a sixth sense when it came to Calla's whereabouts.

"Are you home yet?"

"Just walked in the door."

"How'd you get back?"

"I took the bus."

"I should've been there to drive you."

"You had a hearing, Rae. What were you supposed to do? Ask the judge to postpone?"

"No, but I should've been there."

"You're being silly."

"Do you have any food?"

"Um, yeah," Calla said. "Plenty."

"Calla Hammond." Rae's tone was full of scolding. "You are and always have been a terrible liar. I'm bringing you dinner."

"You really don't need to do that."

"I'll be there by six. Does Indian sound good?"

Calla knew it was no use to argue. "Indian sounds great. Thanks, Rae."

"You're welcome." Rae's tone softened. "How are you feeling today?"

"Pretty good. I'm going to call the library in a minute to see if I can get on the schedule for tomorrow."

"I thought you weren't going back to work until next week."

"I wasn't, but there's no reason to sit around for another three days with nothing to do." She paused before adding, "And I could use the money."

"Oh, honey," Rae sighed. "I had a feeling that might be the case. Do you need some help?"

"No," Calla said firmly, trying to infuse her voice with a conviction she didn't fully hold. "I appreciate the offer, but I'm fine. Really."

"Okay." Rae sounded skeptical but didn't press the issue. She knew how much Calla prized her independence. "I'll see you tonight, then. Love you."

"Love you, too. Bye."

Calla set the phone down and bit her lip. The truth was that she wasn't fine—not on the financial front. Dr. Kraft wanted to run tests at least once a week for the foreseeable future. She was pretty sure her boss would accommodate time off for the study, but fewer hours at the library might make it hard to cover her rent and other expenses.

She didn't want to give up on the study, though. Not yet. Reuben and Dr. Pemmaraju already felt like close friends—something she rarely experienced. Once they'd learned about her health history, they seemed committed to helping her find answers regardless of whether it helped their research or not. And she had to admit it felt good to be a part of a team that might achieve something monumental for the world, even if their goal seemed like the longest of long shots.

She wanted—no, she needed—to do both. She was just going to have to find a way to make it work.

. . .

The following Thursday, Calla arrived at the lab with a dozen freshly baked chocolate chip cookies in hand.

"Omigod," Reuben moaned as he bit into one. "These are amazing. They're still warm! Where did you get them?"

"I made them. I wanted to thank you guys for everything you've done for me."

"I'm pretty sure you've got that backward, Calla, given the amount of blood I've taken from you recently," Reuben said. "But please, feel free to thank us anytime you feel the urge to bake."

Even grumpy Ralph seemed mildly impressed. "Not bad for a lab rat," he said, grabbing a handful of cookies before turning back to his bank of computers.

"Cookie, Dr. Pemmaraju?" Calla asked as the woman in question poked her head into the main room of the lab.

Dr. Pemmaraju's face brightened. "You're right on time!" She waved Calla over to the small examination room. "Let me take a look at your arm first." She glared at Reuben and Ralph. "Save one for me, gentlemen. Or there'll be hell to pay."

"Where's Dr. K?" Calla asked as she took off her shirt and hopped onto the exam table in her bra. She and Dr. Pemmaraju had agreed not to bother with hospital gowns when it was just the two of them.

"He's in a budget meeting with the finance committee." Dr. Pemmaraju gently peeled off the bandage covering Calla's biopsied arm. Dr. Kraft had been right about it being a melanoma—the pathology report had confirmed his suspicion. "We're getting some pretty exciting results from your blood tests, but we'll need more funding if we want to—" She drew a sharp breath. "My god!"

"What?" Calla asked. "Is something wrong?"

"No, no," Dr. Pemmaraju said quickly. "I'm sorry. I didn't mean to frighten you. It's just that the lesion . . ." She probed the back of Calla's arm. "It's gone."

"Gone?"

"Gone." Dr. Pemmaraju pulled over a rolling stool and sat down, her eyes wide. "I need to document this." She stood up as quickly as she had sat down and crossed the room. "I wonder if taking the biopsy provoked an immune response, or if it would've resolved on its own?" she murmured as she rummaged around in a cabinet, her excitement seeming to grow by the second. She turned to face Calla. "Do you have time to meet with Dr. Kraft today? He should be done by two or so, and I know he'll want to examine you. We could grab a quick lunch while we wait."

Calla looked at her watch. "Sorry, but I need to be back at work by then. If I'm going to make the bus, I need to leave by one-thirty."

Dr. Pemmaraju gave her a probing look. "Calla, is your participation in this study making it hard for you to get to work?"

She shrugged. "A little, but I can manage, as long as it's not more than a few hours a week. I work at a library. Doesn't really compare to curing cancer, but it pays the bills."

"Don't minimize what you do," Dr. Pemmaraju chided gently. "Take it from a girl who spent countless childhood hours camped out at her local library; your job is important. But Calla, if I'm being completely honest with you, things could get a lot more intense with the study. And quickly. Last week, we infused six mice with cancerous tumors with your blood. All six are now in remission. We don't understand why yet, but with a little more time and—"

"A little more blood?"

"Unfortunately, yes. We're going to need more samples. And not just of blood. Dr. K wants to run some tests using your bone marrow. An aspiration is a pretty involved procedure. And he's mentioned other tissue biopsies."

"Other biopsies? That's not exactly what I signed up for."

"I know. I get it. We're talking about a lot more of your time," Dr. Pemmaraju said. "But, Calla? No bullshit. We may actually be onto something here."

Calla eyed her for a moment. "My blood really cured your lab mice?"

"So far. It's too early to know anything for sure, but the results are more promising than anything we've seen before." Dr. Pemmaraju opened a drawer and pulled out a camera. "Would it help if we paid you for participating in the study?"

"You can do that?"

"We should be able to."

"Then yes, actually, it would."

Dr. Pemmaraju walked back over to the examination table. "How does this sound? Let me take some photos of your arm. Reuben will do your blood draw, and then you can head back to work. I'll talk to Dr. Kraft when he gets out of his meeting." She held up the camera with an air of determination. "It's time to discuss compensating you. He should be able to afford it if he gets the budget he's asking for today."

. . .

Calla was called back to the hospital a few days later. This time, she was summoned to the office of Jackson Albright, the hospital's assistant general counsel.

"Thanks for meeting with me today, Ms. Hammond," he said as he offered her a seat in one of the chairs in front of his desk. "And congratulations on the good news about your brain tumor."

"Thank you." Calla sat down and glanced at a framed photo on his desk. "You have a lovely family."

Jackson smiled at the portrait of himself, a young woman, and three small boys. "Three can be a handful, but we can't imagine life without them." He cleared his throat. "So, uh, it must have been quite a shock when you woke up from that surgery, huh?"

Calla noticed his fingers silently drumming. "Shock is one word for it."

"Right. Well. The hospital was very pleased with the outcome." He bobbed his head a few times. "Very pleased. And happy that you're recovering so well, of course."

"That's nice of you to say." *What's with all the pleasantries?*

Jackson fiddled with some papers on his desk. "We've also been made aware that your participation in Dr. Kraft's research study has strained your finances."

"Yes, it has."

"Given the unique set of circumstances we're dealing with, the hospital administration feels that there is an opportunity for the parties involved to agree to an arrangement." He paused. "So that we can avoid any disputes down the line."

"You're worried I might file a lawsuit. Because of the surgery."

Jackson didn't deny it. He handed Calla a document. "This is a draft settlement agreement and release of claims. You'll want to have your lawyer look it over, of course."

Calla barely contained a chortle at the idea that she had a lawyer.

"Essentially, it states that you waive any claims you might have against the hospital stemming from your craniotomy. In exchange, the hospital will cover all costs associated with the surgery—past and future—and pay you a sum of ten thousand dollars."

"I'm sorry. Did you just say ten thousand dollars?"

"I did."

"But you know what happened wasn't Dr. Cho's fault, right?"

"This agreement would allow us to bypass the question of fault."

"I see."

"If I may continue—"

"Wait. Dr. Cho's not going to get into trouble, is he?"

"I, uh, don't know." Jackson shifted a little in his seat. "That's not really my department."

"Well, I don't think he should get in trouble. Can we put that in the agreement?"

"I can look into that." He jotted a note down on a legal pad in front of him, then continued. "The agreement also covers your participation in Dr. Kraft's study. The hospital is prepared to pay you a stipend of two hundred and fifty dollars for each day or part of a day you are engaged in work on behalf of the study. Any expenses associated with your participation in the study will be reimbursed." He gave her a wink. "Keep your receipts, okay? The accounting office is strict about these things. Trust me. I know from personal experience."

Calla stared blankly as he continued to speak. *Ten thousand dollars. Daily stipends. Expense reimbursements.* The implications washed over her.

"Calla?"

"Yes."

"I asked if you have any other questions."

"Uh, no, not right now." She gave her head a little shake. "I'm sorry, this wasn't exactly what I expected."

Jackson stood up and buttoned his suit jacket. "I've given you a lot to think about," he acknowledged. "Take a day or two to read the agreement over. Talk to an attorney. I'll check on adding the provision about Dr. Cho. In the meantime, call me if you come up with any questions." He held out his hand.

Calla stood and shook his hand. "Thank you."

Jackson gave her a curious look as she moved to leave his office. "Sure wish I knew what's got everyone so excited about you. I've never drafted a document quite like this before."

Something in his expression gave Calla pause. She shrugged and decided to play dumb. "I don't really understand it myself. All this science-y stuff can be so complicated."

ELEVEN

"TEN THOUSAND DOLLARS seems like a lowball offer to me."

Calla and Rae were sitting on the patio at Empire Cafe, munching on sandwiches and sweet potato fries. The hospital's settlement agreement lay on the table between them.

Rae continued, "I think there's more going on here than just avoiding a lawsuit from the surgery." She tapped the papers in front of her. "This talks an awful lot about the study."

"I noticed that, too," Calla said. "It got me thinking."

"About what?"

"That maybe I should ask for a share of whatever they might make. Not much," she rushed to add. "But something. Just in case."

"In case they're right, and your blood can cure cancer?"

"Well, yeah. I figure, if it's my body they're going to hack to pieces, I might as well get some of the reward. If there is any."

Rae grinned. "That's my girl."

"You think it's a good idea?"

"I think it's a great idea. What have I always told you?"

"That I'm the only one who's gonna look out for me." Calla recited the line dutifully. They'd discussed it about a million times over the years.

"Exactly. You need to protect your interests. And this right here might be your last chance to do that." Rae touched the papers again. "Do you have any idea how valuable your blood might be?"

Calla had done a Google search the night before: How much is a cure for cancer worth? The number it produced was eye-popping. Even a fraction of a percent could be worth millions and millions of dollars.

"*If* they're right."

"That's starting to sound a lot more likely than it did two weeks ago."

Calla had told her about the lab mice and the disappearing melanoma.

"We'll see," Calla said. "Nothing's for sure yet." She touched her cheek and let out a soft laugh. "It's kind of ironic. My skin's caused me problems my whole life. And now, it might hold the key to curing cancer. How crazy is that?"

"I always said you were special."

"Or it could be nothing."

"Either way, you need to cover your bases. I know a lawyer who can help with that. Denise is a real bulldog. She'll make sure you get what you deserve."

TWELVE

A MONTH LATER, Dr. Kraft called to make his weekly scheduling demands. Ever since her settlement with the hospital had been finalized, he'd treated Calla like an employee. She was being paid now; her time was his to command.

"Hey, Dr. K."

"I need to admit you to the hospital for a few days this week." He never troubled with pleasantries.

"Again?"

"Yes."

"Why?"

"Calla, we are this close to a breakthrough." She imagined him on the other end of the line, holding his thumb and forefinger millimeters apart to drive home his point. "But I need more tissue samples. Liver and kidney this time. We'll have to do them under general anesthesia, and I'd like to get at least thirty-six continuous hours of blood samples."

Calla winced. She still had stitches from the last round of biopsies.

"Okay, but could we start on Tuesday? Tomorrow is—"

"Be here tomorrow morning. Eight o'clock sharp."

He didn't bother saying goodbye before hanging up.

It took a while before Calla felt motivated enough to get off the couch and start packing her hospital bag. Rae's friend, Denise, had negotiated a good deal for her. A thirty-thousand-dollar lump sum payment for the not-surgery. The two-hundred-and-fifty-dollar daily stipend. And, after a good deal of back and forth, a quarter of one percent of any profits generated by the study or products derived from the study.

Almost all of the lump sum payment had gone to pay off Calla's half-finished bachelor's degree and some other bills. It was nice to be out of debt for once, but Dr. Kraft's demands on her time and body were starting to wear on her. Promise after promise of his elusive "final proof" left Calla feeling taken apart, piece by piece, drop by drop, with no end in sight.

. . .

The next morning, Calla climbed aboard the bus with a lot less bounce in her step than usual.

"Morning, Charlie."

She handed the driver a bundle wrapped in wax paper.

"Calla, you're too much. You know you don't need to bring me anything."

She waved away his concern. "It's no trouble. I had some fruit to use up, so I made a batch of banana nut muffins last night. Thought you might like one."

Charlie peeled back the paper and sniffed. "Smells delicious." He gave her a crinkly smile. "Thank you."

"You're welcome." Calla took her usual seat in the first row. She'd gotten into the habit of chatting with Charlie during her weekly rides to and from the hospital.

Since their first meeting, Calla had learned he was a retired engineer and a recent widower. He had a son who lived in Portland, but they only saw each other once or twice a year. Charlie was lonely but couldn't bear the idea of giving up the house he'd shared with his wife to move out west. So, he'd applied for a commercial driver's license and started driving for the city. He liked keeping busy and meeting new people. And he seemed particularly fond of Calla.

"If you don't mind me saying so, you're looking a little tired today." Charlie kept his eyes on the road as he steered the bus away from the curb.

"Didn't sleep well last night," Calla said. "It's going to be another long week."

"Another one?" Charlie had given her enough rides at this point to understand that a long week meant she wouldn't be going home for a few days. And that when she did, she'd be exhausted and possibly in pain from whatever tests and procedures Dr. Kraft had ordered.

"Yep."

Charlie shook his head. "You know, I managed to get my wife enrolled in a clinical trial after she was diagnosed, but it was nothing like this thing you're part of."

The bus pulled over to the curb. As a group of new passengers climbed aboard, Calla wondered how Charlie might feel if he knew the truth about the Panacea Project. She'd only shared the most basic details with him, and she hadn't even mentioned that it had anything to do with cancer. Dr. Kraft was becoming increasingly paranoid about what he called "operational security" and constantly reminded the research team not to discuss their work outside of the lab. As far as Charlie knew, Calla was going in for tests and scans that had something to do with her vitiligo—which wasn't a complete lie. She felt sure, though, that Charlie would support the work they were doing, even if whatever good resulted from it would come too late to save his sweet Mary from cervical cancer.

Charlie exuded a warm, paternal air that Calla had never experienced before. It would have been nice to fully share this part of her life with him—to get his advice and possibly some encouragement. But more and more lately, she was glad she hadn't. What would Charlie say if she admitted that her commitment to the study was waning? That the endless grind of tests and scans and x-rays and procedures was becoming too much? Would he still be her friend if he knew that part of her was beginning to wish that none of this had ever happened?

A glance out the window told her the hospital was two stops away. Enough ruminating. Calla pulled her phone out and sent a text to Reuben: Lab rat #1 is three minutes out.

He replied with a thumbs-up emoji.

Charlie caught her eye as she stood to exit and gave her a serious look. "Take care of yourself. I worry about you."

"I'm fine, Charlie. Just a little tired, that's all. See you in a few days."

Ever the gentleman, Charlie tipped his hat and pulled the lever to open the bus door. Reuben was waiting with his ubiquitous wheelchair at the bottom of the steps.

"Seriously, Reuben? Haven't I told you about a hundred times that I'm capable of walking into the hospital on my own?"

"And haven't I told *you* about a hundred times that it doesn't matter? You're precious cargo. And you look exhausted." He patted the seat of the wheelchair. "Sit."

"Fine," Calla grumbled as she complied, trying to secure her bags and muffin tin so they wouldn't slide off her lap.

"Honey, you baked!" Reuben exclaimed in mock surprise.

"When do I not bake?"

"What'd you bring this time?"

"Banana nut muffins."

"Good! Ralph hates those."

"That's a good thing?"

"Yup. It means I don't have to share with that human garbage disposal."

"Don't hold back, Reuben. Tell me how you really feel."

He laughed. "You ready to roll?"

"Ready as I'll ever be."

As Reuben pushed her up the sidewalk toward the main entrance, Calla asked, "What's on tap for today?"

"First stop, imaging."

"What is it this time? CT scan, MRI, x-ray?"

"CT. Dr. K wants to check that spot on your kidney."

Calla tilted her head back and gave Reuben her best stink eye. "Someone's keeping track of all the radiation I'm being exposed to, right? Cuz I'm worried I might start glowing at some point."

"Testy, testy."

Reuben pushed her through a double set of automatic doors and turned left toward the hallway that led to the red elevator bank. Imaging was on the third floor. Calla figured she could get there with her eyes shut at this point.

They slowed to a stop in front of the elevators. Reuben pushed the call button, then leaned back against the wall so he was facing her. "I know you're getting sick of all these tests."

"It's fine."

"No, it's not. It's way more than you signed up for. And it's my fault you're even stuck in this position."

"You? Why?"

He blew out a big breath. "Because I'm the one who told Dr. Kraft about you in the first place. He told me to be on the lookout for any patients that might be helpful to his research. So, when I heard about what happened during your surgery, I told him." His voice was laced with guilt.

"Don't feel bad," Calla said. "You know as well as I do that he was going to find out one way or another." She grabbed his hand and squeezed it. "I'm glad it was you and not some other random person."

The elevator dinged. Reuben gave her a smile. "Thanks," he said, then took up his position behind her chair. "Alright, then. Let's go get you scanned. I've got something fun planned for afterward."

· · ·

An hour later, they were headed to an unfamiliar wing of the hospital.

"Where are we going?" Calla asked for the third time.

"Patience. You'll see soon enough."

They turned a corner and were greeted by a large, multi-colored sign lettered in a playful font: Pediatric Cancer Care Unit.

"Reuben, wait, I'm not so sure about this."

"Relax, love." He steered her into an airy common area where ten kids were gathered around a large table. A red-haired woman was teaching them to make paper butterflies.

Reuben pushed Calla up to an empty spot at the table and leaned down to whisper in her ear, "Just give it a shot. For me. You never know. You might enjoy yourself."

He gave the woman a wave and then skedaddled before Calla could protest any further.

"Welcome," she greeted Calla. "My name's Monica. I'm an art therapist here at the hospital. Would you like to introduce yourself to the class?"

Calla looked around at all the little faces turned expectantly toward her. "Hi," she said shyly. "I'm Calla."

A chorus of voices replied, "Hi, Calla!"

"We're making butterflies for the common room wall," Monica explained. She gestured toward the materials piled in the middle of the table. "The first step is to decorate the wings. They're already cut out, so grab some markers and have fun."

Calla snagged two butterfly wings. As she picked through the marker options, the little girl next to her asked, "Would you like to share mine?"

She slid a set of markers, neatly lined up in a metal case, into an open space on the table between them.

"Are you sure? Those look pretty special."

The little girl nodded. "My grandma gave them to me. I don't mind sharing. Just as long you promise to put them back in the right place when you're done."

Calla smiled. "I promise. Thank you."

She selected a purple marker and started doodling on one of her paper wings. "What's your name?"

"Lizzie." The little girl didn't look up from her work. She was wearing flannel pajamas and a crocheted cap with a big pink flower on it. A nasogastric tube was taped to her left cheek.

"It's nice to meet you, Lizzie. I like your hat."

"Thank you. I have one for every day of the week, all in different colors. My mom made them."

"That was nice of her."

"She doesn't like for me to be cold." Lizzie capped the marker she was using and set it back into the case. She glanced at Calla. "Your hair is pretty. I miss my hair."

A lump formed in Calla's throat. "I bet you do."

"Does your skin look like that because you have cancer?"

Calla briefly marveled at the matter-of-fact way children asked questions. She wished more adults were as direct. "No," she said. "This is just the way I was born."

"So, you don't have cancer?"

"Not right now." Calla tried to think of the simplest way to explain her situation. "I did, but it went away. My doctors are trying to understand why that happened."

"Mine went away for a while, too." Lizzie's attention was back on her project. "But then it came back."

"I'm sorry, Lizzie." She was fighting tears now.

"Me too," the little girl said wistfully. "I had to miss the end of third grade." She bent her head lower over the butterfly wing she was decorating. "I hate cancer."

"I hate it, too," Calla whispered as the lump slid down her throat and lodged somewhere near her heart.

She looked at the little faces gathered around the table and tried to comprehend the enormous toll cancer was taking right in front of her. And this was in just one room, in one hospital, in one city. The true scope of cancer's carnage—the millions of people worldwide afflicted and fighting—was almost unfathomable. If it was within her power to even *try* bringing an end to it, who was she to deny Lizzie or anyone else that chance?

Calla's chest softened as she filled with a renewed sense of purpose and clarity. Temporary inconvenience and a little pain were nothing compared to what these children were going through.

She considered Lizzie, working so earnestly on her butterfly project, and silently vowed: *I will do whatever it takes to make sure you get to go to the fourth grade.*

All too soon, Reuben reappeared beside her. "Time to go."

Lizzie looked up at him. "But she hasn't finished her butterfly yet."

"I know, but I need to take her to the lab for a blood draw," Reuben explained.

The little girl gave Calla a knowing look. "I have to do those a lot, too. I used to be afraid of them, but now they use my port." She patted a spot on her chest just below her collar bone. "I like it better that way. It doesn't hurt as much."

Calla shook her head admiringly. "Lizzie, I think you're the bravest person I've ever met. Would you do a favor for me?"

Lizzie gave her a calculating look. "What's the favor?"

Calla laughed. "Smart girl. Always a good idea to know what you're getting into first, isn't it?" She held out her butterfly wings. "Will you finish this for me and hang it next to yours on the wall?"

Lizzie cocked her head. "That depends. Will you come back to visit me?"

"I'm planning on it."

Lizzie smiled and took the paper wings from Calla. "Deal."

As soon as they were back on the elevator, Calla gave Reuben the stink eye. "You are one manipulative son of a bitch. You know that?"

"Who, me?"

"Yes, you!"

"Don't be mad," he said, sounding concerned she might actually be. "I just thought it might help if—"

"If you reminded me what we're fighting for?"

"Well, yeah, something like that."

Calla let him stew for another second or two before dropping any pretense of displeasure. "Well, you were right. That was exactly what I needed today. Thank you."

"You're welcome." Reuben's relief was evident. "Now, let's get you to the lab. I've got one more surprise for you once we're done there."

THIRTEEN

AT REUBEN'S INSISTENCE, Calla's had her hands pressed tightly over her eyes. She had tried to keep track of the turns they'd taken after exiting the lab, but she suspected Reuben was walking her in circles. They could be anywhere in the hospital at this point.

"Okay, I've paid my blood tribute. What's the surprise?"

"Calla, the defining characteristic of a surprise is the fact that it is unexpected. I'm not about to ruin it by telling you what it is before we get there."

"Where is there?"

"Girl, I swear I'm about to turn this wheelchair around and take you back to Ralph."

Calla giggled.

Finally, the wheelchair slowed. "Almost there," Reuben said. "No peeking!"

The chair stopped.

"Can I look now?"

"Not . . . quite . . . yet." Calla felt him set the brakes on each wheel. "All right. Now!"

She dropped her hands from her eyes and immediately clapped them over her mouth.

"SURPRISE!"

It looked as though the entire day shift of nurses, technicians, and doctors on call for her floor had gathered outside Calla's hospital room beneath dozens of balloons and a huge banner that exclaimed: Happy Birthday Calla!

Rae stood in the center of the group, clutching a huge cake festooned with twenty-three burning candles. She beamed at Calla and then launched into a rollicking version of "Happy Birthday."

Once Calla had blown out her candles and greeted everyone, she turned to Reuben. "How did you know today was my birthday?"

"You're my friend. Friends know each other's birthdays."

"I don't know your birthday."

"It's April twenty-third."

Calla frowned. "Great, now I feel like an asshole."

"Don't beat yourself up. I have to look at your date of birth every damn time I put a sticker on a tube of your blood or some other sample. It's burned into my brain at this point."

"Point taken. Seriously, though, this is the nicest birthday I've had in a long time."

Reuben leaned down and hugged her.

"Just one thing," Calla said once he straightened back up. "Am I allowed to get out of this chair now?"

Reuben laughed and held out his hand. "All right. But only because it's your birthday."

Calla stood up and was immediately grabbed from behind.

"Happy birthday, sweetie!" Rae turned Calla around and pressed a kiss against her cheek. "Would you like to open your present now?"

"You didn't need to get me a present." Calla looked at all the people milling around her—laughing, talking, passing out slices of birthday cake. "This is more than enough."

Rae looked at Reuben and said, "If she doesn't want it, I'll take it."

"She's gonna want it," Reuben said. He tilted his head toward Calla's hospital room. "Come on. I left it on your bed."

Calla followed her friends into the room. She was shocked to find that it was filled with flowers and balloons. "Did the two of you do all of this, too?"

"No, honey," Rae answered her. "These are from people who work at the hospital. You've made quite an impression on the folks here."

"She's right," Reuben said. "Everyone knows you're something special. And I might have let it slip that today was your birthday," he added, "to one or two or maybe twenty people." He handed her a box wrapped in floral paper. "Here. This is from Rae, Dr. Pemmaraju, and me."

"Where is Dr. Pemmaraju?"

"I don't know. She was supposed to meet us here." Reuben pulled his phone from his pocket and checked the screen. "She hasn't texted me. Something must have come up. Go ahead and open it. She wouldn't want you to wait."

Calla ripped off the paper, revealing a sleek white box. "No way," she breathed. It was a brand-new iPad.

"You like it?" Reuben asked, grinning like the Cheshire Cat.

"I love it."

"We all chipped in for a Netflix subscription, too," Rae added. "Now you can binge-watch *The Great British Baking Show* to your heart's content."

"That will definitely make the overnight stays a lot more enjoyable." Calla beamed. "Thank you."

Before she could pull them into a group hug, Dr. Pemmaraju dashed into the room, a wild look in her eye. "It's out!" she cried.

"What's out?" Reuben asked.

"Dr. Kraft just got a call from a reporter at the *New York Times*. Someone leaked a story about the study."

FOURTEEN

CALLA, REUBEN, DR. PEMMARAJU, AND RAE were gathered in Calla's hospital room, their eyes glued to the television hanging above her bed.

"Researchers are using the blood and bone marrow of a local woman to cure cancer in lab animals. Could this lead to the miracle cure so many cancer patients have been waiting for? Tune in to the nightly news at six for more on this breaking story."

The story was spreading like wildfire—promos plastered on every local and cable news station and sensational headlines at the top of nearly every online platform they checked.

"Facebook and Twitter are blowing up." Reuben didn't even bother to look up from his phone. "This is insane!"

Finally, Rae scooped up the remote control and clicked off the television. "I don't understand why this is happening so fast," she said. "Wouldn't most reporters dismiss this as a hoax without some sort of proof? No offense to the work you're doing, but I wouldn't believe it if someone told me they'd discovered the cure for cancer. Not without some pretty convincing evidence."

"That's the problem." Dr. Pemmaraju was curled up in an armchair near the window, staring into space. "Someone leaked a draft of the paper Dr. Kraft and I were working on that summarized our findings so far. And all of the data backing up our conclusions."

"So, what they're saying is true?" Rae pointed at the lifeless television screen. "Calla's blood really can cure cancer?"

"We still have a lot of work to do to verify it," Dr. Pemmaraju said, her voice quiet. "But yes, based on our most recent results, something in Calla's blood or bone marrow can cure some, if not all, types of cancer." She cast an apologetic look at Calla. "I'm sorry you had to find out this way. We wanted to wait until we were absolutely certain."

"Ho-ly shit," Reuben whispered.

"My god." Rae slumped back in her chair.

Calla said nothing. She looked down at her hands, trying to visualize the blood coursing through them, traveling an endless loop from her organs to her arteries and veins and capillaries and back again. What power lay just beneath the surface of her skin? And why had she been chosen to possess it?

"And this was documented in the paper that was leaked?" Rae asked.

"Yes."

"Who had access to the paper?" Reuben asked.

"As far as I know, just Dr. Kraft, me, and . . ." Dr. Pemmaraju frowned.

"And?" Reuben prompted her.

"Ralph. He was the only other person with access to the database."

"Ralph." Reuben spat out the name. "It wouldn't surprise me at all if he did this."

"But why?" Calla asked. "What would he have to gain?"

"I don't know," Dr. Pemmaraju said. "Money?"

"Maybe he thought people should know what you're working on," Rae suggested. "To give them hope."

Reuben snorted. "Doubtful. Ralph Grimes isn't the altruistic type."

"Okay, then," Rae amended, "what if he knows someone who's sick? Maybe he thought getting the word out about your research right now could help them somehow."

"I suppose that's possible," Dr. Pemmaraju mused. "The publication process is pretty slow, even under the best of circumstances. Between peer review and revisions, it can take up to a year before a paper sees the light of day. And we were hitting some roadblocks that threatened to slow us down."

"What kind of roadblocks?" Calla asked.

"Dr. Kraft had put out feelers to editors at some of the major journals, just to get an idea of where the paper might have the best chance of being accepted. We were hoping to qualify for an expedited review process since our research has the potential to dramatically alter the landscape of cancer treatment. But he was getting some pretty intense skepticism in response to his inquiries. A lot of people think we're tilting at windmills. And it doesn't help that he has a reputation for being difficult to work with."

"So, it would be a while before the paper got published," Calla said. "If it got published at all."

"Yes."

"Did Ralph know that?"

"Probably. Dr. Kraft wasn't shy about airing his frustrations in the lab."

"That's for damn sure," Reuben agreed.

"I don't know," Calla said, her tone doubtful. "If Ralph wanted to help someone, why would he risk getting kicked off the research team?"

"Who knows?" Reuben threw his hands up. "Maybe to spite Dr. Kraft. They've never really seen eye to eye."

Calla turned to Dr. Pemmaraju. "What about Dr. Kraft? Is there any chance he's the leak?"

"Absolutely not. Prior publication of a paper is a big no-no for medical journals. Dr. Kraft would never risk a stunt like this."

"How's he taking the news?"

"About how you'd expect. When I left his office, he was on the phone screaming at someone on the legal team about suing the *New York Times* for theft of intellectual property."

An uneasy silence fell over the group.

Rae stood up and glanced out the window overlooking the hospital's main entrance. "What's done is done," she said with an air of quiet finality. "And all this speculating isn't going to help us solve the bigger problem we're about to have on our hands."

"What's that?" Calla asked.

"A news truck just pulled up. I'd bet good money they know the patient they're looking for is somewhere in this building." She locked eyes with Calla. "No one knows it's you, Calla. Not yet, at least." A worry line creased her forehead. "God help us when they figure it out."

FIFTEEN

THE FOLLOWING MORNING, Calla noticed a surge of unfamiliar people—nurses, doctors, even other patients—peeking into her room. The word, it seemed, was out among the denizens of the hospital, and it wasn't surprising. Too many people had heard about her "miracle" surgery not to put the pieces together. But the blatant invasion of her privacy was jarring.

"After all these years, you'd think I'd be used to being stared at," she commented to Rae in a voice she hoped would carry out to the latest pair of gawkers in scrubs.

"That's it!" Rae jumped up from her chair. "I'm shutting the door."

Calla laughed when Rae leaned out the door and called, "HIPAA compliance is a real thing, you know!"

"Thanks, Rae."

"You're welcome." Rae settled back down in her chair and glanced at the cell phone that had been glued to Calla's hand since she'd woken up two hours earlier. "Honey," she said gently, "obsessing over this isn't going to change anything."

"I know." Calla tossed the phone onto her bedside table. "I just feel so helpless sitting here, waiting for my name to be plastered all over the Internet."

"I'm not so sure it'll happen that way. No news organization worth its salt is going to publish your name without permission." Rae shook her head slowly. "I'm starting to wonder if we should be more worried about the wrong person overhearing hospital gossip."

"Oh, come on, Rae. What do you think is going to happen?"

"I don't know," Rae said. "But desperate people do some pretty desperate things." She glanced at her watch. "Crap. I'm late for work."

"Go," Calla said. "I'm good. I promise. Thanks for coming to check on me."

Rae brushed her fingers lightly against Calla's cheek and then stood up to leave. "I'll be back this evening. Call me if you need anything before then, okay?"

"You don't need to come back. Go home and get some rest. And stop worrying! I'm safer here than I would be at my apartment."

Rae did not look convinced. "Everyone involved in this is going to have an angle, Calla. Remember that."

"When did you become so cynical?"

"I was born cynical. Just be careful, okay?"

Someone knocked on the door and pushed it open halfway. "Can I come in?"

"Reuben? Of course!"

He slipped in and closed the door behind him. "I have some news about a certain lab technician."

"Ralph?" Calla asked.

"He just got canned for leaking the paper. Dr. K's so mad he insisted on having two security guards escort him from the building."

Calla let out a low whistle. "Wow. So, he really did it?"

"Yup. From what I heard, he was trying to cover his tracks when the IT guys found evidence that he'd downloaded the paper and a bunch of data onto an external device. They think maybe it was a thumb drive. Something he could stick in his pocket and sneak out of the hospital."

"Unbelievable." Rae shook her head in disgust. "What did he have to say for himself?"

"Not much. Some whiny bullshit about being cut out of the loop. He's just mad that he got caught. Probably can't believe he wasn't able to pull one over on the lightweights in the IT department."

"I never met the man," Rae declared, "but good riddance."

"You can say that again." Reuben bumped fists with her.

"On that note, I'm off." Rae pointed at Reuben. "Take care of her while I'm gone."

Reuben gave her a salute. "Yes, Ma'am."

Once Rae had left, Reuben turned to Calla. "You ready to head down to the OR for your biopsies?"

"Do I have to?"

"Yes. But if it helps, I've got some excellent drugs waiting for you."

"Now you're talking." Calla swung her legs over the side of the bed and gave Reuben her most winsome smile. "Any chance you'll let me walk?"

"Nope." He pulled Calla's wheelchair out from its resting place next to her bed and gestured for her to take a seat.

"You have an unnatural relationship with this thing. You know that, right?"

"How many times do I have to tell you? It's hospital policy."

"Yeah, yeah." Calla sat down and held her feet up while Reuben folded down the footrests. "Ralph turned out to be a real rat, didn't he?"

"I think we all learned an important lesson from our time with Ralph."

"And that is?"

"Never trust a man who doesn't like banana nut muffins."

SIXTEEN

TWO DAYS LATER, Calla felt well enough to get out of bed and go for a walk. The stitches from her surgical biopsies (Dr. Kraft had excised small chunks from her liver and a kidney) still stung, and she was tired as hell but healing quickly.

Calla hadn't forgotten her promise to Lizzie. As soon as she finished her breakfast and struggled into a pair of sweatpants, she set out for the pediatric oncology unit. It was a slow, painful walk. But for once, it was a walk and not a ride in a wheelchair.

When she arrived in the common area, she saw Monica working with a group of three children much younger than Lizzie.

"I don't know if you remember me. My name's Calla. I was here a few days ago working on the butterfly project."

Monica smiled. "It's nice to see you again! Did you come to see the finished product? It looks great."

"And Lizzie. I promised her I'd visit."

Monica's face fell.

"What's wrong?" Calla asked.

Monica turned the children over to a nearby colleague, then took Calla by the arm and led her to a quiet corner of the room.

"I'm sorry to have to tell you this, but Lizzie is in isolation. She picked up an infection, and it turned into pneumonia. They had to intubate her last night."

"But she was fine three days ago."

"I know," Monica said sadly. "Pneumonia can develop very quickly in leukemia patients. Especially during treatment, when their immune systems are compromised."

"Is she going to be okay?"

"I hope so. She's a strong kid. A real fighter."

"Can I see her?"

Monica thought for a second. "If her curtain is open, you might be able to see through her hall window, but you can't go into her room. And she's heavily sedated, so she won't know you're there."

"That's okay. I'd just really like to see her."

"Come with me." Monica walked her past a nurses' station and down a hallway lined with patient rooms. They slowed as they approached a woman standing alone, arms wrapped around herself, gazing into a large window that looked into one of the rooms.

"Anne?" Monica's voice was gentle.

The woman ducked her head and quickly wiped her cheeks before answering. "Hi, Monica." She sounded exhausted.

"Anne, this is Calla. She met Lizzie a few days ago while we were working on an art project." Monica motioned from Anne to Calla and back again. "Calla, this is Anne. Lizzie's mother."

Anne grasped Calla's hand. "It's nice to meet you. Lizzie told me about meeting you. She doesn't have many opportunities to make new friends. Thank you for being so kind to her."

"She was kind to me," Calla replied. "She's a special girl."

"How is she doing today?" Monica asked.

"About the same. I'm hoping that's a good sign, you know, that it hasn't gotten any worse."

Monica placed her hand on Anne's arm. "I hope that, too." She glanced at Calla. "I should get back to my class. Can I get either of you anything before I go?"

"No, thank you," Calla said as Anne shook her head.

"I'll see you later, then."

As Monica walked away, both Calla and Anne turned toward the window. Lizzie looked smaller than Calla remembered, dwarfed by her bed and the tubes and wires crisscrossing her body.

When Anne spoke again, she was on the verge of tears. "She's been fighting for so long. I feel like we're running out of time."

"I'm so sorry." Calla didn't know what else to say. No words could soothe the pain that the mother standing beside her was being forced to bear. She was surprised when Anne reached over and squeezed her hand.

"You're nice to come visit my baby. Not many people do that anymore. She'll be happy when I tell her. When she wakes up."

They stood together in silence, keeping vigil over Lizzie until a nurse came to check the little girl's vital signs. Calla parted from Anne with a hug and a promise to return soon.

Then she headed straight for the lab.

SEVENTEEN

"ABSOLUTELY NOT." Dr. Kraft was adamant.

"Why not?"

"We are nowhere near ready to give your blood to random patients, Calla. There are too many risks."

"What risks? You told me that my blood type makes me a universal donor." Calla glared at him. "And Lizzie is not some random patient. She's a little girl fighting for her life."

"All cancer patients are fighting for their lives. Get used to it."

Calla turned to Dr. Pemmaraju, hoping for some backup. "Why can't we—"

"The answer is no!" Dr. Kraft exploded. "It's bad enough that I have to deal with fallout from the fiasco with Ralph. We cannot afford any more mistakes!"

"But Lizzie's going to die if we don't do something! Don't hospitals make exceptions for people like her? I've read about it. It's called compassionate use, right?"

Dr. Kraft set down his clipboard. "Okay, why don't we indulge this little fantasy you're playing out in your head? Let's say we spend precious hours putting together a presentation to convince the hospital's ethics panel to give this girl your blood. Let's say they agree to our proposal. Let's say it saves her. Then what?

"Are we morally obligated to give your blood to every cancer patient in this hospital? What about the cancer patients in the rest of the country?

What about the rest of the world? You are one human being, Calla, with a limited amount of blood circulating throughout your body at any given point in time. Even if we take just your white blood cells, which your body can replace rather quickly, you would still be hooked up to a machine for two to three hours, at a minimum, every time we needed more, which would be all of the time."

Calla crossed her arms and wondered what Dr. Kraft would say if he could see Anne keeping her desperate watch over Lizzie.

"How do we decide who gets priority? Why is your friend more important than the next patient? How many people will die waiting in line for your blood? And that's assuming your blood cures all of their cancers, which we haven't come close to establishing at this point." His eyes widened. "Are you beginning to comprehend the ethical and logistical dilemmas we are facing here? What we need is time to figure out how your immune system is beating cancer, and then find a way to replicate that in a scalable manner outside of your body, not emotional outbursts."

"And in the meantime," Calla said flatly, "Lizzie dies."

"That is the hard, ugly truth of this. People are going to die before we find a cure. But we are working as fast as humanly possible. And don't forget," he added, "cancer patients still have treatment options."

"Not all of them. Not Lizzie."

Dr. Kraft picked his clipboard back up. "We're done discussing this."

"I'm not!" Calla threw her hands up in frustration. "I don't even know why I bothered coming in here. It's my blood. I'll do what I want with it."

"No, you won't," Dr. Kraft said coldly.

"Excuse me?"

"As a participant in this research study, you won't be able to convince a licensed physician to transfuse your blood into a cancer patient without my blessing, which I will not give. If you recall, you signed an agreement to that effect. Think about what could happen if the transfusion didn't work. What if it hastened this little girl's death for reasons we can't explain? Her parents could sue us. They could shut the study down and destroy any chance we have of finding a cure, all because we were too hasty. As doctors and scientists, our first priority is to do no harm. I will not abandon that principle just because you feel bad for some kid!" He jabbed a finger in the direction of the door. "Walk her back to her room, Juhi. I don't need this distraction right now."

"Come with me, Calla." Dr. Pemmaraju took Calla gently by the arm.

As soon as the door shut behind them, Calla blinked back the tears that were threatening to roll down her cheeks. "It's like he's missing a sensitivity chip."

Dr. Pemmaraju nodded. "I know, but like it or not, it's his study. He's in charge. And he does have a point. However bluntly he made it. We have to follow strict protocols if we want to have any chance of getting a treatment or drug approved for widespread use by the FDA. Those are the rules."

"I know," Calla said. "And don't get me wrong. I know you're doing your best. Dr. Kraft, too," she forced herself to add. "But sometimes it feels like the people we're trying to help get lost in the bureaucracy of it all. The peer review, the replications, the protocols." Her shoulders slumped. "What good is this gift if I never get to use it?"

Dr. Pemmaraju wrapped her arm around Calla as they walked down the hall. "Just be patient. I know it doesn't seem like it right now, but we're making progress."

EIGHTEEN

ANOTHER DAY CAME AND WENT without Calla's name appearing in the news. After the initial frenzy, excitement about the study seemed to be fading without new information to fuel the media's constant need for updates. Calla was just starting to relax when the rug of relative anonymity was yanked out from under her. This time for good.

She had just finished eating dinner in her room when she received a text from Rae. It was short and to the point: Turn the TV on right now. Channel 13.

Calla grabbed the remote and pointed it at the television. Channel 13 was airing its nightly network news broadcast. The anchor was introducing a special-interest segment.

"Earlier this week, the world was transfixed by the news that a Houston woman's blood and bone marrow has cured cancer in lab animals. Is a treatment for humans on the horizon? Vicky Nguyen from our affiliate station in Houston joins us now with an exclusive live interview that may shed some light on this developing story."

The close-up of the anchor's face was replaced by a shot of a female reporter in a navy-blue sheath dress, perched on an upholstered armchair. Calla had watched this woman report the news for years, but never in her wildest dreams (or nightmares) had she imagined being the subject of one of those reports. She sat bolt upright on her bed, eyes glued to the screen, simultaneously curious and terrified about what Vicky Nguyen was about to say.

"Cancer is one of the leading causes of death in the world. Last year alone, over seventeen million new cases were diagnosed worldwide. Nearly two million of those were in the United States. The search for a cure is one of the great medical pursuits of our time. But despite advancements in diagnostic tools and treatments, a definitive cure has eluded doctors and scientists. That may be about to change. Two months ago, a seemingly wrong-patient surgery led to the discovery that one woman's immune system may be capable of not just fighting the disease but eradicating it. Joining me now is one of the original members of the research team that made the discovery and is working to relegate cancer to the annals of history."

The camera zoomed out to reveal Ralph sitting across from Vicky on a matching armchair, looking more dapper than Calla had ever seen him in khakis and a button-down shirt that he'd actually bothered to tuck in.

"Creep!" Calla yelled at the screen.

Vicky continued her narration. "Ralph Grimes is a twenty-eight-year-old medical lab technician. Until recently, he managed a small laboratory investigating a case in which a woman's cancerous brain tumor mysteriously disappeared." She smiled warmly at Ralph. "Thank you for talking with me today, Mr. Grimes."

Ralph tugged on his pant legs. "You're, uh, you're welcome."

Calla noted with a malicious satisfaction that his acne hadn't improved.

Vicky leaned forward, and the interview began in earnest. "Up until a few days ago, you were employed at a research lab that was doing some very interesting work in the field of cancer immunology. Can you tell us about your role at the lab?"

"Sure." Ralph flicked his bangs out of his eyes. "I am—I was the lab tech, so I was in charge of running tests on things like blood and tissue samples, keeping the lab stocked and sanitized, maintaining the database, stuff like that. I also handled most of the IT issues that came up."

"And who were you working for?"

Ralph hesitated for a moment before answering. "Dr. Carson Kraft at St. Peregrine's Cancer Center."

"What type of research was Dr. Kraft doing?"

"At first, he was focused on developing therapies that use the immune system to treat cancer. Immunotherapy. Then he got interested in the spontaneous regression of tumors."

"The spontaneous regression of tumors," Vicky repeated the words. "What does that mean, in layman's terms?"

"It refers to cases where a patient's tumor goes away on its own. With no treatment."

"And what, specifically, was Dr. Kraft's interest in this phenomenon?"

"He wanted to identify patients who had experienced spontaneous tumor regressions. He thought it could be useful to study their immune systems."

Vicky tilted her head slightly, clearly telegraphing her mounting interest. "Was he able to identify any such patients?"

Ralph licked his lips. "One. He found one."

"This would be the subject of a paper that was leaked to the press earlier this week. The one authored by Dr. Kraft?"

"Yes."

"Without revealing any identifiable personal information, what can you tell us about the patient?"

"She was originally diagnosed with a brain tumor. But during the surgery to remove it, the surgeon discovered that it was gone." Ralph paused. "She was exactly the type of patient Dr. Kraft was looking for."

"What happened next?"

"Dr. Kraft recruited her to join his study. She agreed, and we began trying to figure out what had happened to her tumor."

"And what did you find?"

"It was extraordinary. A series of tests charted a rapid decline in tumor markers in the days after the patient's surgery. Her body was literally killing off the cancer cells."

"You're saying her immune system was curing her cancer."

"That's exactly what I'm saying."

"If that's true, you're describing an extraordinary breakthrough in cancer research."

"I am."

Vicky switched gears. "Mr. Grimes, at the beginning of this interview, I mentioned that you were employed in Dr. Kraft's lab until earlier this week. What happened?"

This time, Ralph didn't miss a beat. "I was fired."

"Why were you fired?"

"Because I was the one who leaked Dr. Kraft's paper."

"You admit doing this?"

"I do."

"Why?"

Ralph took a deep breath. "Because I believed the patient's safety was at risk. Dr. Kraft is obsessed with proving his theory as quickly as possible. He was ordering too many blood draws and doing too many invasive procedures to obtain tissue samples."

"I'm not sure I follow. How would leaking the paper to the press protect the patient's safety? Why not file a complaint with the hospital?"

Ralph's voice took on a defensive edge. "I tried talking to Dr. Kraft, but he wouldn't listen to me. No one at that hospital was going to listen to me. They were all drooling over how much money his research was going to bring in. The only way to get anyone to pay attention was to go public."

"What about the patient? Did you share your concerns with her?"

Ralph frowned. "Well, no. I didn't."

"Why not?"

"I guess I didn't want to scare her."

"I see." Vicky glanced down at a piece of paper she was holding in her lap. "You didn't talk to the patient, but you did find time to contact a literary agent, isn't that right?"

Ralph suddenly looked deeply uncomfortable. "How did you—"

"And that agent," Vicky spoke over him, "just closed a seven-figure deal on your behalf with a major publisher. Are you sure that didn't factor into your decision to leak the paper?"

Ralph's eyes darted from side to side. "I, uh . . ."

"Mr. Grimes?"

"Say something, you fucking rat!" Calla cried.

"Mr. Grimes," Vicky repeated. "Do you have a response?"

Ralph's mouth settled into a defensive pout. "Look, I'm just protecting my interests here. Everyone's going to make money off of this. And I've more than earned a share of it." His voice took on a plaintive tone. "But I swear I'm not the bad guy. Dr. Kraft is! He'll do whatever it takes to make sure he goes down in history as the man who cured cancer. If someone doesn't stop him, he'll drain every drop of blood and squeeze every ounce of bone marrow out of her body to do it." He turned and looked directly into the camera. "Listen to me. Someone needs to protect her. Her name is Calla Hammond. She's a patient at St.—"

Vicky's mouth dropped open in shock. "Mr. Grimes!"

Before either of them could say another word, their microphones were cut off. The camera panned away from Ralph and zoomed in on Vicky, who looked furious. Her eyes were fixed somewhere off camera. After a few moments, she nodded.

"Ladies and gentlemen, we are experiencing some technical difficulties in the studio and need to take a short commercial break."

Calla stared blankly at the screen as the image of Vicky's face transitioned to a commercial for heartburn medication. Within seconds, both her cell phone and the landline in her room began to ring.

NINETEEN

"WHAT HE DID WAS ILLEGAL, VALERIE. I want to know what your people are going to do about it!"

Dr. Kraft had been storming around one of the hospital's conference rooms for five minutes, raging about Ralph's many misdeeds over the past week.

Calla leaned over to whisper in Dr. Pemmaraju's ear. "What do you think pissed him off more? The fact that Ralph told everyone my name, or that he basically called Dr. Kraft an asshole on TV?"

Dr. Pemmaraju tittered. "My money's on the second," she whispered back. "Definitely the second."

Calla and Dr. Pemmaraju were huddled at one end of the long table that dominated the room, sitting as far away from Dr. Kraft as possible. At the other end sat Valerie Wright, a petite blonde woman sporting a stylish bob and a black power suit. She had introduced herself as the hospital's director of communications and marketing. Her cool demeanor was a powerful foil for Dr. Kraft's restless anger.

"Legal is working on a strategy, isn't that right, Jackson?" Valerie looked toward a man sitting across the table from her. Calla recognized him from their meeting a month earlier.

"Who the hell are you?" Dr. Kraft demanded.

Jackson sat up a little straighter and adjusted his tie. "I'm Jackson Albright, Sir, assistant general counsel to the hospital. I don't believe we've—"

"Why isn't Patrick here? Is this meeting not important enough for his highness, the general counsel?"

Jackson cleared his throat. "Sir, Mr. Beckham is on a plane headed to Houston as we speak. He's been on a family vacation in Hawaii, but he cut that short after the interview aired yesterday. And let me assure you that we've been strategizing by telephone ever since the initial leak."

"Fine, fine." Dr. Kraft threw himself into the chair at the head of the table. "Just tell me what the plan is."

"Well, first of all," Jackson said, "we'll be coordinating with the OCR about the disclosure of Ms. Hammond's protected health information."

"What's the OCR?"

"The Office of Civil Rights," Jackson explained. "It's the enforcement arm of Health and Human Services. They investigate HIPAA violations. They can impose civil penalties or refer the case to the Department of Justice if they determine there are grounds for a criminal investigation."

"That sounds like it will take a while," Dr. Kraft grumbled.

"It might," Jackson conceded. "But it's the process we have to follow."

Dr. Kraft slammed his hand down on the conference table. "Damn it!" he shouted. "That cannot be our only recourse! Ralph Grimes needs to pay for what he's done!"

"Calm down, Carson," Valerie said. "He wasn't finished."

Calla and Dr. Pemmaraju exchanged a look. No one ever called Dr. Kraft by his first name. It just wasn't done.

Valerie signaled for Jackson to continue.

"We also plan to sue to enforce the non-disclosure agreement Mr. Grimes signed when he started working for you, Dr. Kraft. And if he does publish a book, we'll go after every penny of his advance and any royalties he gets. We will bring the pain, Sir. I assure you of that."

Dr. Kraft did not look impressed. "What about the lies he told? We never argued about Calla's safety. He was just pissed I wouldn't credit him in the paper. Everything he said in that interview was bullshit, and people need to know it! I don't want to wait two years for some lawsuit to work its way through the legal system. I want something done now!"

Valerie rapped the table authoritatively. "That's where I come in. From now on, I'm in charge of messaging. Any contact with the media needs to be run through me. Understood?" She made eye contact with each person sitting around the table. They all nodded their assent. "Good. Now, our first step is to get the two of you," Valerie pointed to Dr. Kraft and then to Calla, "in front of a camera. I'd like to do a live interview during prime time on one of the networks."

"What?" Calla asked.

No one seemed to hear her.

"An interview," Dr. Kraft mused. "I like it." He shot Valerie a calculating look. "Who do we get to do it? And when?"

"I'm still finalizing the details," Valerie said, "but *ABC World News Tonight* has offered us a ten-minute slot on Monday night. In-studio. They'd like to keep the story in the family since it originated with one of their affiliates. And they're the only ones willing to do it on such short notice. Everyone else wanted more time to research and prepare, but I think time is of the essence in this case. The longer we wait to respond to Mr. Grimes' allegations, the more it looks like we're trying to hide something." She glanced at Dr. Kraft. "What do you think?"

"When you say 'in-studio,'" he emphasized the words with air quotes, "where exactly do you mean?"

"New York."

Dr. Kraft frowned. "I hate New York. Why can't we do it down here?"

"They don't want to come down here."

"What if I don't want to go up there?"

"Then there won't be an interview," Valerie said flatly. "Carson, we're talking about less than a day of travel in exchange for taking control of the narrative. You want vindication? This is the fastest way to get it. Do you think you can put on your big boy pants and deal with a little inconvenience for me?"

Dr. Kraft pouted for a moment before answering. "Fine."

Valerie smiled smugly. "Thank you. That gives us two days to prepare. We'll fly up on Monday afternoon."

Calla raised her hand. "What if *I* don't want to give an interview?"

"Excuse me?" Dr. Kraft whipped his head around in her direction. It was the first time he'd acknowledged her presence since the meeting had started. "This doesn't work without you! You have to tell them Ralph was lying!" He looked back at Valerie and Jackson for support. "Tell her she has to give the interview. Isn't this sort of thing required by her agreement with the hospital?"

Jackson opened his mouth to respond, but Valerie held up her hand to silence him. "No, Carson, it's not. Calla's not promoting a movie. She's a participant in a research study who's just had her privacy violated in one of the most public ways possible." She turned toward Calla, her expression serious and sympathetic. "No one will force you to do anything, but I can't deny that this interview won't have the same impact without your participation. Can we discuss your concerns?"

Calla knew she was being handled but decided she preferred Valerie's conciliatory approach to Dr. Kraft's petulance.

"My name's out there now. I know there's nothing I can do to change that. But I'm not so sure throwing my face into the mix is such a great idea."

"It's only a matter of time before someone finds an old photo of you or takes a new one, Calla," Valerie replied. "If it hasn't already happened."

"Okay, fine, but do you really need *me*? It's not like I can answer questions about the study." Calla pointed at Dr. Kraft. "He's the brains of the operation. All I do is supply the raw materials."

"You're more than that, Calla," Valerie insisted. "Much more. You are the heart of this story. People want to see you. They want to hear from you." She paused for a moment. "Did you know that since the story broke on Monday, the hospital has received over a hundred letters and emails about the study?"

Calla shook her head.

"It's true," Valerie continued. "Almost all of them mentioned you. People want to thank you for what you are doing. Many of them are sick or have sick family members. You're a miracle to them. A beacon of hope." She stood up and began pacing up and down the room. "The telephone in the development office has been ringing off the hook all week. Donors are clamoring to pour money into this project. The amounts being discussed would turbocharge the pace of research. But now, thanks to Mr. Grimes, all of that is at risk. People are worried the study has been tainted. That you're being used against your will. We could be looking at an investigation." She slowed to a stop directly across the table from Calla. "We need to get out in front of this story before it's too late. And we need your help to do that." She glanced at Dr. Kraft. "Isn't that right, Carson?"

Dr. Kraft cleared his throat. "Listen, Calla," he said, clearly struggling to inject warmth into his voice. "I know I can be . . . a jerk. Sometimes."

Dr. Pemmaraju snorted. "Sometimes?"

"Okay," he conceded. "I'm a jerk most of the time. I'm selfish. I'm too focused on my work. Is that better?"

"Getting there," said Dr. Pemmaraju.

Dr. Kraft turned back to Calla. "But have I ever done anything to make you feel like you were in danger around me?"

"No," Calla admitted. And it was the truth. Dr. Kraft could be intense, grumpy, and unrelenting, but she'd never actually felt unsafe around him.

"Good, good." Dr. Kraft bobbed his head. "Then help me fix this. Don't let the work we've done go to waste." In a somewhat begrudging tone, he added, "Please."

Calla searched his face, wondering if this was a master manipulation or if she'd just glimpsed a more human side to Dr. Kraft. She decided to give him the benefit of the doubt.

"Okay. I'll go."

Valerie clapped her hands together. "That's settled then. Let's discuss logistics."

As she and Dr. Kraft launched into a discussion about plans for the trip, Calla looked at Dr. Pemmaraju.

"What about you?" she asked in a low voice. "Are you coming, too?"

"I think," Dr. Pemmaraju said slowly, "that it will be better for me to sit this one out. Too many cooks and all that."

"Are you sure?" Calla asked. "Because I think we should at least discuss it."

"I'm sure. Someone needs to keep the lab running while you two do damage control."

Their conversation was interrupted by Valerie, waving from the other end of the table.

"Calla! We need you for a minute."

Calla sighed. "Why do I get the feeling that the next forty-eight hours are going to suck?"

TWENTY

ON MONDAY AFTERNOON, Calla found herself staring out the window of a Cessna Citation XLS on loan from one of the hospital's board members. Valerie settled into one of the cushy leather seats across from her.

"How are you feeling?"

"Tired," Calla said.

"I'm so sorry about your friend."

Lizzie had died at noon the previous day. She'd never gotten off the ventilator. Never had a chance to say goodbye to her mother.

"You probably think it's silly for me to be upset about someone I barely knew," Calla said. "Dr. Kraft does."

Valerie looked serious. "Not at all. The death of a child is never easy to accept. For anyone."

"I should've tried harder to help her."

"I know it feels that way," Valerie said gently, "but she may have been past the point of help. Sometimes, there's nothing we can do."

"I don't believe that," Calla replied. "If my blood can do what everyone says it can do, then we should have tried." She looked back out the window. "Now, we'll never know."

Valerie sighed. "I'm sorry to ask this, Calla, especially right now, but I need to know. Can we count on you today?"

"I'm here, aren't I?"

"I'm afraid that's not good enough." Valerie leaned forward, closing the distance between them. "This interview doesn't work if you're not on board. If we're going to save the study, it's imperative that we restore Dr. Kraft's credibility. We can't do that unless you convince people that you're part of the team. A *willing* part of the team."

"I think you might have mentioned that once or twice over the past couple of days."

Valerie ignored the sarcasm. "Today could be a game-changer, Calla. With strong public support, we can increase funding for the study. Get political backing for expedited approval from the FDA for human trials." She locked eyes with Calla. "We do that, and you'll never have to wonder again if you did enough."

An announcement came over the intercom: "Folks, this is Captain Ibara. We've reached our cruising altitude of thirty-five thousand feet. Looks like we'll have a smooth ride all the way up to Teterboro, so please feel free to move about the cabin. Snacks and drinks are in the small fridge behind the cockpit here. There's a lavatory in the back. Enjoy the flight, and let us know if you have any questions."

Calla and Valerie sat in silence for a few minutes. Finally, Calla said, "Did you know that this is my first time on an airplane?"

Valerie sat back in her chair, looking a little bemused by the change of subject. "I did not."

"It's true. Never been on a plane." Calla laughed softly. "Who am I kidding? I've never been anywhere. Two months ago, I was a college drop-out shelving books at a library. Now I'm flying on a private plane to New York City, and they're talking about me on TV like I'm someone special." She shook her head. "My immune system can cure cancer, but I couldn't use it to save a little girl. Pretty much everything I thought I knew about the world has been turned upside down over the past couple of months, so you know what I'm going to do? I'm going to get myself a Coke and look out this window for a few hours. Because this is my first ride on an airplane, and I need some time to think." She stood up. "We're done prepping. I know what I need to do today, and I'm going to do it. And don't lecture me about the stakes. I know better than anyone else what they are."

TWENTY-ONE

THEY LANDED AT TETERBORO AIRPORT in New Jersey at 4:15 p.m., only twenty minutes behind schedule. A shiny black Suburban was waiting for them.

Dr. Kraft grunted appreciatively as they descended the stairs. "You can't deny that flying private has its perks."

"Let's go," Valerie said briskly. "Traffic into the city is going to be murder."

Calla spent the ride into Manhattan taking in every detail of the landscape whizzing past her. At first, she was disappointed. Lines of warehouses and strip centers gave way to residential areas that didn't look all that different from what she was used to seeing in Houston. But then they crossed the George Washington Bridge, and she caught her first glimpse of the city. The skyline seemed to stretch to infinity in every direction, resplendent beneath a cloudless sky. Calla had never seen such a dense thicket of buildings—it called to mind a vast, manmade forest pulsing with life and energy. They turned onto the Henry Hudson Parkway, and Valerie began to narrate their passage down the west side of the island, pointing out landmarks and giving Calla the general lay of the land. Eventually, they made their way into the city proper and turned north again, past Columbus Circle. (Calla felt a little jolt of recognition when she saw a sign for Broadway.) Finally, they passed Central Park and arrived at the ABC studios on West 66th Street.

As they pulled up to the building, Calla saw a crowd gathered near the doors. A number of people were holding signs with slogans like "Calla = the CURE" and "~~CANCER~~".

"Oh my god," she murmured.

The Suburban pulled over to the curb and rolled to a stop. Nearly in unison, every person on the sidewalk turned to see who had arrived.

"It's her!" someone yelled. "She's here!"

Cheers erupted from the crowd.

"How did they know we would be here?" Calla asked.

"ABC ran a promo about the interview last night," Valerie replied. "But this is . . . unexpected." She paused for a moment to gather her thoughts. "Okay, here's the plan. We get out of the car and head straight for the door to the building. No stopping. No talking to anyone. Got it?"

"Uh, I guess." Calla wasn't sure she was ready for this. She had just spotted a row of people sitting in wheelchairs, all of them bundled up against the brisk October air. Several were children.

Valerie addressed the driver. "If you could go around and get the door for them, we're ready."

She turned back to Calla and Dr. Kraft. "As soon as the door opens, go." She focused on Calla. "Don't be scared. These people are here to support you. Just smile and walk into the building."

They sat in silence for a few seconds, waiting for the driver to fight his way around to the passenger side of the car. The moment Valerie opened the front passenger door, he pulled on the rear door handle. Sound and light burst into the car, startling Calla. The tangy aromas of exhaust and cooked food and people packed together struck her full force.

Valerie grabbed Calla's arm and urged her out of the car. The crowd immediately surged forward, waving and shouting, threatening to engulf her. She tried to smile, but her breath caught somewhere in her chest. She shrank back from the onslaught of reaching hands. Valerie's grip was unrelenting, though, pressing her toward the curb.

"You're doing great," she said, her mouth close to Calla's ear, her voice calm and reassuring. "Just keep walking."

They mounted the sidewalk and had just begun to move past the line of wheelchairs when one of them suddenly rolled forward. A little boy sat in the seat, his legs covered with a blanket and a wool cap on his head. Calla's heart shifted. He looked so much like Lizzie.

"Please!" the woman behind him called out. "Please lay your hand on my son. He's dying!" Her voice was tinged with hysteria.

It seemed like such a simple request—a quick squeeze of a sick child's hand. Calla took a step in his direction. The woman's eyes lit up hopefully, but as Calla began to swing her hand forward, someone wrapped an iron-like arm around her shoulder and steered her away from the boy and his mother.

"Don't," Dr. Kraft said gruffly. "It won't help, and they'll all expect the same if you do it for him. We'll never make it inside."

Calla only had time for a quick glance over her shoulder—long enough to see the woman's face crumple in misery—before she was marched up to a revolving door. A security guard checked their IDs, then stepped aside to let them enter the building. Valerie squeezed into the first opening with Calla and pushed the door around until they were inside.

They were met by a woman holding a clipboard.

"Hi!" she chirped, giving them a megawatt smile. "I'm Mary Ann O'Malley."

Valerie stepped forward first. "Valerie Wright. We spoke on the phone."

"Nice to meet you in person." They shook hands.

"This is Calla Hammond and Dr. Carson Kraft." Valerie gestured to each of them in turn.

"Good to meet you both." Mary Ann exchanged a handshake with Dr. Kraft and then turned to greet Calla, who was still staring at the crowd gathered on the sidewalk. Several people were pressing their faces against the tinted windows, clearly hoping for one more look at the world's most famous cancer patient.

"Are you okay?" Mary Ann touched her shoulder.

Calla jumped a little. "I'm sorry. What did you say?"

"I was just asking if you're okay." Mary Ann followed Calla's gaze out the front windows. "That kind of attention can be disconcerting if you aren't used to it," she said knowingly. "And to be honest, most people never get used to it. Even the big-time celebrities." She wrapped her arm more fully around Calla and started guiding her toward an elevator bank. "Come on. Let's get you up to the green room."

As she led the group through the building, Mary Ann explained that she was the producer in charge of the interview. She would be their liaison while they were at the studio, and if they had any questions, they should come to her first. Calla liked her immediately. Mary Ann exuded competence, simultaneously acting as a tour guide, taking calls on her cell phone, and issuing orders to various people they passed, all while maintaining a brisk walking pace.

"There's the set." Mary Ann pointed to a cavernous-looking area on their right that was jammed with equipment and lights. The actual anchor desk and the backdrop behind it were smaller than Calla had imagined.

"Will we be sitting at the desk?" she asked, wondering how three people would fit behind it.

"No," Mary Ann replied as they skirted the back of the set. "You can't see it from here, but there's a small sitting area with a couch and two chairs on the far side of the anchor desk. That's where you'll be." She slowed down a little as they entered a narrow hallway and approached a door bearing the ABC logo. "This is the green room." She opened the door and ushered them into a room filled with old couches and a few pieces of battered office furniture. "It needs a little sprucing up, but it gets the job done." She pointed to a counter in the far corner. "Coffee's over there, and water bottles are in the mini-fridge. The bathroom is a little further down the hall. Second door on the right. Make yourselves at home. I'll be back in fifteen minutes to take you to hair and makeup."

Calla excused herself and found the bathroom exactly where Mary Ann had said it would be. She locked the door behind her, wet a few paper towels, and pressed them against her cheeks. Her stomach roiled with unease. The crowd outside, the boy and his mother, the lights, the cameras—everything was happening too fast. She felt like a passenger on a runaway train, helpless to stop its momentum. She wished Rae or Reuben were with her. A friendly face, something familiar and grounding would be nice right about now. She threw away the paper towels, checked her reflection in the mirror, and thought about what Rae might say to her in this situation. "Buck up, little camper."

When she returned to the green room, Valerie handed her a bottle of water. "Drink this. I don't want you getting dehydrated."

Dr. Kraft paused his pacing to lock eyes with Calla. "Don't forget what we discussed. You're not in danger. You've never been in danger. You barely knew Ralph."

"Carson." Valerie shook her head sternly. "That's enough. She's ready."

They lapsed into silence. Dr. Kraft resumed his pacing, and Valerie pulled out her phone. Calla sat on a couch, sipping her water.

Finally, Mary Ann returned. "Follow me."

She led them back down the hallway to another somewhat smaller room lined with mirrors and canvas director's chairs. A man and a woman stood behind the chairs.

Mary pointed to the woman first. She was slim, with long, auburn hair. "Calla, this is Toni. She'll be taking care of you. Toni, this is Ms. Hammond."

Calla gave a brief wave. "Call me Calla."

Toni smiled. "Nice to meet you, Calla." She patted the back of the chair in front of her. "Have a seat."

Mary Ann moved down to the next stylist. "Dr. Kraft, you'll be with Leo today."

"Great. Do you have anything that can cover up these grays?"

Calla chortled. Dr. Kraft was clearly enjoying the trappings of his burgeoning fame.

Her amusement faded as Toni studied her face and hair. What was the stylist going to suggest? A thick layer of makeup? Hair styled to cover parts of her face?

"Well, my job is pretty easy today." Toni finally said. "You hardly need me to do anything, Calla. I would like to play up your eyes a bit, if that's okay. Those eyelashes are amazing!"

Calla nodded her assent, then sat back as Toni went to work applying eyeshadow, mascara, and a little powder ("Just a touch, to reduce any glare from the lights").

Once Toni and Leo were done, Mary Ann explained exactly how and when Calla and Dr. Kraft would enter the set. Everything was choreographed down to the second.

"In a minute, we'll get you miked up and you'll take your seats on the couch. Dr. Kraft, you will sit on the inside so your head doesn't block the camera's view of Calla. Absolutely no talking until I signal you that we're on a commercial break. You'll meet with David briefly before we're back on the air. Then, it's go time. The interview will last ten minutes. When it's over, I'll escort you back to the green room. Any questions?"

No one said anything. Mary Ann glanced at her watch. "Okay, let's go!"

She led them to a far corner of the set packed with racks of audio-visual equipment. Two technicians went to work clipping wireless microphones to their clothing and running sound checks. When they were done, Mary Ann motioned for them to stay where they were and to stay silent.

Calla's stomach was doing flip-flops again. *What the hell am I doing here? This is such a bad idea.*

A commercial break was called. Suddenly, the entire set jumped into action.

"This is it, kids," Mary Ann announced. "Follow me!"

Calla turned to look at Valerie. "I'm not sure I can do this," she whispered.

"You're going to be great. It'll be over before you know it."

"Let's go!" Dr. Kraft hissed.

"I'll be right over there." Valerie pointed to an area behind one of the cameras. "Just look over at me if you get nervous, okay?"

"Okay." Calla trailed after Dr. Kraft. He bounded onto the dais where the interview would take place. Once they had both arrived, Mary Ann settled them on a small couch.

"Try to hold these positions," she said as she smoothed down the shoulders of Dr. Kraft's suit jacket. "David will be here in just a moment."

"Hello!" A jovial voice rang out. David de Luca, the anchor of *World News Tonight*, came into view. He was shorter than Calla had expected but just as handsome in person as he was onscreen.

Mary Ann handled the introductions. "David, this is Dr. Carson Kraft and Calla Hammond."

"Great to meet you both!" David shook Dr. Kraft's hand but hesitated for a fraction of a second before taking Calla's. It was only the slightest pause, but it carried a hint of reluctance that Calla was all too familiar with. He was afraid to touch her. She felt a little deflated as she watched him master his discomfort, which (to his credit) he did almost instantly. Everyone else in the studio had been so unconcerned with her appearance that, for a few minutes at least, she had forgotten to feel like she was different.

David took a seat in an upholstered chair opposite the couch and a flock of people immediately surrounded him, touching up his makeup, combing a few loose hairs, fiddling with his mic. They scattered when Mary Ann called out, "One minute!"

David leaned forward. "I know Mary Ann went over this with your folks a few days ago, but just as a recap, I'm going to start with some basics about the study and then shift to the allegations raised by . . . what was the fellow's name?"

"Ralph Grimes," Mary Ann replied promptly.

"Ralph Grimes," David repeated. His eyes widened as he looked from Dr. Kraft to Calla. "Sound good?" He didn't wait for an answer. "Good!"

"Ten seconds!"

Almost magically, all sound and movement on the set subsided.

David worked his jaw a few times, then turned toward the camera with a serious look. "Welcome back. I'm David de Luca. Tonight, I'm joined by a physician–researcher and his subject who are working on a project that might change the face of cancer." He turned toward the couch. "Dr. Carson Kraft, Calla Hammond, thank you for being here."

"Thank you for having us," Dr. Kraft replied. "It's an honor to be here."

Calla blinked. Dr. Kraft's entire persona had transformed. All of a sudden, he was the embodiment of a warm, engaging human being.

David looked at Calla, his eyes signaling her to speak.

"Uh, yes!" she yelped. "Thank you!"

Inside, she cringed. Her voice sounded too loud, her enthusiasm too fake. Out of the corner of her eye, Calla could see Valerie drop her forehead into her hand.

Fortunately, David seemed accustomed to nervous interviewees. He moved on immediately.

"Dr. Kraft, you've spent your career developing what some have called a rather unorthodox theory about the immune system's role in fighting cancer."

Dr. Kraft flashed a humble smile. "That's right."

"Would you mind giving us a brief overview of that theory?"

"Certainly." Dr. Kraft shifted to lecture mode. "In the simplest terms," he said, "cancer is the uncontrolled growth of abnormal cells. Sometimes, these cells create masses that we call tumors. In other cases, take leukemia, for example, the abnormal cells don't form tumors, but they do outnumber and overwhelm healthy cells. Left unchecked, cancer cells of any type proliferate and interfere with the normal functioning of organs and other systems in the body. This eventually leads to death." He paused to take a breath. "The question is, how do we stop this process or potentially prevent it from ever happening? Cancer is a tricky foe. The vast majority of patients are unable to fight the disease on their own. They require medical and surgical interventions. And while we've gotten pretty good at beating back the enemy, even our best weapons—chemotherapy, radiation therapy, surgery—don't always work. Sometimes the disease is too advanced or too aggressive to respond to treatment. Sometimes the treatment causes its own damage, even other cancers. But," he raised a single finger, "there are some people, a precious few, who don't need interventions. We know this because either they are exposed to a carcinogen and escape unscathed, or they develop cancer but manage to recover with little to no treatment. It is my belief—my theory—that these people possess immune systems capable of fighting cancer on their own. And if that is true, it means that our fundamental understanding of cancer is flawed."

"Flawed in what way?" David asked.

"Cancer has always been treated as a group of disparate, yet related, diseases. My theory suggests that there may be a single, underlying mechanism that causes the uncontrolled division of cells. That cancer is, in fact, one disease."

David raised an eyebrow. "And how has that gone over in the oncological community?"

Dr. Kraft chuckled. "Well, given that it calls into question over a century of research and thought about cancer . . . let's just say some people think it's misguided."

"How do you respond to the naysayers?"

"That's where this young lady comes into the story." Dr. Kraft patted Calla on the knee and gave her a warm smile. The man was certainly capable of putting on a good show. "As you can imagine," he continued, "it can be difficult to identify patients who *don't* develop cancer."

David gave a hearty laugh. "Good point!"

"That being said, doctors have reported on cancer patients who experienced so-called miracle recoveries for years. But there hasn't been a serious investigation of the phenomenon. Until now." Dr. Kraft patted Calla's knee again. "A while ago, Calla had a seizure . . ."

Calla's attention began to wander as he recounted the events that had brought them together. She'd heard the story so many times now. Her ears perked up, though, when Dr. Kraft made a slight gesture toward her face and said, "As you can see, Calla has a skin condition called vitiligo."

She stiffened slightly. Out of the corner of her eye, she saw Valerie encouraging her to smile from her perch behind the camera. But it was nearly impossible to relax when the most intimate details about her health were being discussed so publicly.

"Calla has the non-segmental form of the disease, which means that it affects both sides of her body. It is also widely considered to be an autoimmune condition. Essentially, her immune system attacks her melanocytes. Those are the cells that produce melanin, a natural pigment that gives a person's skin its color. When melanocytes are attacked, this causes white patches to form on the skin."

David jumped in. "And you believe there is a connection between Ms. Hammond's skin condition and the disappearance of her tumor?"

"I do. Autoimmune diseases cause the immune system to attack healthy cells and tissue. In Calla's case, a confluence of factors driven by her vitiligo appears to have trained her immune system to attack cancer cells."

Calla said a silent prayer of thanks that he had left out the part about her delayed puberty. There was no reason for the whole world to know about that.

"We believe that's why her brain tumor disappeared," Dr. Kraft continued. "And why a melanoma we found on her arm resolved on its own. And why, every time we infuse her blood and bone marrow into lab animals with various other cancers, their disease is completely eliminated." Dr. Kraft let that statement hang in the air for a moment. "This is a vast oversimplification of the science involved, of course, but once sufficiently triggered by the presence of a malignancy, Calla's immune system eradicates it."

"In other words," David said, "her immune system cures her cancer."

"That's the most interesting part, David. It doesn't just cure *her* cancer. It cures any cancer. Her immune system is ingenious. No matter what we confront it with, it finds a way to shut down the disease. The more we study it, the closer we get to understanding how her immune system is capable of reversing that first cellular error message that launches the uncontrolled division of cells. Once we pinpoint that coding error, if you will, our hope is that we will be able to develop a way to turn it off in other people. And potentially stop it from ever happening."

David uncrossed his legs and leaned toward Dr. Kraft. Calla could sense his building excitement—could see him anticipating the viral glory as clips of this moment repeated endlessly across the social media universe, culminating almost inevitably in a Pulitzer Prize.

"You're not just talking about a cure for cancer. You're talking about a vaccine."

Dr. Kraft dipped his head modestly. Like a master puppeteer, he had engineered the conversation to lead to this exact moment. "That's correct."

David shook his head as if awestruck. "Incredible." Then he rubbed his chin and frowned slightly. "Dr. Kraft, all of this information was made public last week when a research paper you had been working on was leaked to the press. Is that correct?"

A sober nod. "Yes."

"And that leak was traced to a former employee of yours, Ralph Grimes."

"It was."

"Mr. Grimes has since made some fairly serious accusations against you, including the claim that he leaked the paper in order to bring attention to his concerns about Ms. Hammond's safety. Would you care to address those allegations?"

Dr. Kraft laced his fingers together; his expression was solemn. "I would, David, and I thank you for the opportunity. Ralph was my lab technician. He was responsible for running various tests on Calla's blood and tissue samples and logging the results in our database. About two weeks ago, he approached me with a demand that his name be listed as one of the authors of the paper you mentioned, which summarized the results of our research thus far. I refused."

"Why was that?"

"Ralph helped generate some of the raw data for the paper, but he didn't participate in its analysis or in the writing. It wasn't appropriate to credit him as an author. Furthermore, it wouldn't have been fair to my colleague, Dr. Juhi Pemmaraju, who did the lion's share of the work on the actual paper."

For the first time in the interview, Calla gave Dr. Kraft a genuine smile. It was nice to hear him give Dr. Pemmaraju the credit she so richly deserved.

"How did Mr. Grimes react?"

"He was furious. He said I was denying him his rightful place in history. He was very focused on how the study could make him famous. And he . . ." his voice trailed off.

"Yes?" David prodded.

"Well," Dr. Kraft said slowly, "as distasteful as this may sound, he was convinced his role in the study would make him rich. I tried to reason with him, but he stormed out of the lab. The next day, the draft was leaked." He shrugged. "Ralph knew that type of exposure could disqualify my paper from consideration for publication. I can only assume that he wanted to deny me the honor of having it published traditionally, just as I had supposedly denied him a share of the credit. But if he intended to hurt me, he failed."

"Why do you say that?" David asked. "Certainly, your reputation has taken a hit."

Dr. Kraft raised his chin. "This isn't about my reputation or adding another line to my CV. This is about curing cancer." He turned to look at Calla. "All that matters to me is that Ms. Hammond and I are able to continue our work and share what we learn with the world."

This line elicited a silent fist pump from Valerie, and even Calla had to admit that she was impressed. Dr. Kraft was doing his best to expose Ralph as the money-grubbing ingrate he was. Only one hurdle remained.

"Mr. Grimes claimed that you are performing too many tests on Ms. Hammond. That her safety is at risk. What is your response to that?"

Dr. Kraft held up his hands. "The first time I ever heard anything about his supposed concerns was during the interview he gave last week."

David narrowed his eyes. "You're saying that he never raised concerns about Ms. Hammond's treatment?"

"No. Not to me, and not to anyone else involved in the study."

"Did he ever threaten to file a complaint against you with the hospital?"

"Never."

"Just to be clear, was there any basis for his statement that Ms. Hammond's participation in the study puts her in danger?"

Once again, Dr. Kraft turned to Calla. "I think Calla is the best person to answer that question."

Showtime.

David looked directly at her. "Ms. Hammond? Have you ever feared for your safety while under Dr. Kraft's care?"

Calla thought about the answer they had practiced over and over again. *No. I've never felt unsafe while participating in Dr. Kraft's study.* It was simple, and it was true. But suddenly it didn't strike her as forceful enough.

Dr. Kraft was right. This was about more than any one person. This was about safeguarding the study so they could make a difference in the world.

"No. I've never feared for my safety while working with Dr. Kraft. Not once. It's been the honor of my life to participate in this study, and I'm disgusted that Ralph has tried to undermine everything we've accomplished so far for his own personal gain."

"Calla," David pressed, his tone serious. Calla couldn't help but notice that he had switched to her first name as a personal appeal. "Your role in Dr. Kraft's study requires a lot of sacrifices. Lab tests, procedures, scans. You are literally donating parts of your living body to research, and, from the sound of it, none of that is going to end anytime soon." He paused for a moment, long enough for Calla to admire his skill at infusing his words with drama. "Why are you doing this?"

Surprisingly, this was not a question they had prepped, but she'd been thinking about the answer nonstop for two days. "When my brain tumor was diagnosed, I was terrified. Beyond terrified. Over the past two months, I've spent a lot of time in the cancer ward as a patient and as part of Dr. Kraft's study. I've seen a lot of cancer. A lot of pain. A lot of despair. A few blood draws and some biopsies are nothing, *nothing*, compared to the hell most cancer patients and their families go through." Her voice shook a little, thinking of Lizzie and her mother. She took a deep, calming breath. "If I can help save one person from going through that, then of course, it's worth it."

David finally cracked a small smile. "Based on what I've heard tonight, Calla, you may be able to do a lot more than help just one person."

Before she could respond, Dr. Kraft leaned forward and stole the last word. "That's the plan, David," he said. "That's the plan."

Calla glanced over at Valerie. The communications director beamed and gave her two thumbs up.

"Well, we wish you both the best of luck," David said. "Thank you for taking the time to be here tonight."

Calla and Dr. Kraft expressed their thanks, then sat quietly while David handed the broadcast over to the local affiliates. As soon as the all-clear was announced, David shook hands with Dr. Kraft.

"Really incredible work you're doing. I'd love to do a follow-up story at some point."

"Of course," Dr. Kraft said smoothly.

David leaned closer to Dr. Kraft and dropped his voice. "You know, my mother-in-law was just diagnosed with breast cancer." He tilted his head toward Calla. "Is this immune system stuff for real?"

Calla froze. What exactly was he asking?

Before Dr. Kraft could answer, Mary Ann and Valerie stepped onto the dais.

"Great job, you two!" Valerie exclaimed.

David made a show of looking at his watch and then stood up. "I've got a meeting." He pointed at Mary Ann. "Mary Ann will give you my personal cell number." He turned back to Dr. Kraft. "Call me anytime to set up that, uh, follow-up interview." He gave everyone a quick nod and then strode away.

"Well, that's a first," Mary Ann said, casting a quizzical look at David's retreating figure. "He usually guards his personal number like it's a crown jewel." She shrugged. "Let's get those mikes off of you. Then we'll head back to the green room."

They trailed after her, Valerie chatting excitedly about how well she thought the interview had gone. A few minutes later, they were back in the green room.

"Here's David's number," Mary Ann handed a slip of paper to Dr. Kraft. Then she turned to Calla. "And here's my card. It's got all my numbers and my email address." She pressed the card into Calla's hand. "Don't hesitate to reach out if you need anything, okay?"

"Okay," Calla replied, running her thumb over the embossed letters. "Thanks."

"One more thing," Mary Ann added. "I had security scout another exit you can use to avoid the crowd at the main entrance. I'll have them coordinate with your driver if you're interested."

"That would be great," Calla said.

"Works for me," Dr. Kraft clipped. "Let's just get out of here." He had shed the warmhearted doctor act the second the cameras had stopped rolling.

"I'll take care of it," Mary Ann said.

Ten minutes later, they were escorted out a side door. The Suburban was idling at the curb.

"You'd better hurry," Mary Ann urged as she looked up and down the sidewalk. "I think we've been spotted." A group of people was running toward them, waving their hands frantically.

"Thanks for everything," Calla said as they clambered into the back seat of the vehicle.

Mary Ann slammed the door shut.

"Go!" Valerie shouted as people gathered around the vehicle, shouting Calla's name and slapping at the windows. "My goodness, they're tenacious."

Dr. Kraft didn't look up from his phone. "What do you expect, Valerie? You're sitting next to the cure for cancer."

The words hit Calla funny. What was she, exactly, to the people out there? To Dr. Kraft or Valerie or David de Luca? A person? Or a means to an end? She'd meant every word she said in the interview. She was committed to the study. But if the events of the past week had taught her anything, the only person she could really trust right now was herself.

Rae's words from a few days earlier echoed in her mind. "Everyone involved in this has an angle."

TWENTY-TWO

"YOU'RE AN ACTUAL FAMOUS PERSON!" Reuben hooted.

Calla had just finished describing the mob scene outside ABC studios in New York.

"It's not funny," Calla grumbled. "It's crazy. My whole life, people have been afraid to be near me. Now, they won't stop asking to touch me. They think I've got magical powers or something."

Dr. Kraft had insisted on a round of tests before letting her go home, so Reuben was once again carting her from one end of the hospital to the other.

"Anyway, enough about me," she said. "How are things with you? How's Michael?"

Reuben jumped into a detailed account of his boyfriend's first semester of law school, and Calla was grateful for the distraction. The reality of her new normal was starting to sink in, and it left her feeling profoundly unsettled. Everywhere she went, she was recognized. Even in the hospital. She was used to being stared at, of course, but this was different. When people looked at her now, their eyes didn't hold fear but an indignant sort of covetousness, as though Calla had stolen something that belonged to them—the ability to fight a disease that affected almost everyone, either personally or tangentially.

But Calla knew she shouldn't have been too surprised. Not after what Rae had told her about how women with albinism in Tanzania were raped because the attackers were convinced the unforgivable act would cure their AIDS. It was a stark realization—how quickly humanity could be abandoned when death came knocking.

Reuben was in the middle of a story about Michael's torts professor when they approached a woman pushing a man's wheelchair in the opposite direction. The man had no hair, not even eyebrows. His face had the gaunt, hollowed-out look of repeated chemotherapy.

Calla watched recognition creep into the woman's expression. "Oh my god, it's you," she said as they passed.

Reuben started pushing faster. Calla heard the other wheelchair being turned around and footsteps rushing toward them.

"Stop! Please!"

"Go ahead and stop, Reuben," Calla said, her voice low. "It's okay."

"Not a good idea," he muttered but did as she asked.

The woman pulled up beside them. "Thank you, thank you," she panted. "I've been praying for this. For a chance to meet you. I know who you are, of course. All of the cancer patients here do." She was talking a mile a minute. "I'm Debra, and this is my husband, Greg. He's being treated for melanoma. That's one of the cancers you've had, isn't it? I've read all about you. I saw you on TV, too. Could you . . . would you mind just laying your hand on my husband?"

Calla suddenly felt sick to her stomach. She didn't want to give this woman or her husband false hope.

"Please," the woman begged. "We're looking for a miracle. We've got two kids." She scrambled to pull her phone from her pocket. "I can show you pictures—"

"That's okay," Calla said. She knew she was indulging a fantasy. She felt a wave of disapproval emanating from Reuben. But the woman seemed so desperate. Calla took Greg's hand in her own. "I'm so sorry you're going through this," she told him.

"See? That wasn't so hard, was it?" the woman asked. Her smile hardened. "Now, do you think you could find it in your heart to donate a bit of your blood to my husband?"

Calla dropped Greg's hand. "Excuse me?"

"You heard me."

"I—I can't."

The woman's face flushed with anger. "You can't? Or you won't? If I had what you have, I'd share it with everyone!" She shook a finger in Calla's face and glowered contemptuously. "But not you, I guess. You're too selfish. You're not worthy of the gift God has given you."

"Debra, stop," Greg said weakly. His words were lost in the growing turmoil.

Reuben stepped in front of Calla, blocking her from the woman's view. "What exactly do you think she's doing in this hospital, *Debra*? Taking a vacation? Her cancer's gone, but she's still here every week, giving blood and getting carved open again and again so that people like your husband have a chance to beat their disease. She doesn't have to do those things. She *chooses* to do them." He shook his head in disgust. "Shame on you and your so-called faith. Only a fool would call Calla selfish." He whipped around and began pushing Calla's wheelchair toward the closest elevator bank.

"Wait!" Debra called after them. "Come back! I'm sorry! I didn't mean it that way!"

"Follow us, and I'm calling security!" Reuben yelled over his shoulder. "We are not stopping again, no matter what you say," he told Calla.

She didn't respond.

"This is getting out of control," Reuben fumed once they were in the elevator. He pushed the button for Calla's floor. "The hospital needs to protect you from those kinds of people. I'm talking to Dr. K about this."

Calla let him vent. Her head was buzzing. Her whole body felt numb. Was this her life now?

Reuben dropped her off in her room with a promise to return in half an hour to pick her back up for one last blood test.

"Try to relax," he told her. "Get your mind off that horrible woman, okay?"

Calla nodded mutely.

As soon as Reuben was gone, she started digging through her overnight bag for jeans, a long-sleeved t-shirt, and a ball cap—her standard uniform for going out in public. She'd always worn a lot of clothing to cover up her vitiligo, both to discourage people from staring and to protect her skin from the sun. Now, her outfit would serve another purpose: as a disguise that would, hopefully, protect her from unwanted attention while she snuck out of the hospital.

Dr. Kraft would have to survive with one less blood test from her. She needed a break. She needed to go home, sleep in her own bed, and cook in her own kitchen.

She dashed around the room, shoving things into her bag. Luckily, there wasn't much to gather; she hadn't unpacked after the trip to New York. She threw the bag over her shoulder, then slipped out of her room and down the hall toward the stairwell. She couldn't risk running into someone on the elevator.

As she jogged down the four flights of stairs, she thought about how this moment felt a lot like the day when her brain tumor was diagnosed, when her life had been neatly sliced into before and after.

"Before" had now become the time when no one knew her name or her face. When she was still a person who hadn't yet been reduced to a commodity, a finite resource, a rare raw material to be excavated and processed and mass-produced so humanity could hold mortality at bay for a little while longer. A time when she was ignored by the people who now couldn't decide whether to scorn her or sanctify her, so they did both.

She reached the ground floor and cautiously opened the door to the front lobby. Her movement caught the attention of a security guard sitting at the information desk. His mouth dropped open a little when he saw her. *So much for my disguise*, Calla thought. She pressed her finger against her lips, hoping to convey the idea that she wanted to keep a low profile. The guard looked away and busied himself with his cellphone.

She edged out from behind the door and walked straight toward the hospital entrance. Head down and shoulders slumped, she was just a visitor leaving the hospital or a worker heading home after the night shift.

She made it through the double doors and stepped onto the sidewalk that wound down to the street. A man was standing near the curb, yelling into his cell phone.

"Come back right now!" He appeared to be signaling a car on the other side of the semicircular driveway.

Calla locked eyes with the man. There was something a little odd about the way he was dressed. His entire face was covered by a ball cap, sunglasses, and a surgical mask. She gave him a wide berth as she passed, and he made a show of turning his back to her. She heard him murmur something into his phone and wondered if he was embarrassed by his outburst.

Calla saw a bus pulling up to the stop at the end of the sidewalk and started walking faster. The door opened, and she saw Charlie in the driver's seat. He hailed her with a huge smile. She started to wave, but someone grabbed her arm from behind.

"Excuse me."

Calla's heart dropped as she turned to see the man she had just walked past.

"Yes?" She tried to pry her arm from his grasp.

"Are you Calla Hammond?"

"Let go of my arm!"

"You *are* Calla Hammond!" The man's grip tightened, then, "I'm right here, hurry up!" he shouted into his phone.

"Let go of me!"

"Hey, let her go!" Charlie threw the bus in park and started to stand.

A late-model Civic cut in front of the bus and screeched to a halt. The back door popped open. The man shoved Calla forward and pressed her toward the opening. She stumbled and whacked her head against the door frame. Dazed, she fell awkwardly across the back seat as the man tucked in her legs. The slamming door smacked the bottoms of her feet.

TWENTY-THREE

"GO, GO, GO, GO!" the man barked as he jumped into the passenger seat.

The car peeled away, and Calla bounced around the back seat like a pinball.

"Drive!" the man screamed. "Faster!"

"I'm going as fast as I can."

A horrendous sound of metal scraping concrete.

"You're ruining the car."

"Shut up and let me drive!"

The car straightened and accelerated. Things in the back seat settled down enough for Calla to get a better look at her abductors. The female driver was dressed the same as the man—long sleeves, ball cap, sunglasses, surgical mask. Though simple, the disguises were actually pretty smart. After all, face masks were still commonplace since the coronavirus pandemic, especially at hospitals.

The man grabbed something from the glovebox and twisted around to face Calla. "Are you okay?" he asked. "I didn't hurt you, did I?"

Calla was surprised to hear concern in his voice, especially since he was now pointing a handgun at her. "This is only to make sure you do what you're told," he said. "We don't want to hurt you. We just need—"

"Stop talking!" the woman commanded as the car squealed left. "Stay focused."

"Okay, geez!" The man turned back around.

"Keep an eye out for the cops," the woman said. "We might need to change our route to the house if we run into any."

"If you'd stop driving like a maniac, we might not need to worry."

A siren in the distance.

"Fuck," the woman hissed.

"Maybe it's not for us."

The siren grew louder.

"It's for us," the woman said.

Calla managed to sit up and look out the back window. She glimpsed flashing lights in the distance, weaving back and forth.

"Get down!" the woman screamed. "Get her down. We're screwed if the cops see her."

"Get down," the man ordered Calla, brandishing the gun in one hand and grabbing the back of her shirt with the other. He forced her to lay on the floorboard, where she came face-to-face with a toy car and some very old Goldfish. "How the hell did they find us so quickly?"

Charlie, Calla knew.

"I don't know. Hold on."

The car's movements became more erratic as the sirens drew closer. There seemed to be more than one now. The man was forced to remove his hand from Calla's back, freeing her to raise her head slightly and take stock of her surroundings. *Not much to work with*, she thought. But then she took a closer look at the door. A blazing orange strip was visible on the lock. *How could they have forgotten?*

The sirens grew louder.

"Maybe we should pull over and see if they pass," the man said.

"They'll see her, damn it!" She smacked the steering wheel. "You should have put her in the trunk."

"Oh, so this is my fault? I did the best I could, you know. It's not like I had a ton of time to execute your perfect—WATCH OUT!"

Slamming brakes wedged Calla against the seatbacks. The car jolted to a stop. A quick glance told her the man's attention was focused forward.

Don't think. Just go.

She pushed into a crouch as the woman laid on the horn and cursed the stopped vehicle in front of them. "Fucking move!"

Calla grabbed the door handle and threw her body forward. She landed hard on the pavement as a car ripped past in the adjacent lane. A hot breath of exhaust. Her arm burned with pain, and blood dripped into her right eye. She found her footing anyway and kicked the door closed as the man wheeled around, gun in hand.

But a shot never came. Instead, the Civic lurched onto the sidewalk and around the stopped car, then back onto the road, the curb crunching the exhaust pipe.

Cradling her right arm, Calla swayed, unsteady.

Twenty yards ahead, the Civic slammed to stop, its reverse lights illuminated.

Go! Keep moving!

Calla stumbled to the sidewalk and started to run. A few startled pedestrians jumped out of her way. Then, two police cars zipped past, sirens wailing. They screeched to a halt, blocking the street. Four officers leapt out. Three pulled their guns and advanced on the Civic, yelling at the driver to stop. The fourth ran toward Calla.

"We need EMS!" he yelled over his shoulder. "Call it in now!"

He stopped a few feet short of her and held out his hands. "It's okay. Houston police. I'm here to help you."

A keening wail from the middle of the street: "My baby! I just wanted to save my baby!"

Calla felt the world spin at a sickening speed, and once again, the pavement rushed up to meet her.

TWENTY-FOUR

IT TOOK SOME BUREAUCRATIC SCRAMBLING, but Calla was eventually returned to her "home" hospital following the kidnapping attempt. She received three stitches for the cut above her right eye and a sling for her slightly fractured arm. A police officer was now stationed outside her room door. She was channel surfing aimlessly when he stuck his head inside. "You've got a visitor," he announced.

A familiar voice said, "I can come back later if she's resting."

"Charlie?" Calla called out. "Is that you?"

The bus driver stepped into the room. "Hey there, kiddo. I don't want to bother you."

"Are you kidding? Charlie, I owe you my life."

He stared at the floor; his cap was twisted in his hands. "I should've blocked the driveway with the bus." His voice was laced with regret. "Then this never would've happened. I don't know why I didn't think to do that."

"Charlie, look at me," Calla said. Finally, reluctantly, he raised his eyes to meet hers. "You did the only thing you could do in the situation. You called the cops. I'm just glad you knew something was wrong. Everything happened so fast. It took *me* a minute to figure out what was going on. And I can't believe you managed to clock the license plate number. The police said it made all the difference." She beckoned for him to come closer. "You're a hero. Thank you."

Before Charlie could say anything in response, the door swung wide open, and Rae barreled in. "Calla! I was up in Conroe when I got the call. I can't believe how long it took me to get here! There was traffic and then an accident, and I just . . ." She rushed to Calla's bedside and began examining her from head to foot. "What did they do to you? If I get my hands on—"

"Rae," Calla cut her off. "I'm fine. Really."

"You're not fine!" Rae cried. "You were kidnapped, for Christ's sake!"

"Well, lucky for me, Charlie here saw the whole thing go down and called the cops right away." Calla pointed at Charlie, hoping to shift Rae's attention (and emotion) away for a moment or two. She had only just managed to quell her own panic about what had happened.

Rae turned to Charlie. "I know we only just met, but . . ." She kissed his cheek with a resounding smack. "Thank you for saving my baby."

Charlie blushed. "It was nothing, Ma'am."

"Call me Rae, okay?"

"Only if you'll call me Charlie."

Calla watched as they smiled at one another. "I'm glad you two are finally getting the chance to meet."

"Don't change the subject," Rae said sharply, though her eyes were shining a little brighter than Calla had seen in a while. "Now, tell me what happened."

Calla gave her a quick overview (with some color commentary from Charlie). Rae shook her head. "How on earth did they know you'd be walking out of the hospital at exactly that moment?"

"Dumb luck, if you can believe it." A deep voice with a thick Texas drawl came from a hulk of a man in the doorway.

"Detective." Calla waved the man into the room. "These are my friends, Charlie and Rae."

The man shook hands with Charlie. "Good to see you again. We met earlier when I was taking witness statements," he explained to Calla. Next, he turned to Rae. "Ty Decker. I'm the detective assigned to this case. Thought I'd give Ms. Hammond an update before I head back to the station."

"What can you tell us?" Rae asked.

"Quite a lot, actually." Decker pointed at a chair. "May I?" When Calla nodded, he pulled it closer to the bed and sat down. "Looks like a pretty open and shut case. The couple involved gave a full confession."

"So, they were a couple," Calla confirmed.

"Yes, Ma'am. Married five years. They have a three-year-old son. Diagnosed with a brain tumor about six months ago. Not doing so well. They petitioned the hospital for a blood transfusion from you but got denied. So, they started casing the place a few days ago, hoping to grab you and do it themselves. They bribed a security guard to keep an eye out and call them if he saw you."

"I saw him," Calla said. "He was sitting at the information desk, right?"

"That's the one," Decker confirmed. "Guess he was in a bit of financial trouble, so he took the money." He shook his head. "He's in a heap more trouble now."

"And he called those people when he saw me come out of the stairwell?"

"That's right. You happened to walk out right when the husband was walking in to do some recon. Like I said, just dumb luck on their part."

"They confessed to all of this?" Charlie asked.

"Yes, Sir."

Calla frowned. "And they were going to take my blood?"

Decker cleared his throat. "I don't know if we need to get into that right now."

"I want to know," she said firmly. "Please."

"Well, based on their preliminary statements and a search of their residence, they were going to do one or more blood transfusions from you to their son. They had the equipment set up in their guest room, and the wife had watched some videos on YouTube."

Charlie's mouth dropped open in shock. "YouTube?"

"Yessir. It's a brave new world out there. Seems you can learn to do most anything if you've got a screen and an Internet connection." Decker rubbed pensively at the bald spot on his head. "Anyway, they claim they were only going to keep you until they got confirmation that the transfusions worked. Then they were going to drop you somewhere on the other side of town. They'd even bought you a burner phone, so you could call for help."

"How thoughtful," Rae said wryly.

"What about their son?" Calla asked. "What will happen to him?"

"He's with Child Protective Services now. The maternal grandparents live in Houston, so they're evaluating whether it's safe to place him with them. He's quite ill and needs a lot of care."

Calla felt as though a stone had been dropped into her stomach. Another kid in the system. A sick kid. She knew it wasn't because of her, but it still felt that way.

Rae patted her hand and gave her a knowing look. "Not your fault."

"But—"

Rae stopped her. "I'll get in touch with some folks at the office. Make sure he's getting the care he needs, okay?" When Decker gave her a quizzical look, she explained, "I'm a special investigator with CPS."

Decker nodded and stood up. "Well, unless you've got any other questions for me, I'd best be going." He pulled his wallet from his back pocket and extracted three business cards. "I'll be in touch with the two of you soon," he said as he handed cards to Calla and Charlie. "And don't be surprised if you hear from the D.A.'s office. They'll want to talk to you themselves as they sort out what to charge these folks with." He handed the third card to Rae. "Please give me a call if I can be of any assistance with the child."

"Thank you." Rae gave him a grateful smile.

"I've arranged for police protection for the next few days while I conduct my investigation. And I believe the hospital is looking into private security options for the longer term."

That took Calla by surprise. "Private security? Like a bodyguard?"

"Seems prudent, given the circumstances."

"For how long?"

Rae sighed. "Calla, I think you're going to have to get used to the idea that things have changed."

Calla laid back on her pillow and stared moodily at the ceiling. "Everything was going great until Ralph opened his big mouth."

"We'll get you through this." Rae's tone was soothing but not altogether convincing.

"I'm never getting my life back, am I?"

What a stupid question. Of course she wasn't. The events of the last two days—the screaming crowds, the signs, the people demanding her help, brazenly taking what she had for their own—were proof enough. Nothing would ever be the same.

TWENTY-FIVE

SEVERAL HOURS LATER, after a dinner of icky hospital food (Calla was dying to get back to her own kitchen), Calla and Rae were snuggled on the bed together, binge-watching *Arrested Development* on Calla's new iPad. Charlie had gone home shortly after Decker's visit.

"Good evening." Dr. Kraft walked into the room without knocking. He was trailed by Dr. Pemmaraju and Reuben. Valerie brought up the rear a few moments later, her eyes glued to her cell phone.

"How nice of you all to stop by," Rae said drily. "Finally."

"We've been stuck in a board meeting," Dr. Kraft replied.

From the back of the room, Reuben caught Calla's eye and mouthed *Are you okay?* He pointed at Dr. Kraft and made a talking gesture with his hand.

Rae swung her legs over the side of the bed and stood up. "What kind of show are you running around here?" she demanded. "You seem to have zero control over the people working at this hospital." She pointed a finger at Dr. Kraft. "I don't care what kind of agreement Calla signed with you. If you don't start protecting her *today*, I'll yank her out of here so fast it'll make your head spin."

"It's not that simple—"

"Bullshit," Rae cut him off.

Calla made a face at Reuben. You knew things were getting serious when Rae Wiley started swearing.

"She's worth millions to this hospital," Rae said. "Maybe even billions. I think you can spare a little of that to make sure she doesn't have to worry about being grabbed every time she walks out the front door!"

"You're absolutely right," Valerie said smoothly, admonishing Dr. Kraft with a look before stepping in front of him. "I'm afraid we haven't met yet. I'm Valerie Wright. Director of communications and marketing for the hospital."

"Rae Wiley."

They shook hands, then Rae crossed her arms. "So, what's the plan?"

"The board has agreed to move Dr. Kraft's lab to a more secure location in the hospital and to hire a private security team. I've already been in touch with a reputable firm. The principal is former Secret Service and an old family friend. He's headed here now to meet Calla and get the lay of the land."

"When do I get to go home?" Calla asked. "There's no way I'm hiding out at this hospital for the rest of my life."

"I'd prefer to let Bruce explain how this will work," Valerie said as she glanced at her cell phone again. "I asked him to meet us up here . . . ah, good. He just texted. He's on his way."

While they waited for Bruce to arrive, Dr. Pemmaraju and Reuben gathered close to Calla's bedside.

"How are you feeling?" Dr. Pemmaraju asked as she peered at the vital signs monitor above Calla's head.

"Like I jumped out of a car."

"What on earth possessed you to sneak out like that?" Reuben tut-tutted at her. He glanced around to make sure that Dr. Kraft wasn't listening to him, then leaned closer to whisper, "You should've told me that you wanted to leave so badly. I would've taken you home."

Calla sighed. "I know, Reuben. I just needed some space. It was all . . . you know, getting to be too much."

"I'm so sorry," Dr. Pemmaraju said as she examined the bandage above Calla's eye. "About all of this."

"Bruce!" Valerie exclaimed, cutting their conversation short. "Come in."

Calla looked up to see an extremely tall man stride into the room. He was in his late fifties, maybe early sixties, with close-cropped white hair and a military bearing.

"Good evening," he said politely.

"Thanks for coming on such short notice." Valerie presented him to the group. "Everyone, this is Bruce Kendall, the founder of Aegis Security Services." She introduced him to each person in the room, ending with Calla.

"I understand you went through quite an ordeal earlier today, young lady," Bruce said as he clasped her hand.

"Yes, Sir."

"Bruce," Valerie prompted, "what can you tell us about your plan to protect Calla from a repeat of this morning's incident?"

"Based on the information you've given me so far, I'd recommend a three-person team. One to guard the lab and provide perimeter security. A second to provide close personal protection for Ms. Hammond during the day. And a third to provide overnight protection."

"So, Calla will have someone with her around the clock," Rae said.

"Yes, Ma'am."

"Good."

"Do you really think that's necessary?" Calla asked, wondering how she would handle being followed around by a stranger all day, every day.

"From what I can tell, Ms. Hammond, the abduction attempt today was amateur at best. But it proves that even the dumbest criminals get lucky. And that you're vulnerable. So, yes, I think twenty-four-hour protection is necessary right now."

"Can I go back to my apartment?"

"Once you're medically cleared to leave the hospital, I don't see why not. I'll just need the keys to your apartment and your mailbox so that we can make copies and start assessing the situation there."

"My mailbox?"

"Yes. We'll be checking your mail from now on."

"You think people have figured out where I live?"

"People can be incredibly resourceful when they want something, Ms. Hammond, as you learned today. We need to take every precaution to keep you safe." He glanced at Valerie and Dr. Kraft. "If it works for you folks, we'll get started in the morning."

TWENTY-SIX

FIRST THING THE NEXT MORNING, Bruce returned to Calla's hospital room. This time, he was accompanied by a tough-looking young woman.

"Ms. Hammond, this is Kendra Litton. She'll be taking point on the lab and perimeter security. You might not see her often, but she'll be at the hospital every day and at your apartment and elsewhere as needed. She runs a tight ship."

"Thank you, Kendra," Calla said. "Nice to meet you."

Kendra stood with her feet planted slightly apart and her hands behind her back. She gave Calla a crisp nod. "Yes, Ma'am. Nice to meet you, too, Ma'am."

"Please, call me Calla."

"Yes, Ma'am."

Bruce chuckled. "Kendra is a former Army Ranger. All of my employees are former military or law enforcement."

"I see."

"Your close protection should be here any minute." Bruce frowned as he glanced at his watch.

"Knock, knock!" It was Reuben. "Time for that blood draw you missed yesterday." He rolled his wheelchair next to Calla's bedside. "And just for fun, Dr. K tacked on an MRI. Hop aboard the Sanchez Express."

"Seriously?" she asked. "It's been, like, five minutes since the last one."

"You're thinking of the CT we did on your birthday. It's been three weeks since the last MRI."

"Time flies when you're having fun," Calla muttered as she moved from her bed to the wheelchair.

"Can you wait a few minutes until my guy arrives?" Bruce asked. "I'd like for him to accompany you." His phone buzzed and he answered it with a snap, "Where are you?" A long pause. "We'll discuss it when you get up here. Room four-oh-five." He slipped the phone back into his pocket. "Room number mix-up," he explained. "Give me three minutes."

"Sure thing," Reuben said.

Bruce beckoned Kendra. "Hallway. Now."

After they left, Reuben let out a low whistle. "Gee, someone's grouchy."

"Yeah," Calla agreed. "Remind me never to get on his bad side."

A few minutes later, they overheard Bruce in the hall. "Late on the first day. Not a good look. What's going on, soldier?"

There was a low murmuring in response, but Calla and Reuben couldn't make out the words.

"It's not your job to question my decisions!" Bruce barked. "It's your job to keep the client safe."

Reuben gave Calla a look. "Sounds like some serious drama. I'm going to sneak a peek."

"Reuben, no!" she hissed, but it was too late. He had already darted across the room to look out the narrow window in the door.

"Of course not," they heard Bruce say. His voice was lower now, his tone more conciliatory. "That's your decision to make, not mine." More murmuring. "Listen, this is a good opportunity for you, Brandon. For a lot of reasons. You'll be here in town, and there's a lot of flexibility with the three-man rotation. If you need time off, it won't be a problem."

Reuben clapped his hand over his mouth and scurried back to Calla's wheelchair.

"Oh. My. God!" His eyes were as round as saucers. "Your bodyguard is smoking hot. Like, Sexiest Man Alive material. Like—"

Calla elbowed him to shut up just as the door opened.

Bruce strode back into the room. He was followed by a second man who was at least thirty years younger than him, six feet tall, and perfectly built. He was clean-shaven and wore his hair military-style, which accentuated the sharp lines of his cheekbones and jawline. His skin was dark brown, and his eyes were an inviting hazel that might have appeared friendly if not for the stern look on the rest of his face. Reuben wasn't kidding. The man standing in front of them was quite possibly the most attractive human being Calla had ever laid eyes on.

Reuben placed his hand under Calla's jaw and gently closed her mouth, which had fallen slightly open. "Told you," he breathed. Louder, he said, "Gentlemen!"

"Ms. Hammond, this is Brandon Foster. He'll be your daytime close protection. Jimmy McInerney has the night shift. You'll meet him this evening."

"Ms. Hammond." Brandon did not make eye contact.

"Brandon is a former Navy SEAL. The best of the best."

Brandon continued to stare at the wall above Calla's head.

Reuben hastened to fill the awkward silence. "I'm Reuben Sanchez. Calla's nurse. And I hate to say this, but we're late for a blood draw." He got behind the wheelchair and started to push it forward. When he reached the doorway, he looked over his shoulder at Brandon. "You coming with us, or what?"

"Go," Bruce ordered.

Brandon followed them into the hallway. Calla and Reuben attempted some light conversation on the way to the lab, but Brandon's stony silence made things so uncomfortable they eventually abandoned the effort.

"What's his problem?" Calla asked quietly once she and Reuben were alone in the blood draw room. Thankfully, Brandon had stationed himself outside, giving them a few minutes of privacy.

"No idea," Reuben answered as he prepped her arm. "He's definitely no Prince Charming, but hopefully he'll keep the crazies at bay."

"Yeah, hopefully."

After the blood test, they made a silent trip to the radiology department. Reuben left Calla and Brandon alone briefly in the empty waiting room while he went to grab Calla's oral contrast. When he got back, they were sitting on opposite sides of the room, doing their best to completely ignore one another.

"Bottoms up," he instructed Calla as he handed her a large plastic cup. She gulped it down. "How long is the wait for this one?"

"Thirty minutes to coat your GI tract." His phone buzzed. He pulled it from his pocket. "Crap. Dr. K needs me." He called over to Brandon, "I've got to run up to the lab for a few minutes. Can you stay with her?"

Brandon gave him a sour look. "That's my job."

"Right," Reuben said drily. "Thanks."

"Don't leave me here alone with him." Calla tried to keep her voice as low as possible.

Reuben knelt next to her. "You're gonna have to get used to having him around," he whispered. "Ask about his hobbies or something."

"Are you insane? That's not going to work."

"I'll be back as soon as possible."

"Reuben . . ."

He stood up and gave her a pat on her shoulder. "Call me on my cell if you need anything."

Calla stared daggers at his back as he walked away. The door clicked shut, and she was once again alone with Brandon. She hopped up from the wheelchair and checked out the magazines on a nearby side table to see if any had been updated since her last visit. She grimaced when she saw the latest copy of *Time Magazine*. The cover bore a close-up of her face. It was a stark black-and-white image. Her eyes were focused somewhere distant, and her expression was either fierce or frightened. Across the page sprawled the words: Is She the End of Cancer?

"That's got to be weird."

"Excuse me?" she asked, looking up in surprise. *He speaks.*

"Nothing," Brandon said, and then, as though he was fighting an urge to stay silent, "It's just got to be strange. Being on the cover of *Time* and all."

Calla looked at the cover again and let out a grim laugh. "Yeah, it is. Especially since I have no idea when this photo was taken." Maybe by a photographer outside the television studio in New York? But if it had happened then, how had the magazine printed it so quickly?

"You didn't pose for that?" The tone of his question was skeptical at best.

"You think I want my face plastered on every magazine and newspaper in the country?"

"I don't know. Maybe. Some people would."

Calla shook her head firmly. "Not me. I've never liked—" She didn't need to go there.

"Never liked what?"

Calla turned the magazine face down and walked back to the wheelchair. "Forget about it."

"Suit yourself."

Calla realized she probably shouldn't pass up on an opportunity to keep him talking. "I've never liked having my picture taken." She pointed at her face. "Obviously."

"I don't see anything wrong with your face."

Calla stared at him for a moment. No one said things like that to her. "That was nice of you to say. Thank you."

"You're welcome." His tone was still serious but less irritable.

Okay, maybe he just takes a little while to warm up.

She searched for a way to keep the conversation going. His job seemed like a safe topic.

"Have you known Bruce for a long time?"

"Couple of years. A buddy of mine in the Navy hooked us up after I left the SEALs."

"Why'd you leave? Were you injured?"

Brandon stiffened. "It's personal."

"Sorry," Calla said. "I didn't mean to pry."

"Don't worry about it."

Silence again.

Calla felt like she'd lost every inch and then some of the progress she'd made with Brandon. She checked the time on her phone, then muttered, "Cancer is a waiting room."

Brandon gave her a sharp look. "What did you say?"

"Huh? Oh, it's just this thing Reuben and I say to each other sometimes. That cancer is a waiting room."

"How so?"

"Well, cancer has these huge, scary, life-altering moments. Like the day you get diagnosed. But the rest of the time, *most* of the time, you're stuck in a waiting room. Waiting to see the doctor. Waiting to take tests. Waiting for the results from those tests. Then more waiting to see if the cancer's back so you can wait to take another round of tests. Even me, the so-called girl with the immune system that can cure cancer. I'm still looking over my shoulder, wondering if this is all some huge mistake and that one of these days, they're going to tell me the cancer's back, and this time I'm screwed."

For the longest time, Brandon looked at her without saying anything. Finally, he stood up and headed toward the door. "I'm going to check in with Kendra. I'll be right outside if you need anything."

The door snapped shut behind him.

Great job. Way to scare the guy off.

Calla buried her nose in an issue of *Good Housekeeping*, searching for new recipes she could try when she finally got to go home.

Brandon didn't come back into the room until Reuben returned from the lab.

"Calla?" he said as Reuben started to wheel her away.

"Yeah?"

"I think you're right."

"About what?"

"About cancer being a waiting room."

Calla studied him for a moment. "Is that your way of apologizing for being so grumpy earlier?"

He waved for Reuben to keep moving. "Hope the scan goes well. I'll be here when you're done."

TWENTY-SEVEN

AFTER THAT FIRST DAY, Brandon wasn't exactly warm and friendly, but he did talk and, on occasion, smile (which Reuben claimed gave him palpitations every time it happened). Reuben wasn't the only one charmed by Calla's bodyguard. Within twenty-four hours of his arrival, every nurse on her floor had a crush on him. Calla was just grateful that he kept anyone who wasn't directly involved in her care at a safe distance. The initial shock of the kidnapping attempt was beginning to wear off, but she was still jumpier than usual and deeply distrustful of strangers.

On the third day after the unexpected extension of her stay at the hospital, Dr. Pemmaraju had some good news for Calla.

"You can go home." She smiled when Calla started doing a little happy dance in her bed. "Your injuries are healing nicely, and there's no reason to keep you here now that your, uh, new friend is on the job." She tilted her head toward the door to Calla's room. Brandon had stepped out so they could have some privacy while Dr. Pemmaraju examined her. "By the way, he's kind of hot."

"*Kind of* hot?"

"Okay, gorgeous."

"Uh-huh."

Dr. Pemmaraju did a little shimmy. "Bet you wish he worked night shift."

They both laughed, but Calla's skin tingled at the thought.

"Seriously, though," Dr. Pemmaraju said. "We all feel a lot better now that you've got some protection."

"I do, too."

Dr. Pemmaraju stood up. "One more thing. I talked Dr. K into giving you next week off."

"Wow. A whole week? What'd you do, promise him your firstborn or something?"

"He'll survive. We've got more than enough data to keep us busy for at least that long. I don't want to see you here until next Friday, and preferably the following Monday, okay? Doctor's orders."

Calla felt a rush of gratitude. "You're the best."

"You know I've got your back." Dr. Pemmaraju winked. "Now, take it easy and call me if you need anything." She started to make her way out of the room, then looked back over her shoulder. "Or if you decide to run off with that bodyguard of yours."

"Hush!" Calla protested in a loud whisper. "He's right outside."

Dr. Pemmaraju grinned slyly and pulled open the door. "She's all yours," she told Brandon. "Take good care of her." She gave Calla a wave. "See you in a week."

"Did you hear?" Calla asked Brandon as soon as he stepped into the room. "I get to go home."

"I heard." Brandon looked amused by her enthusiasm. "Why don't you start packing up? Kendra's driving us to your apartment."

"Do you think we could stop at a grocery store on the way? I'd love to grab a few things."

"Make a list. Kendra will pick up whatever you need."

Calla pursed her lips. "Why can't I go myself?"

"Because it's only been a few days since someone tried to kidnap you. We need more time to complete a threat assessment, and we're still waiting for the police to finish their investigation. Until then, we need to limit your exposure."

"Meaning I'm going to be stuck in my apartment."

"For now."

"Great. So, I'm basically trading one prison for another. Way to rain on a girl's parade, Brandon."

"Would you rather stay here? I'm sure that can be arranged."

"No. I'll pack."

She started to gather up a collection of hand-made cards and drawings from her bedside table.

"Where did those come from?" Brandon asked.

"I took an art class with some of the kids in the pediatric ward a few weeks ago. Their teacher dropped these off yesterday. I guess they heard about what happened to me." She held up a picture of two hands cupping a heart. "It's beautiful, isn't it?"

Brandon frowned. "Those are from kids who have cancer?"

"Yes, why?"

Brandon made a disapproving sound.

"What?"

"I just don't think it's a good idea to give people too much hope. Especially kids."

Calla traced the outline of the heart on the drawing she had shown him. "I know it's not fair that I'm well and they're sick. And I would never intentionally rub that in anyone's face. But I've been sick, too. And I know how powerful hope can be." Carefully, she placed the drawing into her bag with the others. "Sometimes, it feels like the only thing there is."

. . .

An hour later, Kendra, Brandon, and Calla were pulling up to the front of her apartment building when Calla spotted a familiar figure leaning against a bright blue Porsche.

"You have got to be kidding me!" she cried. "Stop the car!"

Kendra hit the brakes. The SUV lurched to a halt.

"What's going on?" Brandon asked. "Who is that?"

Before Brandon or Kendra could stop her, Calla flung her door open and jumped out.

"What the hell are you doing here?" she yelled.

Ralph turned when he heard her voice. He stared at her for a moment before stammering, "Calla, hi. I—I've been trying to get in touch with you."

"So, you just show up at my apartment?"

"I thought it would be better to see you in person. I've been coming by for the past couple of days."

"Oh, okay. That's not creepy at all." Calla gave him a scathing look. "How do you even know where I live?"

"Well, uh, there's this website—" He was suddenly distracted by something behind her.

Calla turned and saw Brandon striding toward them.

"What's going on here?" he demanded as he placed himself between Ralph and Calla. His voice was low, but he was clearly furious. "Who is this, Calla?"

"Only the guy who ruined my life." Calla leaned around Brandon to glare at Ralph. "What the fuck do you want, anyway?"

"I—I—" he sputtered, then fell silent.

"What, Ralph? Spit it out!"

He hung his head. "I heard about what happened. About those people who tried to kidnap you. And I just wanted to say that . . . I'm sorry." He looked up at her, his expression beseeching. "I swear I was trying to protect you, Calla."

Calla stepped out from behind Brandon. "That's such a crock! We both know you made up that bullshit story to justify what you did. And to make Dr. Kraft look bad."

"That's not true! You have to believe me. I really *was* worried about how he was treating you." Ralph's eyes bulged. "There's something wrong with him. Mentally. He's obsessed, Calla. One of these days, he's going to go too far, and then . . ."

Calla wasn't buying it. "Dr. Kraft might be obsessed, but he would never hurt me. You, on the other hand, have already proven that you don't give a shit about anyone but yourself." She pointed at the Porsche. "Be honest. You were just looking for a payday."

"I know it looks that way, but—"

"It *is* that way." Calla shook her head in disgust. "Come on, Brandon. I'm done talking to this asshole."

As they started to walk away, Ralph called after them, "If it makes you feel any better, I'm being investigated for a bunch of HIPAA violations. My lawyer says that all of this may go away. I could even face jail time."

Calla whirled around to see him staring longingly at the Porsche. "Gee, why do I not feel bad for you?" She tapped her chin. "Oh, that's right. I got kidnapped by lunatics because of you. I can't go anywhere without people trying to touch me because of you." She jerked her thumb over her shoulder at Brandon. "I need a freaking bodyguard now because of you. Jail might be a nice break from the crap I'm dealing with. I hope you enjoy your time there." She turned and stalked away.

"Just be careful!" Ralph called after her. "Okay, Calla?"

"Go to hell, Ralph!"

Calla yanked open the entry gate to her apartment complex and marched inside.

"The nerve of that guy," she said as she mounted a set of rickety stairs to the second floor. "Showing up in a Porsche."

"Calla." Brandon's voice sliced through her monologue.

She turned to look at him. "I mean, he thinks an apology will make it all better? Seriously?"

"What happened just now was completely unacceptable."

"I know, right? What the hell did he—"

"Not him. You."

She stopped short. "Excuse me?"

"I cannot do my job effectively if you do things like jump out of cars to yell at people."

"I'm perfectly capable—"

"Even if, *especially* if, the person in question is the one who's responsible for leaking your name to the media. I don't think you appreciate how vulnerable you are. Now, let's keep moving."

Calla turned with a huff and continued climbing. They made it to the third floor and turned left.

"If I'm going to keep you safe," Brandon said, "we need to establish some ground rules. Rule number one: when you're riding with me, you don't get out of the car until I say it's safe. Understood?"

Calla stopped in front of her apartment. "Am I allowed to open my own door?" she asked tightly.

"Actually, no." Brandon moved her aside gently. "Rule number two: I go first when we enter an uncleared space. You stay right behind me."

"And they say chivalry is dead."

"Just doing my job." Brandon pulled a set of keys from his pocket. He quickly scanned the walkway around them before unlocking the door. "Right behind me," he repeated. He pushed open the door and took a step inside in one smooth motion. Calla saw that his right hand hovered near his waist, ready to grab his handgun if necessary. A few more steps, and they were fully inside the apartment.

Calla made a show of looking around. "Unless some bad guy is hiding in my tiny ass bathroom, I think we're okay."

"Shut the door and wait here while I look around," Brandon instructed. Mostly to himself, he muttered, "Should've had Kendra come up with us."

"I kind of think two of you in my apartment would be overkill," Calla said as she closed the door.

"Not after what just happened," Brandon called from the bathroom. He stepped out. "How did that guy know where you live?"

"He said something about finding it on a website."

"Great." Brandon put his hands on his hips and surveyed the room. "Kendra mentioned the place had some issues, but this is . . ." He scratched his forehead.

"This is what, exactly?" Calla asked. She winced as she started to ease herself down onto her futon.

Brandon crossed the room in two strides and helped her sit. "Calla, is the hospital compensating you?"

"Not that it's any of your business, but yes."

Brandon glanced around the room again. "Not enough."

Calla gave him a hard look. "You know, I've always been kind of proud that I have my own place. It might be a dump, but at least it's mine."

"That's not what I meant."

"Then what did you mean?"

Brandon stood up straight and looked down at her. "I can give you ten reasons why this apartment isn't safe for you anymore, starting with the cheap deadbolt on your front door. And that's just for starters. That hospital's probably going to make a ton of money off of you. Which makes me wonder why they aren't taking better care of you."

"Maybe they are. Maybe I just like living here."

"Kid yourself much?"

"Fine. You're right. I hate this place. The paint's peeling and the kitchen sink leaks. But I can't afford anything else right now. At least, not until I pay off my yacht. You know how it is."

Brandon snorted. "You're a funny bird, Calla Hammond."

"Sarcasm's essential for someone like me. I've been the butt of way too many cosmic jokes."

"I wouldn't call this situation a joke."

"Can we talk about something else?"

Brandon looked like he wanted to discuss it further but said, "How about food? Make a grocery list for Kendra, and I'll order some pizza." He pulled his phone out of his pocket. "Pepperoni okay with you?"

Calla cocked her head. "You're staying late? What about Jimmy?"

"He called in sick, and we don't have anyone who can fill in for him tonight, so I'm covering his shift."

"Is he okay?"

"He caught the flu from one of his girls. He was more worried about getting you sick than anything else."

Jimmy McInerney was Calla's nighttime close protection officer and all-around solid guy. He was a giant of a man—nearly half a foot taller than Brandon—and a bit scary-looking. But underneath his scowl and tattoos, he was a total softie. He had three little girls at home who, along with his wife, were the loves of his life.

"Are you sure about this?" Calla asked. "I think you should go home and get some sleep. I'll lock the cheap deadbolt *and* wedge a chair under the knob. It'll be fine, really."

Brandon looked like he was trying not to laugh. "I've dealt with worse than a night without sleep. And you won't be fine. Any bozo with a computer and a few bucks to spare can look up your address." When Calla opened her mouth to argue further, he said, "This is non-negotiable. I'm staying."

. . .

By seven that evening, Calla's refrigerator was restocked, and she, Kendra, and Brandon had polished off an extra-large, double pepperoni pizza from Pink's.

"I'm gonna head out," Kendra announced as she carried her plate into Calla's kitchen. "Are you sure you're okay on your own here tonight?" she asked Brandon.

"One hundred percent," Brandon assured her. "Go home. Get some rest."

"I'll be back to relieve you at oh-eight-hundred."

"Sounds good."

"Thanks for getting groceries," Calla said as she accepted the plate from Kendra. "And for picking up the pizza."

"It was my pleasure, Ma'am."

"Any chance I can talk you into calling me Calla?"

"Probably not, Ma'am."

Calla laughed. "Have a good night."

Once Kendra was gone and the dishes were done, Calla fought to suppress a yawn. "You know, I've thought of another problem with you guys staying here every night."

"And that is?"

"This is a studio apartment. What are you going to do? Sit at the kitchen table and watch me sleep on the futon?"

"No, I'll be outside."

"All night?"

"All night." He looked a little amused. "You understand this is what I do for a living, right?"

"I know. I just hate for you to be uncomfortable because of me."

"Think of all the overtime I'm charging to the hospital, and then you'll stop worrying about it." He grabbed a chair from the mismatched set around Calla's battered table. "I'll be right outside if you need me. Lock the door, but don't deadbolt it. Just in case I need to come back in."

Calla followed him to the door. "Is there anything else I can get you? Some water, maybe?"

"Nope."

"Well, okay then. Good night, Brandon."

"Good night."

He started to pull the door closed, but she stopped him. "I—Nothing. Just . . . thank you."

Brandon flashed a rare smile. "Sleep tight."

TWENTY-EIGHT

IT WAS 3:00 A.M. WHEN CALLA finally gave up on trying to sleep. She'd been tossing and turning for hours, her mind racing with questions. She had always felt safe in her apartment, but Ralph's impromptu visit and Brandon's frank assessment of her vulnerabilities had unsettled her. Was she really as exposed as he seemed to think she was? It was reassuring to know that he was right outside her door for the night, but how long could she count on the hospital to foot the bill for a private security team? And did she even want a bodyguard standing watch every hour of every day? She wasn't going to live under a cloud of threat forever, was she?

Calla threw off her blankets and switched on the lamp next to the futon. She thumbed through a book for a while, hoping it would take her mind off things, but her thoughts remained locked in an anxious loop. She pulled out her phone and scrolled the Internet for a while without anything catching her interest. She considered inviting Brandon in for a chat, but for some reason, the prospect of a prolonged conversation with him proved a little too intimidating. Instead, she headed into her minuscule kitchen and started pulling out bowls and spoons and ingredients. She needed something to occupy both her mind and her hands. She needed to bake.

Soon, the scent of yeast and flour filled the apartment and wrapped around her like a warm embrace. It had been a while since she'd made bread, but the recipe was a simple one, and the acts of mixing and kneading were therapeutic. She sipped on chamomile tea while her dough rose and then, after another round of kneading, rose again. The sun was just beginning to rise when the finished loaf came out of the oven. While it cooled, Calla whipped up some scrambled eggs and started a pot of coffee.

She quickly set the table and then poked her head out the front door before she lost her nerve. Brandon was sitting on his borrowed kitchen chair, looking alert as ever, scanning the courtyard below.

"Good morning," Calla said quietly, hoping not to startle him.

"You're up early."

"I couldn't sleep. Can I interest you in some breakfast? I made toast and eggs, and I've got a fresh pot of coffee almost ready."

"You didn't need to do that."

"I wanted to." Calla beckoned him inside. "Come on. The eggs will get cold."

Brandon stood up and grabbed the chair. He followed her into the apartment and inhaled deeply.

"Smells amazing."

"Thanks. Sit down and help yourself. I'll grab the coffee. Do you take cream and sugar?"

"Just a little cream, thanks."

When Calla returned to the table with two steaming mugs, Brandon was finishing his first piece of toast. "This is delicious," he said. "I didn't know you baked."

"Yeah. I find it relaxing."

Brandon buttered a second piece. "My grandmother used to make bread like this."

"Yeah? What was she like?"

"Sweet. Funny. Spoiled the heck out of me and my sister with her cookies and cakes. It used to drive my mom crazy, all the sugar she fed us."

"That sounds nice."

"What was yours like?"

"Mine?"

"Your grandmother."

"Oh. Well. I . . ." Calla suddenly felt hot. "You know what? I forgot the jam." She jumped up from her seat and bolted around the corner into the kitchen. She was just about the open the refrigerator when she felt movement behind her.

"Calla?" Brandon's voice was quiet. "Did I upset you?"

She shrugged and kept her eyes on the refrigerator door. "It's not your fault. I just don't have any family, and it's always made me feel . . . I don't know. Different. Alone." She turned to look at him. "I don't really remember my mother. I have no idea what my father even looks like. Never met any grandparents. Did I get this," she motioned toward her face, "from one of them? Could their blood do what mine can do? It's just hard sometimes. Not knowing where you come from."

Brandon stayed silent, but his eyes were on her. He was listening.

"Anyway." Calla was suddenly eager to change the subject. "Jam. I was getting the jam."

Before she could turn back toward the refrigerator, Brandon took a step closer to her. He reached his hand up and brushed her cheek with the tips of his fingers. Calla sucked in a surprised breath.

Brandon looked equally surprised. "You, uh, had a little flour there."

"Oh."

A soft buzzing sound filled the space between them. Brandon pulled out his phone and glanced at the screen. Frowned. "Hm."

"Is everything okay?" Calla asked.

"Kendra's here. She's just a little earlier than I expected." He put his phone away, his tone suddenly more business-like. "Thanks for breakfast."

"You're welcome."

"I'll be back in a few hours."

"I'm not going anywhere."

Brandon gave her an earnest look. "Don't worry. It won't be like this forever."

For the briefest moment, that thought was disappointing. She wouldn't mind eating breakfast with him every morning.

"Right," she said quickly. "I know that."

A knock on the front door.

"That's Kendra."

He stepped around the corner to let his co-worker into the apartment. Calla heard them exchange a few words, and then he was gone.

Alone in her kitchen, Calla couldn't decide if she was hurt or relieved that he had left without saying goodbye.

TWENTY-NINE

A FEW DAYS LATER, just when Calla was about to lose her mind from the tedium of being stuck in her apartment twenty-four hours a day, she received a phone call that changed everything.

"Well, Calla, I hope you're happy. I managed to pull a rabbit out of a hat for you."

"Valerie?"

"Though I would have preferred you share your concerns with me before sending your bodyguard over here to plead your case."

"What are you talking about?"

"The board voted last night to amend your contract. From now on, in addition to your stipend, the hospital will provide you with a furnished apartment. Rent, utilities, cable, and Internet will all be covered."

"What?"

"Isn't this what you wanted?"

"I mean, that's . . . incredibly generous, but I never asked anyone to talk the hospital into getting me a new apartment. Certainly not one of my bodyguards. Who was it?"

"Apparently, Brandon Foster has some serious concerns about his ability to keep you safe in your current apartment," Valerie said coolly. "He talked Bruce into getting on the agenda at last night's meeting and didn't mince words. I believe he said something about you living in squalor while the fat cats get rich off of you."

"He said that?"

"He did. He also mentioned that Mr. Grimes visited you the other day and that a stiff breeze could probably knock down your front door. But I think it was the fat cats comment that persuaded them. These are not people who enjoy having their integrity questioned."

"I see." Calla tried not to laugh.

"It's not funny!" Valerie scolded. "Okay, it might be a little bit funny," she admitted, her tone softening momentarily before returning to its usual briskness. "Anyway, I've found a place that should make the board and the bodyguards happy. That leaves you. Do you have time to take a tour today?"

"Hold on, let me check my schedule," Calla said. "And . . . yes, it looks like I can squeeze you in between thumb-twiddling and staring at the wall. I'll just need to be home before *Jeopardy!* starts."

"Cute. I'll text you the address. Meet you there at three?"

"Sure. Can I, uh, bring a friend with me?" Calla had a feeling she could use some moral support. Valerie seemed pretty peeved about this whole thing.

"Bring anyone you like."

That was how, four hours later, Calla found herself standing in an apartment on the fifteenth floor of a swanky high-rise in the heart of the Texas Medical Center.

"It's gorgeous!" Rae gushed. As luck would have it, both she and Reuben were available to join Calla for the tour. Kendra was serving as her close protection; Brandon had requested a couple days off for personal reasons.

Valerie surveyed the living room with a slight frown on her face. "It's a little smaller than I expected."

Calla laughed as she took in the open floor plan, the quartz countertops, and the floor-to-ceiling windows that commanded a breathtaking view of the downtown skyline. "You're joking, right? This kitchen is bigger than my entire apartment."

Valerie brightened a little. "So, you like it? Mr. Foster said to make sure it had a decent kitchen."

Calla felt a little flutter in her stomach. "He did?"

Before Valerie could answer, Reuben burst out of the bedroom. "Calla! You've got to see this bathroom!"

"There's another bathroom?" She'd already spied one in the hallway across from the kitchen.

"Yes. In the bedroom." He grabbed her hand and pulled her through a spacious bedroom into a well-appointed bathroom. "Check it out!"

Calla took in the glassed-in shower, huge soaking tub, and two sinks. "Reuben, this is crazy."

He gave her a stern look. "This is the least they can do. Money is pouring into the hospital right now because of you. They're talking about building a new research wing. Don't you think you deserve a little piece of that pie?"

Calla cracked a smile. "I do like pie."

"That's the spirit!" Reuben wrapped his arm around her shoulders and gave her a quick squeeze. Then he turned and called out, "Rae! Come see Calla's new walk-in closet!"

As Rae and Reuben oohed and aahed over the closet, Calla wandered back into the main room of the apartment.

"What do you think?" Valerie asked as soon as she caught sight of her.

"Are you sure about this?"

Valerie nodded. "This unit is well within the budget the board approved. And it's got the blessing of Bruce and his team—right, Kendra?"

"Yes, Ma'am. This location is much more secure and a lot closer to the hospital, which will make the commute back and forth easier for us."

"So, you'll take it?" Valerie looked at Calla expectantly. She clearly wanted to wrap this matter up quickly.

Calla hesitated. Everyone seemed to think this move was a good idea. And she couldn't deny that it was a definite improvement over her current accommodations. "I'll take it."

"Great!" Valerie whipped her phone out of her purse with an air of relief.

Calla took another look around the living room and shook her head.

"I've never had this much space to myself. My futon's barely going to make a dent in here."

Valerie didn't look up from her phone. "You're getting a furniture allowance, too. I'll set up a meeting with the designer we use for our corporate apartments. She should be able to get enough basics in here to get you moved in by the end of the week. That'll get Bruce off my back." Her phone buzzed. "Excuse me. I need to take this call."

As Valerie stepped away, Kendra smiled at Calla. "You're going to love it here. There's a pool and a twenty-four-hour fitness center on the tenth floor. We can take a look at those on our way out." She chuckled. "You might never want to leave!"

"I know, right?" Calla tried to mirror Kendra's enthusiasm, but she couldn't help but wonder if this new apartment was a piece of the pie, as Reuben had said, or a gilded cage.

THIRTY

TRUE TO HER WORD, Valerie had Calla moved into the new apartment within forty-eight hours—with new furniture to boot. Calla didn't move much out of her old place, just a few boxes of clothing, books, and some things from the kitchen. The rest she donated or discarded. She figured it was as good a time as any for a fresh start.

Brandon returned from his time off more subdued than usual. He was diligent in helping Calla sort and pack her belongings but brushed off her gratitude when she tried to thank him for convincing the board to cover her living expenses. "It was the right thing to do," he'd said gruffly, hoisting a box before marching out the door.

The following Monday, it was back to business as usual.

Dr. Kraft summoned Calla to the lab bright and early for a round of bloodwork. Kendra dropped Calla and Brandon off in front of the hospital. As they walked inside, Calla watched a team of workers unfurl an enormous banner that stretched from the roof of the building nearly to the ground. It bore a photo of Dr. Kraft from the waist up. He was standing at an angle to the camera with his arms folded and a serious expression. The bottom half of his body was covered with the words *The Innovators Gala: Engineering the Cure for Cancer, Honoring Dr. Carson Kraft, Saturday, November 1.*

Calla's mouth dropped open. "They're throwing him a gala?"

"Looks that way," Brandon said.

"Because he needs an even bigger ego?"

"Pretty sure it has more to do with money."

Given this new information, it wasn't a huge surprise to find Valerie waiting for them in the lab.

"Good morning!" she chirped. "How are you liking the apartment?"

Calla was immediately on guard. In her limited experience, Valerie was only ever this bubbly when she wanted something. "It's great. Thanks for hooking me up with Lauren." The interior designer Valerie sent over had proven both friendly and good at her job.

"I'm so glad we were able to do that for you."

"Hey, Reuben," Calla greeted her friend as she wriggled out of her jacket. It was still a bit of a chore with the brace on her arm.

"Hey," Reuben said, tugging on her sleeve. His mood was positively somber compared to Valerie's.

"What brings you to the lab this morning, Valerie?" Calla asked. "I've never seen you in here before."

"I came to see if you would do a little favor for me." Valerie smiled widely. "Fundraising is going extremely well right now. The folks in the development office and I would like to capitalize on the moment."

"By throwing a gala."

"To raise money for the hospital," Valerie said. "And we'd like you to attend. As a sort of . . . guest of honor."

"I thought Dr. Kraft was the guest of honor. I saw your banner outside."

"He'll be receiving an award at the event," Valerie acknowledged. "But the people attending want to see you, too. After all, you play a vital role in his work."

"What about Dr. Pemmaraju? She's pretty vital to the study, too."

"That's a damn good question," Reuben muttered under his breath.

For the first time in the conversation, Valerie looked uncomfortable. "Of course, Juhi will be invited. And I'm sure Carson will acknowledge her contributions to his work. But the folks in development want the event to focus on him since he originated the study."

"And they want to parade me around like a mascot."

To her credit, Valerie didn't dispute the characterization. "It's only for a few hours. And it would mean a lot to the hospital."

Calla knew she was trapped. "Right. And how could I possibly say no after everything the hospital has done for me lately?"

"Thank you." Valerie pulled out her ever-present cell phone, presumably to share the good news with the folks in the development office.

"What exactly am I supposed to wear to this thing?" Calla asked. She'd never been to a gala.

"It's black tie," Valerie informed her.

"What does that even mean?"

Valerie started to answer, but Reuben cut her off. "It means we're going shopping." He held out his hand. "And if y'all want to use Calla as your sideshow attraction, you'd better foot the bill."

Valerie gave him a calculating look. "I suppose you have a point." She rummaged around in her purse and pulled out a credit card. "Take her to Tootsies and ask for Mimi. And Reuben?" There was a twinkle in her eye. "Have fun."

• • •

Friday was shopping day.

"You've got an appointment with Mimi at eleven," Reuben told Calla over the phone that morning. "Rae's meeting us there. Then we'll all grab lunch."

"Whoever heard of making an appointment to go shopping?" Calla asked.

"People with personal stylists."

"This is going be interesting."

"This is going to be fun," Reuben declared.

Two hours later, Brandon escorted them through the lofty entrance to one of Houston's most storied boutiques.

"Am I dressed up enough for this place?" Calla whispered to Reuben.

"Hush. You look fine."

A man with a close-cropped beard and an expression of barely disguised incredulity approached them as though he wasn't quite sure what to do with the trio standing before him. "Can I help you?"

"Yes!" Reuben flashed a confident smile. "We have an eleven o'clock appointment with Mimi."

"You do?" The man did nothing to hide his skepticism.

Reuben's smile slid from his face, and he narrowed his eyes at the man. Before he could respond, though, a woman bustled up to them.

"Reuben Sanchez?"

"Yes," he said stiffly.

"Mimi Khoury." The woman smiled and held out her hand. "It's a pleasure to meet you." She turned to greet Calla. "And you must be Calla. Valerie told me all about you!"

"Nice to meet you," Calla replied.

Mimi greeted Brandon, who was standing slightly behind the group, scanning the area around them. "Hi there! I'm Mimi."

"Brandon Foster."

"Calla's bodyguard," Reuben explained.

The man with the beard suddenly looked much more interested in helping them. "I was just about to give you a buzz," he said to Mimi. "Can I get you anything?"

"Why don't you bring us some sparkling waters, Ricky," Mimi instructed crisply. "We'll be over in formal wear."

As soon as Ricky trotted off, Mimi leaned close to Calla and Reuben. "He's a bit of a snob," she said in a low voice. "But a genius with shoes." She eyed Calla from head to toe. "Valerie says you're attending a gala?"

Calla squirmed a little. "Uh-huh. Am I a hopeless case?"

Mimi threw her head back and laughed. "Not at all! I have a feeling you're going to look great in pretty much anything I put you in." She waved. "Follow me. I've already got a few things in mind for you to try."

Calla and Reuben followed her across the store to the section designated for evening gowns. Brandon walked behind them, keeping a close eye on the handful of other customers in sight. Mimi got them settled on a low-slung couch and started peppering Calla with questions about her favorite designers, colors, and styles.

"I'm sorry, but I have absolutely no idea what I should be looking for," Calla finally admitted. "Would you mind making some suggestions for me?"

"I'd be delighted to!" Mimi said. "And don't apologize. I just wanted to get a feel for what you might like. I'll be right back with some options."

As she bustled away, Calla leaned over to Reuben. "Where's Rae? I sound like an idiot."

"She's on her way, and no, you don't." Reuben looked up as Ricky arrived with a tray of sparkling waters. "Thank you," he said coolly.

"You're welcome." Ricky gave them a deferential half-bow as he set the tray down on the table in front of them. "Let me know if there's anything else I can do for you." His gaze flickered over to where Brandon was standing, then back to Calla.

Reuben dismissed him with a tight smile. "Mimi's got us covered. Thanks, Ricky."

As soon as Ricky was out of earshot, Reuben shook his head. "Kiss ass."

"Do you think he knows who I am?" Calla asked as she grabbed a bottle of water.

"No," Reuben grumbled. "I think all he cares about are appearances. And to him, you appear loaded." He pointed at Brandon.

Calla shrugged. "Oh well. I guess that's better than being harassed for a blood sample."

A few minutes later, Mimi returned. "Okay, Calla, I have a dressing room ready with a first round of options. If you'll come this way."

When Calla stood up to follow her, Brandon fell in step behind her.

"You are *not* coming into the dressing room with me," she told him.

"No," he conceded. "But I am going to stand right outside the dressing room door."

"Is that necessary?"

"Yes." His tone made it clear that he would brook no opposition on this point.

Calla exhaled noisily. "Fine. Let's get this over with."

"Don't forget!" Reuben called after her. "I want to see them all!" Then he added, "*On* you!"

Calla complied—reluctantly. It was against every one of her instincts to draw attention to herself. But once she got over her initial discomfort, it was fun modeling the various dresses Mimi had selected.

"I told you she would look good in anything," Mimi crowed as Calla showed off a black Oscar de la Renta mini dress.

"Yeah," Reuben agreed. "This is going to be hard."

Once Rae arrived, they were able to narrow the choices down pretty quickly.

"I think it's between the red satin and the twinkly navy-purple number with the high-low hem," she declared after seeing Calla's favorites.

"I vote twinkly," Reuben said.

"I lean that way, too," Rae agreed.

Calla had on the twinkly dress in question. She examined herself in the mirror. It was sleeveless with a plunging V-shaped neckline and a black satin tie waist. It had the benefit of looking amazing and being comfortable. "I do like it," she admitted. "But are you sure I shouldn't cover up my arms?"

"What do you think, Brandon?" Rae asked.

Calla looked up. She hadn't realized that Brandon was gazing at her from the archway that led to the dressing rooms.

He blinked a few times. "I, uh . . ."

Reuben and Rae exchanged smiles. "Twinkly," they said simultaneously.

"Okay," Calla said. Then she looked at the price tag. "Oh, hell no."

"What is it?" Rae asked.

Calla looked around to make sure Mimi wasn't nearby. "It's way too expensive," she hissed.

Reuben jumped up and took a look at the tag. "Hell yes. We are buying this dress, Calla."

"I can't spend that much on one dress!"

"You aren't. The hospital is," he reminded her. "Valerie said to spare no expense. And we could get ourselves into *way* more trouble than this. I'm pretty sure the red satin was twice as much."

"Seriously?"

Reuben flagged down Mimi. "We'll take this one."

Thirty minutes later, they walked out of Tootsies with the dress, new shoes, a handbag, and a pair of killer earrings.

"Not bad for a day's work," Reuben declared as they handed off their purchases to Kendra for safekeeping in the car. "Who's hungry?" He pointed to a restaurant that was in the same shopping center as Tootsies. "Pondicheri is amazing."

"Sounds good to me," Rae said.

Calla looked at Brandon. "Are you okay if we go there?" Over the past week, he and Kendra had started to loosen up some of the restrictions they'd placed on Calla's movements.

"Sure. As long as Kendra and I can join you."

Calla smiled. "I'd like that."

They waited for Kendra to return from the car and then walked over to the restaurant. At the request of the group, Reuben, being the most familiar with the menu, ordered dishes for everyone to share. The food was delicious, and conversation flowed easily around the table. For the first time since the kidnapping, Calla felt at ease. She was laughing at one of Reuben's jokes about Dr. Kraft when she felt a hand on her shoulder.

"You're Calla Hammond."

Calla looked up. A man was staring down at her, a fanatical gleam in his eyes. She heard the sounds of chairs scraping against the concrete floor and was suddenly aware that Brandon and Kendra had jumped to their feet.

"Sir," Kendra said, her voice calm but commanding. "Please remove your hand from her shoulder."

"But I just want to talk to her," the man said, tightening his grip.

Brandon and Kendra slowly moved closer to Calla.

"Sir," Kendra said again, "I need you to step back."

"No!"

The restaurant fell silent.

The man slid his hand up Calla's neck and wrapped it around a section of her hair. "I just need a piece of her," his voice was raw with emotion. "Please."

Calla's heart thudded. The man yanked on her hair, jerking her head back. A soft whimper escaped her lips. Out of the corner of her eye, she saw a blur of motion.

Brandon rushed the man, grabbing the wrist of the hand that was holding Calla's hair and pinning the other one behind his back.

"Let go of her," he growled.

This time, it was the man who whimpered in pain. He released Calla's hair.

"I've got Calla!" Kendra slipped her arm around Calla's back.

"No!" Brandon barked. "I've got her. You cover him."

Without waiting for an answer, he released the man, lifted Calla out of her seat, and began marching her toward the nearest exit. Behind them, Calla heard the man howl, "No!"

Brandon half-carried her out of the restaurant, down the sidewalk, and through the parking garage to the SUV. His left arm kept her pressed securely to his side. He kept his right hand free, ready to grab his handgun if necessary.

"You're okay," he kept assuring her. "You're safe. I've got you."

As soon as they got to the car, he buckled Calla into the passenger seat, dashed around to the driver's side, started the engine, and backed out of the parking space.

"What about the others?" she asked.

"They're with Kendra," he replied. "You're my priority right now."

"Where are we going?"

"To the apartment."

They lapsed into silence as Brandon threaded the vehicle through the light, mid-afternoon traffic. He kept shooting concerned glances in Calla's direction.

"Are you okay?"

"I'm fine." She wasn't fine.

"Damn it!" Brandon shouted, smacking the steering wheel.

Calla closed her eyes and tried to calm her roiling stomach. She was such a fool. For a few precious hours, she'd convinced herself that she could enjoy a slice of normal life. But normal for her was an illusion. A fantasy. A bubble that burst at the slightest touch.

In so many ways, it always had been.

THIRTY-ONE

IN THE WAKE of the hair-pulling incident, Brandon and Kendra were more circumspect than ever about Calla's movements beyond her apartment or the hospital. Especially Brandon, who seemed to consider it a personal failing that the attacker had even gotten within ten feet of Calla.

"What have you decided about the gala?" she asked one evening as Brandon handed off his duties to Jimmy, who was back on night duty after finally kicking the flu.

Calla dreaded the idea of attending the gala, now just two days away. She would have no problem if her security team declared it out of the question from a safety standpoint.

Brandon's jaw tightened. "It's on for now."

"And you're okay with that?"

He shrugged. "It's a private event with a registered guest list, so it's more of a controlled environment than a restaurant or a store."

Calla must have looked disappointed because Jimmy asked, "Why so blue?" He mimed straightening a bowtie. "You'll get to see me in a tux." He winked. "And I don't dress up for just anyone."

"You're going to be there?"

"Helping Kendra with perimeter security."

"What about you?" she asked Brandon.

"I'll be your close protection, as usual."

Calla frowned. "Are you sure it's worth all this trouble? I'm okay skipping it." She could return the fancy dress and shoes, couldn't she?

"Well, the hospital's not." Brandon's expression was grim. "Unless there's an active threat against you on the day of, they want you there. So, we just have to make it as safe as possible."

. . .

Saturday dawned crisp, sunny, and with zero threats to Calla's safety, so she accepted her fate and allowed Rae to come over for a late-afternoon primping session.

"Perfect." Rae took a step back to admire her handiwork. She had kept Calla's makeup simple, focusing primarily on her eyes and lips. Her hair was piled high on her head in a loose bun, with a few curls artfully framing her face.

Calla looked at herself in the mirror. A stranger looked back at her. A beautiful stranger. She felt transformed. "Thank you."

There was a knock on the bedroom door, and they heard Brandon announce, "Time to go."

"Be right there," Calla called out.

She hugged Rae and grabbed her new handbag.

"Try to have fun, okay?" Rae fussed with one of Calla's curls.

"I'm not sure fun is the word I'd use."

Rae gave her a gentle push. "You know what I mean. Now go."

Calla walked into the living room. "I'm ready," she said as she poked through her bag to make sure her phone was inside. When Brandon didn't answer right away, she looked up and added, "Sorry I kept you . . . what?"

Brandon was staring at her.

Seized with panic, Calla looked down at the skirt of her dress, her shoes. "Is something wrong?"

"No, nothing at all," he said quickly. "You look . . . beautiful."

Calla's heart skipped a beat. "Oh. Thank you." She took a closer look at her bodyguard. He looked impeccable in a classic tuxedo. "So do you." She caught herself. "I mean, not beautiful, but, you know, really . . . nice. Better than nice. Great."

She felt like a moron.

He smiled. "Thanks." He pulled open the door to her apartment. "Shall we?"

"Where are Jimmy and Kendra?" Calla asked.

"Waiting downstairs with the car." Brandon nodded in Rae's direction. "Have a good evening, Ma'am."

Rae's eyes were shining with some unidentifiable emotion. "You, too. Both of you."

Calla and Brandon rode the elevator in companionable silence, punctuated from time to time by the exchange of shy smiles. Jimmy was waiting for them outside the car. He looked equally dashing in his tuxedo. Kendra was behind the wheel in a simple, black, one-shoulder gown.

"Everyone looks so nice," Calla said as she buckled herself into the back seat.

Kendra smiled over her shoulder. "It's fun to change things up every now and then."

Jimmy smirked. "Where exactly do you put your gun in a get-up like that?"

"None of your business, tiny."

Kendra and Jimmy continued their banter throughout the drive downtown to the Marriot Marquis, where the gala was being held. There was a long line of cars waiting to drop off passengers under the hotel's porte cochere.

"The glitterati sure are out tonight," Kendra said as they watched a group of tuxedo-clad men and women in floor-length sequin gowns climb out of a Mercedes in front of them.

"Jimmy, you're with Calla and me until Kendra's got the car secured," Brandon instructed. "Kendra, did you talk to hotel security about parking out front?"

"Sure did, boss," Kendra confirmed as the car inched closer to the entrance. "It's all squared away."

"Good. Stop here." Brandon tapped Jimmy on the shoulder. "Let's move."

"Yes, Sir." Jimmy jumped out of the car with an ease that belied a man of his size and pulled open the rear passenger door.

Brandon took Calla by the elbow and guided her with a gentle firmness out of the car. As soon as they stepped out of the vehicle, Brandon and Jimmy moved Calla toward the front door of the hotel, their eyes in constant motion as they scanned the crowd for any sign of danger.

Once inside, Brandon handed Calla off to Jimmy and began leading them across the massive lobby.

"This place is huge," Calla said as she took in the high ceilings and marbled floors.

"Sure is," Jimmy said. "Brandon's been scouting it out the last couple of nights."

"He has?"

"Yeah. He likes to be prepared."

A short elevator ride later, they emerged on the hotel's fourth floor, where a pre-gala cocktail party was in full swing.

"What do we do now?" Calla looked around nervously, recognizing no one.

Brandon pointed to a table lined with notecards. "Let's get your table assignment."

They fought their way through the crowd to the check-in table.

A perky brunette smiled up at Calla. "Name?"

"Calla. Calla Hammond."

The young woman tapped on the screen of an electronic tablet. "Hammond. Hammond. Ah, there you are. Table number . . . one." She looked up at Calla, her eyes wide. "Oh. You're—"

"There's my VIP!" Valerie's voice cut through the chatter around them. She strode toward Calla, resplendent in a curve-hugging emerald column dress. Her hair was twisted into a chic knot, her ears adorned with diamond drop earrings.

She pressed her cheek against Calla's and made a kissing sound. "I see your trip to Tootsies was a success. You look smashing. Isn't Mimi a genius?"

"Um . . ."

Valerie didn't wait for an answer. "You need champagne," she decreed. She grabbed Calla's arm and angled her toward a nearby bar. "I've got some people who are dying to meet you." She threw a glance in Brandon's direction. "You don't mind if I steal her for a few minutes, do you, Mr. Foster?"

"No, Ma'am."

As Valerie whisked her away, Calla caught a glimpse of Brandon speaking to Jimmy, who nodded and then melted into the crowd. Brandon began following in Calla's wake, keeping her in sight but giving her space. She almost swore he gave her a little wink when he caught her looking back at him.

A few minutes later, drinks in hand, Valerie led Calla over to a small knot of men.

"Gentlemen!" Valerie broke into their conversation. "I'd like you to meet Calla Hammond."

"Ms. Hammond," the tallest and broadest of the men said in a booming voice. "We finally meet." He held out a meaty hand. "I'm Nate Dennings. CEO of the hospital. I've sat in many meetings where your name's come up."

Calla wasn't sure what the proper response to such a statement was, so she opted for something simple. "It's nice to meet you."

Valerie introduced the other men in the circle. "This is Bob Bishop, Bob Owens, and Evan Lewis. They are some of the hospital's top supporters. And, of course, you know Dr. Kraft."

Calla shook hands with the two Bobs. She noted with some amusement that both men were wearing cowboy boots with their tuxedos. Then she turned to Evan, who appeared to be the only member of the group under the age of forty. He surprised her by brushing his lips against her knuckles.

"Fascinating," he said, lifting her hand closer to his face to examine it. He ran his thumb over her fingers. "To think of the power running through these veins."

Calla felt a quiver of revulsion snake up her arm.

Dr. Kraft reached over and plucked her hand from Evan's grasp. "Her blood is only powerful if you know how to harness its potential."

Evan lowered his head slightly, his eyes glittering with annoyance at Dr. Kraft's rebuke.

"And how is the harnessing business going these days, Carson?" the taller of the two Bobs asked.

"Quite well," Dr. Kraft said stiffly. "I'm making progress on a number of fronts."

"Come on now, Carson." The shorter Bob chuckled and took a swig of his drink. "Don't you think we deserve a little more detail than that? Rumor has it you're moving into the pre-clinical phase with a vaccine candidate. How's the animal testing going?"

Dr. Kraft shot an angry look at Nate. "I'm not at liberty to discuss that."

"You know how it is, Bob," Nate interjected. "Even with all of the advances we've seen since the pandemic, vaccine development can still be tricky. Carson is having a lot more luck on the treatment side of things."

Shorter Bob winked knowingly. "So, you'll still have to diagnose and treat patients."

"We'll be *curing* patients," Dr. Kraft corrected.

"How convenient." Evan's mouth twisted into a sardonic smile. "It's nice to hear that the new hospital wing you're asking us to pay for will be put to good use."

Dr. Kraft glowered. "What exactly are you implying?"

"Just that treating a disease, even curing it, is so much more . . ." Evan waved his beer airily. "Profitable," he drew the word out, "than completely eradicating it."

Nate let out a nervous laugh. "Well, now, I wouldn't put it that way at all." He pounded Dr. Kraft on the back. "If anyone can figure out this vaccine puzzle, it's Carson. And in the meantime, no one can argue that finding the cure for cancer isn't a hell of an achievement."

Evan turned to Calla. "And what about you, Ms. Hammond?"

"Me?"

"We wouldn't be standing here if it weren't for you. There's quite a lot of money to be made from this. What do you think? Should you have a financial stake in Dr. Kraft's work?"

Calla lifted her chin. "Yes, I think I should. And I do."

Evan grinned as the Bobs turned questioning looks to Nate Dennings. "Oh, I *like* this one," he said.

Valerie grabbed Calla's arm. "I believe those are the chimes for dinner," she said loudly. "Shall we find our seats?"

"Excellent idea, Valerie." Dr. Kraft inclined his head briefly at the rest of the group. "Gentlemen, it's been a pleasure. As always." His voice dripped acid.

He strode toward the ballroom where the main event was taking place. Valerie followed him, Calla trailing in her wake.

"Carson!" Valerie hissed. "You cannot antagonize this hospital's largest donors."

"Evan Lewis is a pot-stirrer."

"Agreed, but he's a very wealthy pot-stirrer. You need to play the damn game."

"I know what I'm doing, Valerie."

"Then do it," she commanded. "Now, play nice with your tablemates. I've got to go make sure your little pissing match didn't cost us the Bobs' support."

She peeled away from them at the entrance to the ballroom. Conversation buzzed as people streamed inside to find their tables. The room was dotted with round tables, each designed to seat ten people. At the front, a raised stage had been erected. It was equipped with an enormous projection screen and a podium.

"My god," Calla breathed as she took in the scene. "How many people are here?"

"Over two thousand."

Dr. Kraft took her arm as they began weaving through the tables toward the front of the room. People stared as they passed by. A few even called out greetings to Dr. Kraft. He acknowledged them with a dip of his head but did not stop to chat. Finally, they reached their table.

"You're sitting next to me," he declared.

"What about Dr. Pemmaraju? Is she sitting with us, too?"

"I have no idea." He led her around the table to a chair that faced away from the stage. It was positioned in such a way that Calla's visibility to the rest of the room would be maximized. "Sit."

She cut her eyes at him. "I'm not a dog."

"That's not—"

"Dr. Pemmaraju!" Calla waved as she caught sight of her other doctor. "Over here!"

Every eye in the vicinity seemed to turn their way as Dr. Pemmaraju approached the table. She was breathtaking in a Banarasi silk sari—lapis blue with a fuchsia top and opulent gold embroidery. Her wrists were adorned with stacks of delicate gold bangles. Her face bore an expression of fierce determination.

"Dr. Kraft." She greeted her colleague with an icy smile.

"Dr. Pemmaraju. I didn't think you were coming."

She skewered him with a look. "And miss your big night?"

"Well." Dr. Kraft cleared his throat. "If you'll excuse me." He turned and disappeared behind a group of people massed around a neighboring table.

"It's not right," Calla said. "Him getting all of the credit."

"No, it's not," Dr. Pemmaraju agreed. "For all the advances that have been made in the sciences, research medicine is still a bit of a boys' club." She blew out an aggravated breath. "But I refuse to sit quietly and wait my turn, as they like to say. Screw that."

"They'll have a hard time ignoring you tonight," Calla said. "You look amazing."

"So do you. Though I wish we could evolve beyond flashing our feathers to get the attention we deserve."

"Amen to that."

Dr. Pemmaraju flagged down a nearby server who was toting a tray of wine glasses.

"Cheers." She and Calla clinked two glasses of red. "To a better and brighter future. For everyone."

They sat down, and Calla glanced around the room, trying to locate Brandon. It took a few moments, given the size of the crowd, but she finally spotted him hovering next to a service cart near the wall closest to her. He gave her a nod when she made eye contact.

The other seats at the table began to fill up. Nate Dennings and his wife, Caroline, sat on the opposite side so they could see the stage without craning their necks. Valerie set her purse down to reserve the spot next to Dr. Pemmaraju, then dashed away to work the room until dinner was served. The rest of the seats went to people Calla presumed were major donors and their spouses. She smiled and shook their hands, but the din in the room had grown so loud that their names were impossible to hear, much less remember.

She was glad when the hospital's director of development (a woman she had never met) invited a local pastor to the stage to bless the proceedings and finally kick off the dinner. Calla picked at her food while talk swirled around her. Occasionally, she snuck a glance at Brandon. He remained alert at his post, head on a swivel, continuously scanning the room.

Finally, after a signal from Valerie, Nate stood up and buttoned his tuxedo jacket. "Time for me to go to work," he announced to the table before mounting the stage and calling the room to order.

"Ladies and gentlemen, I'm Nate Dennings. CEO of St. Peregrine's Cancer Center. It is my honor to welcome you to our first ever Innovators Gala. Tonight, we celebrate an extraordinary achievement, discovering a cure for cancer." He paused to allow an enormous round of applause. "And the man behind that discovery, Dr. Carson Kraft." Another round of applause, this time even louder. "It is also my distinct pleasure to introduce the young woman whose partnership with Dr. Kraft has made all of this possible." Nate thrust his hand in Calla's direction. "Calla Hammond!" The applause now was deafening. People began to stand, either to express their admiration or to catch a glimpse of the woman in question.

"Stand up!" Valerie exhorted Calla. She threw a look at Dr. Kraft. "You, too! People want to see both of you!"

The applause continued. Dr. Kraft stood, but Calla remained pinned in her seat, overwhelmed by the moment.

Dr. Pemmaraju slipped a comforting hand into Calla's and squeezed. "It's okay."

Slowly, Calla got to her feet.

"Smile," Dr. Kraft instructed as he beamed and waved at the crowd. He leaned closer to Calla. "Remember," he said through his smile, "there's a lot of money here tonight."

Calla's throat felt dry and constricted. Every single eye in the room seemed to be focused on her. Beneath the sound of clapping, she could feel the hum of whispered words—about her dress, her skin, her blood. The expressions on the faces that surrounded her seemed to stretch and distort from polite smiles to avaricious leers. Her heart pounded frantically in her chest, and her breathing grew shallow. Finally, she and Dr. Kraft took their seats as the applause died down.

Nate continued talking, going through the order of events for the evening, but Calla didn't hear him. Everything around her was a jumble of sound and color that threatened to engulf her. The walls of the room seemed to creep toward her. Her rising panic was interrupted by the arrival of a server.

"Coffee?" the young woman asked.

"N—no, thanks," Calla stammered. "Excuse me." Legs shaking slightly, she stood up again.

"Are you okay?" Dr. Pemmaraju asked.

"Bathroom." Calla rushed toward the nearest exit.

Brandon intercepted her near the outermost table.

"What's going on?"

"Can't. Breathe," she rasped.

Brandon guided her toward the door. "Come with me."

As they walked, he spoke into his collar. "Jimmy, bring a bottle of water to the alcove next to the northeast bathrooms."

In less than a minute, he had her settled on an upholstered chair in a small sitting area just off the concourse. Jimmy arrived thirty seconds later, water bottle in hand.

"Thanks," Brandon said. "Can you make sure we have some privacy?"

"Sure thing, boss." Jimmy stationed himself near the entrance to the alcove.

Brandon knelt in front of Calla and unscrewed the cap on the water bottle. "Take a sip."

Hands shaking, Calla took the bottle from him and pressed it to her lips. She managed to choke down a small amount before handing it back.

"Good," he said, his voice soothing. "Now, I'd like you to close your eyes and focus on slowing down your breathing." He took her hands in his and began rubbing circles with his thumbs on the insides of her wrists. "You're having a panic attack."

Calla kept her eyes closed. "How do you know?"

"I've had some experience with them."

"Oh." Calla took a shuddering breath. "From when you were in the SEALs?"

It was a moment before Brandon answered. "No," he said slowly. "My ex-wife used to get them."

Ex-wife? Calla's mind exploded with questions, but it wasn't the time to ask them. She concentrated on her breathing. In, out. In, out. In, out. Slowly, the pounding in her chest receded, and the crushing sense of doom began to fade.

She opened her eyes. Brandon was still kneeling in front of her. He handed her the water bottle again.

"Thank you."

"Do you want to talk about what happened in there?" he asked. "You don't have to, but sometimes it helps."

Calla took another sip of water. "It was like I was trapped. The people and the walls . . . they were closing in on me. I didn't feel like *me* anymore. I felt like nothing was real." She looked away from him. "That sounds stupid, doesn't it?"

"Not at all."

"The only reason anyone in that room gives a shit about me is because I have something they want. And people take what they want. Especially when it comes to . . ."

"When it comes to what?"

"Sickness. Death." A tear rolled down her cheek.

Brandon reached into his pocket and pulled out a handkerchief. "Here."

She dabbed at her watery eyes. "I didn't think people carried these anymore."

"You can thank my dad. He never left the house without one. Taught me to do the same."

When Calla tried to hand the handkerchief back, he waved her off. "Keep it. I've got more at home."

Calla played with the folds of the cloth square. "I don't want to go back in there."

"I'll call Kendra to bring the car around."

He made a move to talk into his radio when Calla blurted out, "I don't want to go home, either."

"Are you hungry?"

"A bit."

"Do you like Turkish food?"

"I don't know. I've never had it."

"I know a place. It's close to the med center. And the food's way better than the rubber chicken they served in there."

"But I thought it wasn't safe to go to a restaurant."

"I think tonight qualifies for an exception. And it'll be quiet there. Not too busy this time of night."

Calla suddenly felt foolish. She didn't want his pity. "Never mind." She shook her head. "You don't need to do this."

"I know. I want to." He gave her one of his devastating half-smiles. "And I'm hungry, too."

THIRTY-TWO

WHEN THEY ARRIVED AT THE RESTAURANT, Brandon instructed Jimmy to ride with Kendra back to her own car. She'd clocked a fourteen-hour shift by that point and was due for a break. He would then return to take them back to Calla's apartment.

"Have a good night," Calla said to Kendra.

"Save me some dessert!" Jimmy called out from the passenger side window.

As the SUV backed out of the tiny parking lot, Brandon escorted Calla through the narrow opening of an ivy-covered trellis. A young man stood at the host stand, wiping down menus. He smiled when he saw them. "Brandon! Good to see you!"

"Good to see you, too, Jalil."

"How's Sydney?"

Brandon hesitated for a fraction of a second. "She's fine." He pointed to a back corner of the patio. "Could we sit over there?"

"Of course!" Jalil scooped up two menus. "Follow me."

"Why don't you sit here?" Brandon pulled a chair out for Calla. She sat down, facing away from the other tables on the patio. Brandon took the chair opposite her, so he could easily see anyone who approached them.

"Can I get you started with something to drink?" Jalil asked as he set the menus in front of them.

"Water for me," Brandon replied.

"I'll have water as well," Calla said. "And a Diet Coke, please."

"Certainly."

"Bring it in a can with a cup of ice, okay?" Brandon said.

Jalil nodded. "I'll be right back."

Calla gave Brandon a funny look. "That was oddly specific."

"It's my only complaint about this place," Brandon explained. "Their soda machine is way too syrupy. I've learned the hard way it's better to get a can."

"So, you're a regular."

"I guess." Brandon toyed with the edge of his menu. "I come about once a month or so."

"With Sydney?" She tried to keep the question as light as possible, but it still came out like prying.

"Yeah." He smiled. "It's her favorite."

Calla's gut twisted a little. She wondered what it was like to have someone smile like that when they thought of you.

"So," she said, trying to choose her words as carefully as possible, "is she your, uh, girlfriend?"

Brandon threw his head back and laughed. "No, but she'll get a kick out of that question!"

"I'm sorry." Calla's cheeks burned. She stared down at the table. "I shouldn't have asked. It's none of my business."

"Don't worry about it. Really. I only laughed because Sydney's my daughter."

Calla's head popped back up. "Your daughter?"

"She's ten."

Jalil returned with their drinks. "Two waters and a Diet Coke." He popped the can of soda and poured it into a glass of ice for Calla.

"Thank you," she said.

"My pleasure. Are you ready to order?"

Calla looked at Brandon. "Any recommendations?"

"Do you like hummus?" he asked.

"Sure."

"Let's start with an order of hummus, then," Brandon said to Jalil. "With some tabbouleh and a side of feta, too. Okay?"

"Coming right up."

As Jalil bustled off, Calla took a sip of her drink, wondering how to fill the silence he'd left in his wake. Brandon must have been doing the same thing because they both ended up talking simultaneously.

"So—"

"What—"

Brandon dipped his head politely. "You first. Please."

"I was just going to ask what else you and your daughter like to do together." She smiled. "Besides going out for Turkish food."

"Let's see. She likes to play board games. Kills me every time we play Monopoly. And we ride bikes when we can."

"That must be hard. Sharing custody."

"It's . . . complicated. My ex's parents help out a lot. We're making it work."

Calla took another sip in the silence that followed. She felt like she was tiptoeing through a conversational minefield.

"Are you feeling any better?" Brandon asked.

"Much better," Calla said. "Thanks for getting me out of there."

"You're welcome."

Brandon cleared his throat. "I've never asked you what you used to do. Before, uh . . . this."

"You mean before I became a professional lab rat?"

Brandon laughed. "Your words, not mine."

"I used to work in a library."

"You're a librarian?"

"I wish. Maybe one day, if this health stuff calms down and I'm able to finish my degree. No, I was just an assistant."

"How'd you get into that?"

"I got bounced around to a lot of foster homes when I was a kid." She touched her face. "I wasn't exactly anyone's idea of a dream child."

Brandon's expression darkened. "That's awful."

"Yeah." Calla sighed. "Anyway, public libraries are free and never all that crowded, so books became my best friends. When I was eleven, I hung around the local branch so much one summer that the librarian put me to work shelving books. She gave me something to do every day. A sense of purpose." Calla looked down at her arms. "And, I got to be inside, which helped, you know, protect my skin."

"Are people really that prejudiced against vitiligo?"

Calla was touched that he knew the name of her condition. "I think," she said slowly, "most people fear what they don't understand. They don't like it when a person doesn't fit neatly into the little boxes we use to classify ourselves. Black, white. Male, female. Gay, straight. If you stray outside the lines, there must be something wrong with you. I've had people point at me, laugh at me, call me names, refuse to touch me when they're handing me change at the grocery store." She shook her head. "My whole life, all I ever wanted was to be normal. To look normal. To be able to walk outside wearing shorts and a tank top without using up a whole bottle of sunscreen or worrying about someone yelling at me to cover that shit up. To hold hands with someone who wasn't afraid of 'catching' something from me." She paused. "But you know what I wish now?"

"What?"

"I wish I'd known how good I had it back then. I can't tell you how nice it would be to go back to being stared at and just getting on with my day. Now, not only do I have to deal with people who think it's fine to comment on how my appearance offends them, I have to deal with the fact that they think it's their God-given right to tear me apart and take pieces for themselves." Calla traced her finger around a design on the tablecloth. "One of the donors asked me tonight if I think I'm entitled to a share of whatever they make from the study. Everyone cares so much about the money. Don't get me wrong; money's nice. I just want to make sure they actually do what they say they can do with all those little pieces they keep taking from me."

"What's that?" Brandon asked quietly.

"Cure cancer. Wipe it from the face of the earth. And not just for the people who can afford it. For everyone."

"I'm sorry, Calla."

"Why? You're one of the good guys. You're keeping me safe."

"For what you've been through. What you're going through."

Calla cast around for a change of subject. "Enough about me. Tell me what you were like as a kid."

Brandon thought for a moment. "Different from you. I was never much of a reader. I liked being outside. I was a big kid, competitive, always getting into trouble. My high school guidance counselor suggested the military, so I joined the Navy right after graduation. The lifestyle fit me like a glove. After a few years, a friend talked me into SEAL training. Second proudest day of my life was the day I earned my Trident."

"What was the first?"

"The day Sydney was born."

"She's lucky to have you."

"I don't know about that," Brandon said. "I screw things up all the time."

"Everybody does, but you're around. That's what really matters to a kid. Trust me. I know."

This time, the silence that swelled between them was charged with intensity. Brandon reached across the table. His fingers brushed the tops of hers. "Calla, I—"

"Hey! Have y'all ordered yet?" Jimmy called from across the half-empty restaurant. Brandon withdrew his hand from Calla's so quickly that she wondered if she had imagined the whole thing. Jimmy approached and plopped down in the seat next to Calla.

"Just a few appetizers," Brandon said, sliding a menu to Jimmy.

"Great! I'm starving."

Calla forced herself to look down at her own menu. Her heart was pounding, and her stomach churned with a nervous, hopeful feeling. She'd liked guys before, but this felt different. This felt . . . reciprocated. Maybe? She felt like an idiot for even thinking such a thing. And yet, when she dared to glance across the table, she saw Brandon looking back at her so intently that she felt certain about at least one thing. She was more than just a job to him.

When he looked at her, she felt like a person.

THIRTY-THREE

"YOU LEFT EARLY THE OTHER NIGHT."

"Dr. Kraft! You startled me." Calla pressed her hand against her chest. She had assumed the lab was deserted. But there was Dr. Kraft, perched on a rolling chair, studying her with the air of a king surveying his domain.

He sniffed. "A lot of people were disappointed they didn't get to meet you."

"I wasn't feeling well."

Dr. Kraft glared at her. He clearly expected more of an explanation, but Calla had no intention of giving him one. She grabbed her coat from a hook near the door. She'd spent the past two hours allowing a dermatologist to take punch biopsies from various areas of her body. The numbing medicine was beginning to wear off, and she felt a little testy.

"I need a blood draw," Dr. Kraft announced as she leaned down to pick up her purse.

"We just did one this morning."

"Wasn't enough." Dr. Kraft pulled on a pair of gloves. "Take a seat."

"You're doing it yourself?"

"I am."

Calla eyed him curiously. Dr. Kraft never stooped to perform lowly tasks like blood draws. He preferred to leave that type of work to others, and Calla was fine with that. There was a distinct art to drawing blood in a way that wasn't painful to the donor, and she didn't have much faith in Dr. Kraft's abilities. "Why don't we call Reuben?" she suggested as she hung her coat back up. "I'm sure he's available."

"No need. I can handle this."

"Are you sure?"

"Calla." Dr. Kraft's voice was now tinged with impatience. "Let's just get this over with."

Reluctantly, she crossed the room and sat down in the blood draw chair. Dr. Kraft rolled up her sleeve and tied a tourniquet around her upper arm. He rubbed the crook of her elbow vigorously with an alcohol-soaked cotton pad, then uncapped a needle and jabbed it under her skin. Calla winced. As she suspected, Dr. Kraft wasn't very good at this. He swore softly, pulled the needle out of her arm, and jabbed again. This time, he managed to hit a vein. With his foot, he pulled a stainless-steel table closer to Calla's chair. Two empty bags and a length of tubing lay on a sterile pad. Dr. Kraft connected the tubing to the needle in her arm. She watched as her blood flowed through the tube and began filling the first bag.

"How much are you taking?"

"Two units."

"That's a lot, isn't it?"

Dr. Kraft watched as her blood slowly filled the first bag. "I don't recall asking for your input on how to run my lab."

"Whatever." Calla leaned back in the chair and closed her eyes. She was tired and wanted to go home. "Just leave enough for me to live on."

THIRTY-FOUR

NOW THAT THE GALA WAS OVER, Calla's life fell back into a routine. Of sorts. Most days, she went to the hospital for tests or scans. The rest of the time, she was at her apartment. Occasionally, she was allowed a quick trip to the grocery store or Target (either very early in the morning or as late at night as possible—always heavily disguised). But her contact with the outside world was limited. No more working at the library. No walks along the bayou that ran behind her new apartment building. No dinners out—not even with the security team in tow. She was too exposed.

There appeared to be an inverse relationship between Calla's media coverage and her freedom of movement—the further her story spread, the smaller her "sphere of safety," as Brandon called it, became. Interest in Calla and the study increased daily. Requests for live television interviews, podcasts, print stories, and photo shoots poured in from all sides. At Calla's request, Valerie turned each one down. But that didn't stop the stories from being written, the photos from being taken, or the speculation from circulating. Calla rarely strayed from the narrowing confines of her world, but every time she switched on the television or checked online, there she was. Everywhere, and at the same time, nowhere.

"Hey."

Calla jumped at the sound of another human voice. She'd been alone for most of the afternoon.

"Brandon? What are you doing here? Kendra said you took a personal day."

"Brought you some dinner." He was holding a pizza box. "Double pepperoni from Pink's. Your favorite."

"Where's Jimmy?"

"Gave him the night off."

"Is everything okay?"

Brandon set the pizza down on the coffee table. "Yeah. He just wanted to tuck the girls in. My ex's parents are in town from Austin, and they offered to take Syd to the movies, so I figured I'd, you know," he paused and scratched his head in a self-conscious way, "check on you."

Calla's heart thumped. She hadn't spent time alone with Brandon since the night of the gala. She'd wondered if he was avoiding her. Maybe not.

She scrambled up from her perch on the couch. "I'll get some plates."

"How are you liking the new place?" Brandon asked as he folded a slice in half and took a bite.

"It's, um, it's great." Calla tried to force some enthusiasm into her voice. "Really beautiful. And big."

"Uh-huh." Brandon cut her a skeptical look. "You sound thrilled."

"It's kind of lonely."

He set his pizza down. "I know it's hard. Not being able to go out much right now. But there's no reason you can't have friends over. Wouldn't that help?"

She shook her head. "Reuben and Michael have better things to do than babysit me all the time." Before her current lockdown, Calla had gone out several times with the couple. But she didn't want to press her luck with them. Reuben saw her enough as it was. He deserved a break from work.

"I was thinking of other friends," Brandon said, a hint of amusement in his voice. "Maybe people who don't work at the hospital?"

Other friends. What a novel concept.

"Not a whole lot of those to choose from at the moment." Calla leaned forward, trying to cover her embarrassment by snagging a piece of pizza.

"I'm sorry."

"It's not like I've never had friends," she rushed to explain. "I have. It's just that I've never had a lot of them. Never needed a lot. I made a few in college, but when I kept getting sick and had to drop out, they stopped calling after a while." She stared across the room. "I think they didn't know what to say. People sometimes don't. When you're sick."

Brandon moved a little closer to her on the couch.

Great, now he's feeling sorry for me.

"I don't have a ton of friends either," he said. "Didn't help when we had Sydney so young. Can't just go out for a beer anytime you want when you've got a kid at home."

"Guess not," Calla replied. She appreciated the attempt to make her feel better, but it was hard to imagine someone like Brandon in the same social bracket as someone like her. She decided to change the subject. "How is Sydney?"

He heaved a sigh. "I'm taking her to Boston tomorrow. My folks are driving up from Providence to meet us. We haven't seen them in a while."

"That should be fun."

"Yeah, I guess."

Calla laughed at his morose expression. "Now you're the one who doesn't sound thrilled."

"No, I am." He cracked a small smile. "Syd wants to visit Harvard. Girl's got big dreams." The smile faded.

"But?"

Brandon shrugged. "Things have been awkward with my parents since Christy left."

"Christy?"

"My ex."

"Oh."

"They wanted me to move up north to be closer to them, but I didn't want to take Syd away from school, her friends. Unlike you and me, the kid's a social butterfly."

Calla made a disbelieving sound.

"What?"

"It's just kind of hard to believe you weren't the captain of the football team. The prom king. The center of everything."

"I was. Until I got the head cheerleader pregnant our senior year in high school. Amazing how fast people scatter when they realize you fuck things up just like everyone else."

"People suck, don't they?"

"Not all of them," Brandon said quietly. "You're pretty great."

"Yeah, right." Calla deflected the compliment. "All anyone sees when they look at me is"—she waved her hand in front of her face—"this."

Brandon grabbed her hand, his expression almost angry. "That's not true, Calla. Most people turn tail and run when things get tough. Trust me, I know. But not you. You're strong and brave and, and . . . selfless." His voice softened. "And this?" He tipped her chin up with his other hand and traced a finger around the bright white skin that surrounded her lips. "This is beautiful."

Calla could hardly breathe. No one had ever touched her like this—in a way that made something she'd always thought of as ugly feel attractive. Time seemed to slow down as Brandon gazed at her with a fierce possessiveness she'd never seen on another person's face. Her eyes closed as he leaned in and pressed his lips to hers. As his mouth began to move against her mouth, a surge of feeling—like electricity—jolted through her.

She broke away.

"Sorry," she gasped. "I—"

"No," Brandon cut her off. "I'm sorry. I should've asked you before I did that."

He slid away from her, distress spreading across his face. Calla reached out to stop him. "It's okay," she said. "I just got a little . . . I don't really know what I'm doing. The last time someone kissed me, I was twelve, and it was on a dare."

"I don't know what I'm doing either." The words had an edge that threatened to cut her deeply if it wasn't for the touch of his hand on her cheek. She pressed her face gently against his palm, savoring the warmth.

"I should go." Brandon pulled his hand away and stood up. "Syd will be home soon."

Before Calla could think of something to say, he was gone, and she was alone again.

Alone and wondering what the hell had just happened between them.

THIRTY-FIVE

CALLA WAS GLAD SHE DIDN'T have to see Brandon for a few days after their impromptu dinner date. She was a jumble of conflicting emotions. Hurt when he didn't call to check on her but relieved to have some space to process their kiss.

The only thing she was sure about was the wisdom of his suggestion to bring some of the outside world into her progressively smaller one.

"I'm having some people over for Thanksgiving," she announced one afternoon as Kendra drove her home from the hospital. Brandon was riding shotgun. It was his first day back after his Boston trip. He'd been preoccupied all afternoon, wrapped up in his thoughts, barely saying more than a few words to Calla. His behavior was bewildering. They'd kissed. Or, more accurately, he'd kissed her. There was obviously something between them. Was he just waiting until they had a moment alone to talk about it? Or was he ignoring her?

"I'd love for you to be there," Calla continued. "Both of y'all."

"Dang." Kendra frowned. "I'm gonna be in Nevada that weekend. Sorry to miss it."

"What about you?" Calla asked Brandon. "Jimmy's coming with his wife and girls. We talked about it last night." A pause. "You could bring Sydney if you like."

No answer. She wondered if she'd crossed a line.

Finally, he said, "Sydney's spending the week with her mother's side of the family."

"Oh, okay."

Brandon seemed disinclined to elaborate, so she let the subject drop.

They were a few blocks from her apartment building when he spoke again. "Jimmy's going to be there?"

"Yeah."

"I might be able to stop by."

"Fine." Calla did her best to match the evenness of his tone, but it was difficult. There was no misreading these signals. Brandon was giving her the cold shoulder, plain and simple. The only question that remained was why.

THIRTY-SIX

CALLA SPENT THE NEXT FEW DAYS knee-deep in preparations for her Thanksgiving dinner party, which had expanded to include Rae, Reuben, Dr. Pemmaraju, Charlie, and various plus ones. The work kept her mind off Brandon, who still hadn't made an effort to talk to her. She was seriously contemplating disinviting him to dinner when Valerie summoned her to the hospital for something she described vaguely as an "executive meeting."

"Please don't tell me you have another gala you want me to attend," Calla said when she caught sight of the communications director.

"Not exactly." Valerie looked grim. She pointed to a chair at the opposite end of the lab's conference table. "Why don't you have a seat? We need to talk."

Calla took a closer look at the other people gathered around the table: Dr. Pemmaraju, Reuben, and Jackson Albright from the hospital's counsel office. Nate Dennings' presence was unexpected. What was the hospital's CEO doing here?

No one greeted her; their expressions were somber. Calla sat down. "What's going on?" she asked. "Where's Dr. K?"

A man Calla had never seen before was sitting next to Valerie. He cleared his throat. "Ms. Hammond, my name is Patrick Beckham. I'm the hospital's general counsel. Let me get right to the point. Did Dr. Kraft take two units of whole blood from you on Monday, November third?"

"I, uh, don't know the exact date, but I remember that blood draw. It was kind of weird."

"Weird in what way?"

"He did it himself. Reuben usually does the blood draws. He's a lot better at them. And . . ." she hesitated, unsure how much to disclose.

"And?" Patrick prompted.

"Well, he took more than usual."

"More blood?"

"Yes."

"Did Dr. Kraft tell you what the blood would be used for?"

Calla huffed. "What do you think?"

"Yes or no, did he tell you what the blood was being used for?"

"No." Calla narrowed her eyes at the lawyer. "What's this all about?"

Valerie leaned forward to speak. "On Wednesday, November fifth, two unusually large cash donations were made to the hospital. They were specifically earmarked for the study. This alone wouldn't normally have raised any suspicions. But yesterday morning, the development office got a call from a third donor who had also just made a substantial contribution to the study. He was calling to confirm the hospital's receipt of his wire transfer." She paused. "And he had a question about where to bring his wife for her transfusion."

"Her transfusion?"

Dr. Pemmaraju picked up the story from there. "I happened to be in the lab when the call was transferred over." Her voice was tight with anger. "The donor got upset when I didn't know what he was talking about. He said he wanted to make sure he got the same deal for his wife that the others had gotten. When I asked him what others he was talking about, he gave me the names of the first two donors."

"Let me guess," Calla said coldly. "They're cancer patients?"

"One is being treated for multiple myeloma. The other for pancreatic cancer. The third one's wife was just diagnosed with stage three breast cancer."

"And they got my blood."

Dr. Pemmaraju nodded. "We're pretty sure the first two did, Calla. There's no record of the blood samples from the November third draw in the lab's database."

"Did it work?"

"Did what work?"

"My blood. Did it cure their cancer?"

"We don't know. We're trying to get that information. But it seems likely, based on my conversation with the third donor."

"That hypocritical bastard!" Calla exploded. "After all of his lectures about ethics and protocols. After he refused to help Lizzie. He was selling my blood?"

Jackson chose that moment to jump into the conversation. "The good news is we were able to shut this down as soon as we heard from the third donor."

Calla shot him a look of contempt. "Oh, *that's* the good news?"

Patrick silenced his underling with a glare. "We haven't had time to conduct a full investigation, but it appears that Dr. Kraft may have had a number of other donors lined up for transfusions. Needless to say, those won't be happening."

"You're damn right they won't," Calla snapped. "Because I'm not giving you people another drop of my blood unless you make some serious changes around here."

Nate Dennings held up his hands in a calming gesture. "Let's not be hasty. I know this news is upsetting, but we're taking steps to address what's happened."

"Like what exactly?"

"First of all, Dr. Kraft is no longer employed by this hospital. We've filed a complaint with the state medical board. It's likely he will lose his license."

"Okay. That's a start. What else are you going to do?"

Nate exchanged a look with Patrick. "We're developing new protocols to ensure better oversight of your blood and tissue samples. These are very unique circumstances. The potential for corruption is on a different level than anything we've ever dealt with before."

"More protocols," Calla said wryly. "I guess that's sort of inevitable. Who's taking over the study?"

"The hospital will form a search committee to appoint a suitable replacement. In the meantime, Dr. Pemmaraju will run the lab."

"In the meantime? How about you skip the search committee and just put Dr. Pemmaraju in charge for good?"

Nate gave her a patronizing smile. "I'm afraid that's not how these things work, Ms. Hammond."

"Well, *I'm* afraid that's how things need to work if you want me to remain a part of the study."

Dr. Pemmaraju caught Calla's eye. *What are you doing?* she mouthed.

Nate's smile hardened. "We shouldn't lose sight of the bigger picture here. We all want this research to succeed. We all want to cure cancer."

"Yes, we do. And that's why Dr. Pemmaraju needs to run the study," Calla said firmly. "She's the only person I trust to do the job. She gets it, or I walk."

"But your contract—"

"Does not preclude her from withdrawing from the study at any time," Valerie said sharply. "Nate, I don't see the problem here."

Nate looked at Patrick, who shrugged and said, "She's right."

"Fine," Nate conceded. "Dr. Pemmaraju, you're in charge of the study, but you report directly to me. Understood? And if I get one whiff of something out of the ordinary, you're gone." He stood up and planted his hands on the table. "This hospital cannot handle any more scandals."

THIRTY-SEVEN

"AND THEN CALLA SAID, 'Well, *I'm* afraid that's how things need to work if you want me to stay in the study.' It was classic. Classic!"

It was Thanksgiving Day, and Reuben was re-enacting Calla's showdown with Nate Dennings for Michael, Rae, and Charlie. They were all nestled comfortably on Calla's new living room couches.

"It wasn't nearly as exciting as he's making it sound," Calla said as she set a platter of cheeses, nuts, olives, and dried fruits on the coffee table.

"Yes, it was," Reuben insisted. "You were a total badass!"

Calla laughed. "Anyone need more wine?" When no one took her up on the offer, she said, "Whenever you're ready, there's red on the counter and white in the fridge."

There was a knock on the front door.

"I'll get it!" Calla trotted across the apartment. So far, she was thoroughly enjoying playing hostess at her first dinner party.

"Dr. Pemmaraju, come in." She stepped aside as the doctor entered. "And you must be AJ," she said to the man following behind. "It's so nice to meet you."

Calla took their coats and led them to the living area, where everyone else was gathered.

"Who let in this riffraff?" Reuben stood up to hug Dr. Pemmaraju.

"Takes one to know one," she laughed in reply.

"Charlie," Calla said, "I don't think you've met Dr. Juhi Pemmaraju yet. And this is her husband, AJ Broussard."

Dr. Pemmaraju elbowed her. "When are you going to start calling me Juhi? I've only asked about a hundred times."

"It feels weird calling you that! You're my doctor."

Reuben held up his glass. "And our new fearless leader!"

"Hear, hear," Rae joined him. "A toast to your well-deserved promotion. I never liked that other guy."

Dr. Pemmaraju took a seat next to Michael. "Thank you, Rae. And I'd love some," she said to Calla, who was holding up an empty glass and a bottle of red wine.

"How's the new job going?" Michael asked.

Dr. Pemmaraju made a so-so gesture with her hand. "It's a little more political than I expected."

"Political?"

"There's a lot of people at the hospital with ideas about what direction the research should be going. But it's early days, and I'm an unknown quantity to a lot of the higher-ups. I guess they just need to get to know me a little better." She sighed. "I've always been more focused on the pure science, but I'll adjust." She seemed eager to change the subject. "Charlie, Calla tells me you're a retired aerospace engineer."

"She would be correct."

"Were you with NASA? AJ's a flight systems engineer there." Dr. Pemmaraju gazed proudly at her husband.

Charlie leaned forward. "Are you on the Mars project?"

"Most of the time," AJ replied. "I coordinate with the lunar team every now and then as well."

They were launching into a discussion about the future of the space program when there was another knock at the door.

Calla jumped up. "Be right back."

Her heart beat a little faster as she crossed the apartment again. Nearly all of her guests had arrived. Brandon hadn't confirmed he was coming, but he hadn't backed out either. Part of her hoped he wasn't about to make an appearance. She was having a perfectly nice evening without him.

There was a tremendous amount of chattering in the hallway. Definitely not Brandon.

"Sorry, we're late!" Jimmy boomed when Calla opened the door. He ran his hand over his mostly bald head. "My hair took forever."

The woman standing next to him laughed. "Don't listen to him. He's covering for me." She held out a foil-covered plate. "It took me longer to bake the pie than I planned."

Calla took the plate and peeled back a corner of foil. "Ooh! Pecan! It looks delicious. Thank you."

Jimmy put his arm around the woman's shoulders. "Calla, this is my wife, Lucia." He held out his other hand toward the three tow-headed girls lined up beside him in descending height order. "And this is Cora, Charlotte, and Claire."

"It's nice to meet all of you," Calla said with a smile. "My name is Calla."

"Do you spell it with a C?" Cora asked.

"I do."

"That's just like our names!" Charlotte said.

"I'm three!" said the littlest one, Claire.

Calla laughed. "Well, that's the perfect age to help me with something." She held the door open a little wider. "Come on in."

As the family filed inside, Calla pointed the grown-ups in the direction of refreshments. Then, she led the girls to her new dining room table. It was already set for dinner, but she'd held off on decorations.

"I was hoping you might like to decorate the table." She held up a bag full of crafts she'd bought during a late-night Target run with Kendra and Jimmy.

Cora started looking through the bag. "What are these?" she asked, holding up a small package.

"They're called place cards," Calla explained. "You write people's names on them and then put them on the table where you want each person to sit."

"We can be in charge of where everyone sits?"

"I'd appreciate it," Calla said. "I've got a lot to do in the kitchen."

Cora's face lit up. "Cool!"

"Let me see what's in the bag." Charlotte craned her neck for a look inside.

"Here." Cora thrust the bag at her younger sister. "But I'm doing the cards." She gave Calla a serious look. "I'm the only one who knows how to write."

"I can write!" Charlotte protested. "I'm in pre-K. I know all the letters."

"I draw unicorns." Claire seemed oblivious to the disagreement brewing between her older sisters.

"Don't be stupid, Claire." Cora rolled her eyes. "It's Thanksgiving. You can't draw a unicorn. You have to draw a turkey or something like that."

"Mo-om!" Charlotte called across the room. "Cora called Claire stupid!"

Claire slipped her hand into Calla's. "You have pretty skin."

Cora looked horrified. "Claire! Daddy said it's not nice to talk about how people look."

"Girls?" Lucia hurried over to the dining room table. "Please tell me you aren't fighting. Do you remember what we said about being on our best behavior today?" She turned to Calla. "I'm so sorry."

"They're fine!" Calla assured her. She gazed down at the girls, who had dumped out the shopping bag and were dividing up the contents. "They seem like so much fun."

"Fun and exhausting," Lucia said with a laugh. "It was nice of you to invite us today. We don't have any family in town."

"I was a little worried Jimmy wouldn't want to spend his day off at work," Calla confessed.

"And miss your cooking? Never."

Calla jumped a little at the mention of food. "Oh god, the turkey!"

She left Lucia with the girls and dashed over to the oven. To her great relief, the turkey looked fine (even with an extra ten minutes of roasting). She set it on the counter to rest while she popped a few sides into the oven to warm. She'd spent the last three days prepping and cooking and baking—and had loved every minute of it.

"Hey Michael?" she called across the room.

He jumped up from the couch and walked over to the counter that divided the living room from the kitchen. "You rang?"

"Reuben says you're the man to see about carving my turkey." She held up a large knife. "Do the honors?"

"I'd be delighted."

Michael carved, and Calla arranged slices of meat on her brand-new serving platter. She ladled the gravy into a turkey-shaped gravy boat, then placed the rest of the sides she'd so painstakingly prepared—green bean casserole, mashed potatoes, sweet potatoes stuffed in orange peels and topped with chopped candied pecans, dressing, macaroni and cheese, ginger-spiced cranberry sauce, and freshly baked rolls—on her kitchen island.

"Dinner is served!" she announced. "Grab a plate from anywhere at the table and help yourselves." She caught Cora's eye and gave her a wink. "Just make sure you sit in your assigned seats once you're ready to eat."

Everyone crowded into the kitchen, talking and laughing, tasting bits of food. Calla poured herself a glass of wine and soaked in the moment. A big family holiday was something she'd always wanted. It hadn't exactly come about in the way she'd imagined (a white picket fence, a spouse, children of her own), but the ties that bound her to the people in this room were that much sweeter and stronger because of the circumstances that had brought them into her life.

"You left the front door unlocked." A deep voice startled her out of her reverie.

"Brandon!" She nearly choked on her wine.

He narrowed his eyes. "You should be more careful. Anyone could walk in here."

"Good thing I've got a bodyguard here, then, isn't it?" she said coolly.

They looked across the kitchen at Jimmy, who was holding Claire in one arm and attempting to prepare a plate with the other. Charlotte stood next to him, pointing out her preferences for various foods.

"Looks like he's got his hands full."

"He's doing just fine." Calla took a sip, hoping it would settle the swarm of angry butterflies in her stomach. "So, if that's all you're worried about, we're good here. No need for you to stay."

"Calla." Brandon lowered his voice. "I know you're mad at me."

"Really? How perceptive of you."

"We need to talk."

She snorted. "You've had over a week to talk to me."

"I know."

"And you think this is the right moment?"

Before he could answer, Cora approached with a blank place card and marker in hand. "Name?" she asked briskly.

"I, uh—"

Calla shook her head. "In case you haven't noticed, Brandon, it's Thanksgiving, and we're about to eat. Give the young lady your name and make a plate." She pursed her lips, considering. "We can talk after dinner."

She stalked away before she could change her mind.

"A toast!" Reuben raised his glass as she swept past the dining table, seemingly oblivious to the drama that had just unfolded in the kitchen. "To our lovely and talented hostess. Thank you for this amazing feast!"

A round of "Cheers!" rippled around the room. Everyone clinked their glasses.

Calla forced a smile. "Thank you."

When everyone looked at her expectantly, she realized she needed to make a speech of some sort. She swallowed hard and tried to collect her thoughts. "It's kind of hard to believe that just a few months ago, I didn't know most of you. Except Rae, of course." She held her glass out to Rae. "Poor woman's been stuck with me for more Thanksgivings than I can count." Laughs rang out around the table. Calla continued, "I've never had a big family. No little brothers or sisters." She smiled at Jimmy's girls. "And not nearly so many friends." She kept her eyes fixed firmly on anyone but Brandon. "I'm grateful to each of you. For your help and your love. For your protection and your support. Thank you. For being here today and for being—" her voice faltered a little. "For being my family."

"To family," Dr. Pemmaraju echoed.

"To family," everyone replied in unison.

"Now dig in," Calla said. "Please."

"Everything's delicious," Rae said after a few bites. "And I love the decorations." She held up a cardboard cutout near her plate. "Is this a purple unicorn turkey?"

"Uh-huh," Claire said. "I drew it."

"Well, you did a lovely job."

The meal unfolded in a pleasant fashion. Once she got her own plate of food, Calla relaxed a little and took part in the conversation and laughter. After everyone had enjoyed seconds (and even a few rounds of thirds), they spread out across the apartment to rest before diving into dessert.

Calla was about to join Rae and Charlie in the living room when Brandon pulled her aside. "Can we talk now? In private?"

Calla blew out an irritated breath. "Fine."

"Where? Your bedroom?"

"Yeah, no. I don't think so." She gestured for him to follow her. "Come on. No one's on the balcony."

The cool night air was a bit of a shock after the cozy warmth inside the apartment. Calla wrapped her arms around herself.

"Are you cold?" Brandon asked. "Can I get you something?"

"I'm fine," she said brusquely. "What do you want to talk about?"

He gripped the balcony railing and fixed his eyes on the distant skyline. "I've been talking to Bruce. We need to make a change."

"A change?"

"Jimmy's been asking to take over the day shift. Permanently. The overnights are hard on his family."

"Oh. I hadn't thought about that." Of course nights would be hard for Lucia, all alone with three small children. "And this is why you've been ignoring me?"

"No." He turned to face her. "Calla, I can't be on your security detail anymore."

"Can't, or won't? Is this because we kissed?"

A painful pause. "Yes."

Calla's cheeks burned with humiliation. "Was it really that awful?"

"No, Calla. It wasn't awful. Not even close." His voice was steady, his tone serious. She believed him. "But it is a problem."

"Why?"

"Because you're not like anyone I've ever known. Because every day I spend with you, you remind me that there's still goodness and honor and beauty in this world. Because I—" He stepped closer and placed his hands on her shoulders. "Because I'm falling in love with you."

Calla's heart swelled. "I don't understand. If you feel that way, why are you leaving?"

Brandon released a deep, bone-weary sigh. "There's something you need to know about me. Something I should've told you a long time ago."

He slipped his hands into his pockets and turned back toward the skyline.

A finger of fear snaked up Calla's back. "What is it?"

"My—"

Brandon's cell phone buzzed. He grabbed it from his pocket and looked at the screen. Then he looked at Calla, regret etched across his face. "I have to take this."

He swiped the screen and raised the phone to his ear. "Is everything okay?"

Calla watched as Brandon listened.

"What? Where?" A note of barely controlled panic in his voice. He listened for a few more seconds. "Okay, I'll be there as soon as I can."

He shoved his phone back into his pocket. "I have to go."

Calla reached for his arm. "Brandon, wait. You can't just tell me you love me and leave. What happened? What's going on?"

He drew her to him and pressed his mouth against hers. Their second kiss. When he pulled away, all he said was, "I'm sorry. I'll call when I can."

Her lips burned as she watched him stride through the sliding glass doors, past the open mouths and questioning looks of her friends. She couldn't bear to meet their eyes. Instead, she wheeled back around and set her gaze on the buildings in the distance, as Brandon had done.

It felt like the cruelest joke—to discover love and lose it in the same instant.

THIRTY-EIGHT

"ANY WORD FROM BRANDON?" Reuben asked as he helped Calla onto her stretcher.

She bit her lip. "No."

It was the Monday after Thanksgiving. Calla was scheduled for a lung biopsy because Dr. Pemmaraju needed a tissue sample for replication purposes. Once that was done, she had promised to cut Calla loose until after Christmas.

Calla had no idea how she would fill the empty hours over the next few weeks.

"Nothing at all?" Reuben pushed.

"I texted him a couple of times. Okay, more than a couple of times. But he hasn't answered."

Reuben blew out a frustrated breath. "Men."

Jimmy stuck his head into the curtain surrounding Calla's bay in the pre-op area. "Everything okay in here?"

"Yep. About to start her IV," Reuben reported.

Jimmy held up his phone. "I just got a text from Kendra. There's a problem in the lab. Can you hold down the fort for me?"

"Sure."

"Thanks, man." Jimmy pointed at Calla. "I'll only be gone a few minutes. You should be fine. Access back here is pretty restricted. Keep this closed, though, okay?"

Calla gave him a thumbs-up, and he slid the curtain shut.

"I guess he's officially switched to the day shift?" Reuben asked as he prepped Calla's IV.

Her shoulders slumped. "Guess so."

"Did he say anything about why Brandon took off so fast at Thanksgiving?"

He pushed up the sleeve of her hospital gown and began probing her hand for a good vein. Calla was so used to the process that she hardly paid attention as he placed the tourniquet and sanitized her skin.

"He doesn't know for sure. He thinks it's a family thing, but Brandon's pretty private. Jimmy didn't even know he had a kid until I mentioned it." She winced a little as Reuben slipped the needle into her hand.

"All done," he announced. He withdrew the needle and taped the tube in place, then covered the insertion site with a clear plastic film. "That's kind of weird, isn't it?" He gathered up a few wrappers and empty packaging. "Haven't they worked together for a while?"

The curtain ripped open before Calla could answer, and two men entered the bay. They were dressed in scrubs. Surgical masks covered their faces. They closed the curtain behind them.

"Back already, Jimmy?" Reuben turned his back to throw away the used IV kit. "That was—"

The man closest to the bed whacked the back of Reuben's head with the butt of a pistol he'd pulled from his scrubs. Reuben slumped to the floor, silent and still.

"Reub—"

The second man clamped his hand over Calla's mouth.

The first man thrust the pistol back into his scrubs, then reached into a fanny pack and pulled out a syringe. He uncapped it and plunged the needle into the injection port on Calla's catheter. She watched in horror as he depressed the plunger.

A strange sensation immediately swept over her body. She couldn't move. Even her vocal cords were paralyzed—her screams reduced to strange, gurgling sounds.

The second man removed his hand from her mouth.

The first man looked at his watch. "Thirty seconds," he said in a low, commanding voice. His accent was unfamiliar, something Eastern European.

He stepped outside the curtain and returned pushing a wheelchair. Quickly, efficiently, the two men lifted Calla from the stretcher and placed her in the wheelchair. They fixed a mask over her face and a surgical cap over her hair and then moved the chair to the side.

Out of the corner of her eye, Calla watched as the men picked up Reuben's prone figure and dumped him onto the stretcher in her place. His head flopped to one side; his hair was soaked with blood.

Tears poured from Calla's eyes and slid down her paralyzed cheeks. She tried again to scream, but she was completely mute and immobilized now. There was nothing she could do to help her friend.

The first man looked at his watch again. "Time." He threw back the curtain and glanced right and left. The second man took up a position behind the wheelchair. At a signal from the first man, they exited Calla's holding bay into the main walkway of the pre-op room.

The chair stopped briefly, and Calla heard the curtain close behind her. How long would it be until someone looked inside? Until Jimmy returned? *Hang on, Reuben. Hang on.*

The wheelchair rolled through the pre-op area toward a back exit. They passed one nurse. The first man gave her a friendly wave. Calla tried desperately to signal her distress but to no avail. The nurse waved back, then returned to her computer screen.

They reached the exit. As the first man held the door, the second pushed the wheelchair into a deserted hallway. They marched in silence—no hesitation in their movements. They knew exactly what they were doing and where they were going. Halfway down the hallway, they entered a room that was empty except for a metal stretcher. It had the feel of an abandoned operating room.

A large, white plastic bundle was folded on the end of the stretcher, next to a black canvas bag. The first man unfolded the bundle and laid it out along the length of the surface. Terror sliced through Calla. A body bag. The first man unzipped it and folded the flaps open. Then he grabbed under her arms as the other man clutched her feet. They lifted her from the wheelchair and into the waiting bag.

As the second man tucked her in, the first man opened the canvas bag and unpacked its contents. He removed Calla's surgical mask and replaced it with an oxygen mask. Next, he unwound a length of plastic tubing, connected the mask to a small silver tank, and turned the valve. Calla felt a flow of cool gas wash across her face. The man checked a gauge, then slipped the tank into the bag next to Calla's thigh. He reached into his fanny pack and pulled out a second syringe that he plunged into Calla's IV.

"She'll be out in ten seconds," he informed the second man. He placed his hand on Calla's forehead and peered down at her. The gesture felt oddly solicitous until she looked into his eyes. They were gray-green and cold, calculating, emotionless. He didn't care for her well-being; he was simply concerned about keeping his schedule.

Calla felt darkness eat away at her consciousness. The last thing she saw was the zipper being pulled over her face. Her last thought was of Reuben and the awful possibility that her best friend was dead.

THIRTY-NINE

CALLA WOKE WITH A START.

What a horrible dream.

She blinked a few times, trying to beat back an overwhelming grogginess.

"Reu-ben?" The word took its time coming out. What kind of drugs had they given her? She'd never felt this incapacitated after anesthesia before.

As her vision cleared, she realized she was lying face down on a white leather bench. She rolled over and saw that the ceiling was low and curved, with light streaming in from a series of round windows. The couch jostled once, then again, and she was suddenly aware that her body, everything around her in fact, was moving at a high rate of speed.

"You're on an airplane," a smooth, cultured voice informed her.

Calla struggled into a sitting position. "Who—who are you?"

A man was seated in a leather chair across the aisle from her. He appeared to be of medium height with a wiry build. His hair was light brown with silver patches near the temples, cropped close to his head. His face was unfamiliar to her, except his eyes. Gray-green and slightly menacing.

"You put me in that bag."

"I did."

"Why?" Calla asked. "What do you want with me?"

"Who I am and what I want are of no real concern to you," he said. "I am simply responsible for delivering you to a person who has taken an interest in you."

Calla eyed him suspiciously. "An interest? They sure have a funny way of showing it. Attacking my friend. Drugging me. Kidnapping me. Who exactly is this person?"

"I'm not at liberty to say."

Somewhere nearby, a toilet flushed. A door opened, and a large man squeezed out from the narrow frame.

"Goddamn airplane bathroom," he growled. His accent was distinctly American. He was much larger than his companion, with a barrel-shaped chest and thick, muscled arms. His eyes fell upon Calla. "Sleeping Beauty's finally awake, huh?" He laughed. "Actually, I take back the beauty part."

"Fuck you." Calla turned back to the first man, who she had decided to think of as the German. "Why did you have to hurt Reuben?"

"Who is Reuben?"

"You mean that girly little nurse of yours?" The American sneered at Calla. "He's probably dead, for all we know."

Calla launched herself at him. "You bastard!" she screamed. "He's my friend!"

The American easily warded off her blows. "She's a feisty one, isn't she?"

He wasn't nearly as amused when Calla took a swipe at his face. Her nails dug into his cheek, leaving a trail of deep scratches. "Bitch!" he roared, slapping her.

The blow knocked Calla back onto the bench. The American lunged forward to hit her again, but the German jumped up to intervene.

"That's enough," he said coldly. "He told us to deliver her unharmed."

"Yeah?" The American spat in Calla's direction. "Well, maybe you'd better put her on a leash, then." He touched his cheek and winced. "Fuck!"

"There's a med kit in the closet by the cockpit. Go clean yourself up."

"Whatever, man." The American lumbered off toward the front of the plane.

The German knelt in front of Calla and took her face into his hands. "I apologize for my colleague's language and behavior," he said as he examined her cheek. "He is new to our organization and not yet familiar with our protocols. We do not abide bad tempers."

Calla sucked in a sharp breath as he probed the stinging skin under her eye. "Pretty sure he's not going to last very long, then."

He narrowed his eyes. "We do not abide them in anyone. Including you." He released her face. "You have the good sense to see there is nowhere to run. For that reason alone, I have not restrained you. But I did leave your IV in place." He tapped her left hand. "And I will, if necessary, give you another sedative."

Calla pursed her lips. He was right. She couldn't exactly jump out of the airplane. It would be better to stay conscious and hope for an opportunity to escape when they touched down. "I'll pass on the sedative."

"Good choice. I will bring you some water and an ice pack for the swelling. We land in about two hours."

As he stood to go, Calla grabbed his arm. "Just tell me, please. Where are you taking me?"

"To the last place you'll ever call home."

FORTY

IT WAS MID-AFTERNOON when the plane landed. Calla stared out a window, trying to glean any information she could about where she had been taken. The airport was small, with just a single runway. Wide, snow-dusted plains stretched into the distance toward a line of mountains. They had obviously traveled north and possibly west, but she couldn't be certain. There had been no announcements during the flight. The German had gone to the cockpit several times to converse with the pilots. Each time, he'd left her in the company of the American, who stared balefully at her while rubbing his wounded cheek, but otherwise left her alone.

As the plane taxied toward a row of hangers, the German approached Calla. He was holding a piece of black fabric and a cable tie.

"Hold your hands out in front of you, please."

"Why?"

"If you do not give me your hands, I will have to ask my associate for assistance. I assure you he will not be as gentle as I will."

Calla held out her hands. "I thought he was supposed to control his temper."

The German wrapped the cable tie around her wrists, slipped the end through the head, and pulled it tight. "I may have to make an exception if you start giving me trouble."

Next, he unfolded the fabric. It was a bag. He lifted it toward her head.

Calla leaned away. "Is that really necessary?"

"I'm afraid so. My employer does not want you to see the airport or the route to the compound."

"Oh, come on!" Calla cried. "We're obviously in the middle of nowhere. What am I going to see? And where could I possibly go? I don't even have shoes on!" She was still wearing just two hospital gowns (one open to the back, the other open to the front) and a pair of bright yellow, hospital-issued socks with gripper bottoms.

The German sighed impatiently. "It's this or the body bag again. Your choice." He gave the bag a little shake. "Make up your mind."

Calla glared at him. "Fine." She leaned forward and allowed him to slip the bag over her head. She braced for a foul smell, but it actually had a brand-new, slightly chemical odor—a small positive in an increasingly hopeless situation.

This was nothing like the first kidnapping attempt she had experienced. These people were highly disciplined and well-funded. Someone very powerful was involved. More than ever, Calla needed to keep her wits about her.

Deprived of sight, her other senses were sharpened. She felt the plane roll to a stop. Heard movement near the front of the cabin, then the sound of the door opening accompanied by a blast of frigid air. Calla shivered and wondered how long she'd have to endure the elements without any protective clothing.

"Time to move." The German grabbed her elbows and pulled her to a standing position. "Up you go." She felt him drape a coat over her shoulders. She was grateful but resisted the urge to thank him.

"We're going to exit the plane now," he explained as he led her forward. "There are five steps down to the ground. The car is very close."

Calla followed his lead without comment. As soon as they stepped out of the plane, she was struck by the stillness around her. Apart from the engines spinning down, there were no other sounds. Just a sense of vast, untamed land. She really was in the middle of nowhere.

The ground was ice-cold beneath her feet. Calla was glad when the journey to the car proved short. The German pulled open a door and helped her climb into the vehicle. Given its height off the ground, she surmised it must be an SUV of some sort.

"Slide to the middle of the bench," he instructed.

Calla did as she was told. She was dismayed when she pressed against the body of another person sitting in the left-hand seat.

"Watch it," she heard the American grunt.

She immediately slid back to the right, colliding with the German, who had climbed in after her. Clearly, they weren't taking any chances. There would be no daring leaps from the car this time around.

Two doors slammed shut.

"Let's go," the German commanded to someone in the front seat.

Without a word, the driver shifted the car into drive.

There was absolute silence for the entirety of the trip. Calla wasn't sure how long it took. Twenty minutes? Thirty? She lost track of the ups and downs, the twists and turns. Finally, the vehicle slowed and crunched onto a gravel road. After another minute, it stopped. Cold air rushed in as the back doors opened.

The German guided Calla from the vehicle. The gravel cut into her stockinged feet until she was ushered onto a smoother surface and then into a building. The floors inside were hard but not cold. Wood, perhaps. The air was warm and clean, laced with the scent of logs burning and a hint of citrus. It was quiet, too, lending the space a lonely feeling.

Calla was led down an endless series of corridors. *This place is huge.* Finally, they slowed, and she heard a door being opened. She shuffled into a room where the German removed the bag from her head. Calla blinked a few times, her eyes struggling to adjust to the sudden brightness. As the German cut the cable tie from her wrists with a utility knife, she took in her surroundings. She was in a large, well-appointed bedroom. It was decorated in a high-end, rustic style with a huge platform bed made of natural wood, a vintage kilim rug, and hammered metal lamps.

"Wait here," the man told her. "Someone will be in to speak with you shortly."

He signaled to the American, and they exited the room. As soon as the door shut behind them, she ran over to test it. Locked. No big surprise.

Resigned for the moment to her confinement, Calla began to explore the room. The wall across from the bed was lined with shelves from floor to ceiling. Books and knickknacks artfully decorated each one. No photos, though. Nothing of a personal nature that might help her identify her captor (or captors). Next to the wall was a sitting area. Two leather club chairs and a side table were positioned to enjoy the view from a large picture window that looked out onto a snow-covered valley. The same mountains she had noticed at the airport loomed in the distance.

She examined the window, finding it thick and heavy and unable to be opened from the inside. The bathroom was just as nice as the bedroom, with a large shower and heated floors, and she discovered a closet stocked with several outfits—sweaters, loose pants, t-shirts—all of which appeared to be her size. A search of the chest of drawers yielded underwear and socks, and even a pair of gray New Balance running shoes and some cozy slippers. At least she wouldn't have to walk around in socks anymore.

"Not too shabby, is it?" a familiar voice asked.

Calla spun around. She hadn't heard the bedroom door open.

"You!" she hissed.

FORTY-ONE

DR. KRAFT STOOD BEFORE HER, a smirk on his face. The German and the American lurked behind him. "Did you miss me?"

Calla lunged toward him. "You bastard!"

The German and the American quickly stepped in front of Dr. Kraft, grabbed Calla's arms, and began dragging her back toward the bed.

"Careful!" Dr. Kraft barked. He took a step forward and peered at her face. "Why does she have a black eye?" he demanded. "I specifically instructed you not to harm her."

"She got a little out of hand on the airplane," the American said.

"Oh really?" Dr. Kraft put his hands on his hips. "Is that why your face is bandaged? You let a little girl like her get the best of you?"

"She's fast," the American muttered. "She took me by surprise."

"I see," Dr. Kraft sneered. "You're incompetent *and* slow."

"That's not—"

Dr. Kraft flicked his hand toward the doorway. "Get out."

"Sir," the German warned, "with all due respect, I don't think that's a good idea."

"I don't care what you think, Jean-Paul. Calla won't hurt me." Dr. Kraft gave her a tight smile. "We're old friends, aren't we?"

Calla had never wanted to spit in someone's face more than she did at that very moment.

Jean-Paul exhaled loudly. "Sir, we've discussed this. No names."

"Oops. Sorry about that, *Jean-Paul*," Dr. Kraft said coldly. His gaze shifted to the American. "And you, too. It's Greg, right?"

"Sir!"

"Enough!" Dr. Kraft yelled. "I'm sick of all the secrecy bullshit. The hard part is over. She's here, and this place is a fortress. She's not going anywhere." He pointed a finger at each man in turn. "And if she does manage to escape, I'm certainly not taking the fall by myself. So do your damn jobs and keep us all out of trouble."

Jean-Paul looked like he wanted to argue the point further but shrugged instead. "As you wish." He beckoned to Greg. "Let's go."

As soon as the door shut behind them, Dr. Kraft pointed at the club chairs. "Shall we sit?"

Calla didn't move. "How could you do this to me?"

"Calla, please," Dr. Kraft clucked disapprovingly. "Be reasonable. Sit down. I'll explain everything."

"Be reasonable?" A hysterical laugh bubbled up in her throat. "Do you know what I've been through today? I don't have to be anything for you!"

"Fine," Dr. Kraft said breezily. "Then I'll have to call that brute, Greg, back into the room. And, as you're already aware, he's not nearly as nice as I am."

Calla scowled and sat down in one of the chairs.

"Smart girl." Dr. Kraft sat down next to her and crossed his legs. "So—"

"Could you stop calling me that?"

"Calling you what?"

"A girl. You've done it twice now. It's insulting. I'm an adult."

"Then start acting like one." He leaned toward her. "Let's be honest, Calla. Life as you knew it ended the moment Dr. Cho opened up your head and discovered that your tumor was gone. At least listen to what I have to say. I brought you here to finish what we started. I'm offering you an opportunity to make history. To change the world."

Calla crossed her arms. "We were already doing that until you started selling my blood."

A muscle pulsed in Dr. Kraft's cheek. "I did exactly what the hospital told me I had to do to fund my research. Raise money. Hand over fist. And what did I get in return? My reputation destroyed. My life's work stolen from me. I was supposed to be a Nobel laureate. The Einstein of my generation. They *took* that from me! And what do you think happened to the rich assholes who got your blood?" He leaned closer to her. "I'll tell you what. A little slap on the wrist. Asked to resign from some boards. Big fucking deal. They're cancer-free now, thanks to me. But were they willing to lift a finger to help the man who made that possible? No. They had what they wanted. To hell with my reputation or my vaccine. And it wasn't just them. It was everyone. That's the part you need to understand, Calla. No one wants a vaccine."

"What are you talking about?" Calla had never seen Dr. Kraft so on edge.

"Think about it. What would the eradication of cancer mean?" He didn't wait for an answer. "It would mean the end of cancer hospitals. The end of drug companies that develop cancer treatments. The end of non-profits that fund research and support patients. They won't admit it, but none of them really want a world without cancer."

"That's a sick thing to say! There are people all over the world who spend their lives trying to cure cancer, and you know it."

"Of course there are. No one has a problem with finding a *cure* for cancer. A cure doesn't threaten the system. Patients would still need to be diagnosed and treated. Then followed up with to make sure there aren't recurrences. Everyone stays in business. Everyone wins. But a vaccine?" He shook his head slowly.

"You're wrong."

"No, I'm not. People are selfish. They fear change. That's why I had to do this." Dr. Kraft motioned around the room. "It was the only way."

"The only way to do what?"

"To end cancer. It will be the greatest discovery in the history of mankind. And *I'm* the one who will do it. But I had to have you to make it work." He shrugged. "So, I made a deal with the devil."

Calla felt a frisson of unease work its way up her spine. "What devil?"

"My business partner."

"What exactly is your deal with him?"

"We each have something the other one needs. His son is sick. Leukemia. Quite advanced. I am going to cure him with your blood. In exchange, my partner has agreed to fund my research. You and I will continue where we left off. You will provide me with blood, bone marrow, and tissue. I will develop my vaccine. We will fund my work by soliciting payments from wealthy parties in exchange for access to cutting-edge cancer treatments."

"You mean access to my blood."

"Precisely."

"And you think that's going to fix your reputation?"

"It's the only way."

"Dr. Kraft, please. You kidnapped me. Anything you accomplish here will be tainted by that. If this is really about your legacy, you have to let me go."

Dr. Kraft smiled. "You're so naive, Calla. Once I have my vaccine, people will be so desperate for it that they won't care how I got it."

"And what makes you so sure this partner of yours will let you walk away with your vaccine?"

"Because I'm going to give it to him. He'll have sole control over the most valuable vaccine known to man. It'll make him the richest person on earth. I don't care about the money. All I want is the credit."

"And what about me? What happens to me?"

Dr. Kraft studied her for a moment. "I suppose he'll do whatever he likes with you. I won't need you anymore."

"Jesus." Calla suddenly felt nauseous. "Ralph was right. You are insane."

"Ralph Grimes said that about me?" Dr. Kraft chuckled. "That weaselly little sneak. He really was worried about you, you know. But he hated me more than he cared about you. That's why he leaked my paper instead of filing a complaint with the hospital. It was quite a stunt he pulled. Trying to kill two birds with one stone. For a few days, I thought he'd ruined everything. But it turns out his leak was just what I needed. No one was going to publish my work. Not in a reasonable amount of time anyway. Ralph gave me a shortcut past all of that to the people I needed to reach.

The people with the money. People like my partner." He laughed again. "I guess it's true what they say, isn't it? There's no such thing as bad publicity."

Watching him, Calla realized that if she didn't do something drastic, something violent, something *right now*, she wouldn't make it out of this situation alive. She glanced around for something that might function as a weapon. Her eyes lit on a polished rock holding down some magazines on the small table between their chairs. If she could incapacitate Dr. Kraft, even for a few minutes, she might be able to escape. She had to try.

Her heart thudded in her chest. She took a deep breath. *Do it*, she urged herself. Her hand crept toward the rock, but before she could grab it, the bedroom door opened. The moment passed.

A tall, very thin man walked into the room. Everything about him was gray and washed out—his hair, his dead-fish eyes, even his skin had a ghostly pallor. His clothes—slacks, button-down shirt, and a cashmere sweater—were simple but of the highest quality. He was neither good- nor bad-looking. He was utterly forgettable. Terrifyingly mundane.

He was followed by Jean-Paul and Greg, who took up positions next to the open door.

Dr. Kraft leaped to his feet. "Calla, this is—"

"No names." The man held up a remonstrative finger. "I've been informed that you are having trouble following this rule." His accent was like Jean-Paul's, though Calla still couldn't quite place it.

"I hardly think it matters if she knows the names of some low-level security guards." Dr. Kraft glared at the two men in question.

"Well, I do," the man said firmly. "These are my rules. You will follow them, or you will leave. Am I clear?"

Dr. Kraft waited a beat before muttering, "Whatever."

Calla watched the exchange with interest. Despite Dr. Kraft's insistence that this man (whoever he was) was his partner, it was clear who called the shots.

The man turned to Calla. He examined her from head to foot with a detached, clinical air, then turned to Dr. Kraft. "When can we start the transfusion?"

"As soon as you like," Dr. Kraft said stiffly, his pride wounded.

"Well, then," the man's eyes bored into Dr. Kraft's, "what are you waiting for?"

Dr. Kraft snapped his fingers at Jean-Paul and Greg. "Take her to the lab."

The man's eyes flicked over to Calla once more. "You'd better work."

Three words. That was all it took to reduce her from a person to a thing—a tool to be used and then discarded. Dr. Kraft might be insane, but Calla felt certain that this man was pure evil.

She stood up and got in his face. "My name is Calla Hammond," she told him. "I'm twenty-three years old. I was born in—"

"Get her out of here!" The man ordered. His face twisted into a grimace, revealing a crack in his carefully controlled demeanor. He was clearly disgusted by Calla's nearness. She pressed closer to him but was stopped by Jean-Paul and Greg, who rushed forward to grab her under the arms.

She began to scream as they dragged her from the room.

"My name is Calla Hammond! Calla Hammond! Don't do this to me!"

FORTY-TWO

"STOP THAT." Jean-Paul gave Calla a shake.

She was still sobbing her name over and over again while he and Greg forced her to walk down the hall.

Calla took a ragged breath and looked up at the two men. "Don't do this," she begged them. "Please."

"Shut up," Greg said brusquely. "Or I'll shut your mouth for you."

Jean-Paul opened a door, and Greg shoved Calla into an enormous room—white-tiled from floor to ceiling, filled with long benches and equipment. Just beyond a glass divider, she could see what looked like an operating room. Everything in it felt sterile, antiseptic, clinical.

"Welcome to my lab," Dr. Kraft said as he walked in behind them. "You should feel honored, Calla. This was all built for you. The very best money can buy. And believe me, it cost a pretty penny to set it up so quickly."

"Guess that means it's time for you to start earning your keep," Greg whispered in Calla's ear. She scowled and tried to jerk her arm from his grasp, but he tightened his grip and gave a menacing leer.

Dr. Kraft frowned at their scuffling. "Take her over to the transfusion center." He pointed toward a section of the room near a large window that overlooked a paved terrace and what appeared to be a swimming pool that had been covered for the winter. Beyond that, a snowy landscape stretched into the distance. A pair of padded recliners were angled to enjoy the view.

Greg marched Calla across the room and forced her onto one of the recliners. He held her in place while Jean-Paul called over to Dr. Kraft.

"Do you want her restrained?"

Dr. Kraft walked toward them and gave Calla a penetrating look. "It's up to you, Calla. This will all be much easier if we don't have to tie you down." He glanced meaningfully from Jean-Paul to Greg. "It's not like they're going to let you go anywhere, so you might as well cooperate."

Calla crossed her arms and stared defiantly out the window. "Just get it over with."

"Good." Dr. Kraft pointed at Jean-Paul. "Tell Anya I'm ready."

"Yes, Sir," Jean-Paul said and left the room. Greg took a few steps back but hovered nearby in case he was needed.

"Who's Anya?" Calla asked Dr. Kraft.

"My nurse."

Calla made a contemptuous noise.

Dr. Kraft cut his eyes at her. "What?"

"You had a nurse. Reuben. Remember him? Those two animals attacked him when they kidnapped me. He might be dead because of you."

"Whatever happened to Reuben isn't my fault," Dr. Kraft said. "I had nothing to do with the extraction. Someone on your security team came up with the plan."

Calla's stomach filled with ice. "What are you talking about? Who?"

"I don't know." He waved a dismissive hand. "Someone with money problems, family problems, something like that. Everyone has a price."

His words landed like physical blows. *Everyone has a price.*

Who had betrayed her? Jimmy? Kendra? *It couldn't possibly have been . . .*

Calla slumped in her seat, despondency settling over her like a blanket. Had Brandon done this to her? She couldn't imagine it—not after he'd told her how he felt about her—but it could explain why he left so quickly on Thanksgiving Day. And why he hadn't reached out to her since.

Calla felt the last shreds of whatever hope she'd been clinging to—to escape, to be rescued, to survive—flutter away like a tiny bird squeezing through the bars of its cage out into the vast wilderness just beyond the thick panes of glass in front of her, leaving behind nothing but resignation.

She watched Dr. Kraft bustling around the lab, looking sickeningly cheerful and unaware of the effect his offhand comment had had on her. She felt a fresh surge of disgust for him.

"Anya." Dr. Kraft raised a hand as Jean-Paul reentered the lab with a woman in tow. She was stout and severe-looking. She wore crisp, navy blue scrubs, and her reddish-brown hair was pulled back in a tight bun. She acknowledged Dr. Kraft with a frown.

"We're ready to begin the leukapheresis," Dr. Kraft said. He didn't bother to introduce Calla.

"Leuka-what?" Calla asked uneasily as Anya pushed back the sleeves of her hospital gown and began inspecting both of her arms. "I thought this was a transfusion."

"It is a transfusion," Dr. Kraft replied as he rolled a large, boxy, white machine next to her chair. It was covered with funny-looking lines and dials. "But only of your white blood cells. This machine withdraws whole blood from one arm, separates the white blood cells, and then returns the remaining red blood cells, plasma, and platelets through the other arm."

"Why not just do it the normal way?"

Dr. Kraft looked simultaneously irritated and amused. "Always full of questions, aren't you?"

Calla shrugged. She might not have any control over fate at this point, but she still wanted to understand what was happening to her.

"Carry on." Dr. Kraft signaled for Anya to continue prepping Calla's arms, then he sat down on the edge of the recliner next to her, unable to resist the temptation to pontificate. "Two reasons we're not taking your blood the 'normal' way." He used air quotes for emphasis. "The first is that I don't need whole blood. I haven't isolated the exact mechanism or process just yet. But I do know that your immune response to cancer is driven by your bone marrow and, by extension, the white blood cells it produces. I only need those cells.

"Second, even though the process takes longer than a standard blood draw, taking only your white blood cells is more efficient in the long run. White blood cells don't live very long, so your bone marrow is constantly replacing your body's supply faster than red blood cells get replenished. We can boost that production even more by giving you certain medicines. Faster replacement of white blood cells means we can do transfusions more often than we could with whole blood. More transfusions mean more clients. More clients mean more money."

Calla's face twitched at his indifferent tone.

"The only drawback is the short shelf life I mentioned. Once collected, white blood cells only live about twenty-four hours. We have to transfuse them on-site. We can't send them out to patients. They have to come here. That's why we invested so much in the lab and the house. It's a treatment center of sorts."

"Do you offer massage packages, too?"

"We do actually have a masseuse on call—oh, you were being sarcastic."

"Picked up on that, did you? Ow!" Calla glared at Anya, who was digging around in the crook of her left arm, trying to find a vein for her needle.

Anya glared back at her. "Hold still," she instructed.

Calla watched the woman closely. Like Jean-Paul, Anya was not American. She must have been brought to this place by Dr. Kraft's mysterious partner. And, if Calla was picking up on her signals correctly, Anya wasn't too happy about the situation. Was she a prisoner, too? Or just grumpy by nature? It was too soon to tell, but Calla already knew one thing for sure—patient comfort was not high on Anya's list of priorities. Calla gritted her teeth as the nurse set to work locating a vein in her other arm.

· · ·

Two hours and a pint of white blood cells later, Calla was unhooked from the machine. Even though she hadn't moved from her recliner, she felt strangely drained by the process. She was grateful when Anya handed her a box of apple juice and a couple of graham crackers. She hadn't eaten in almost twenty-four hours. She savored the snack while watching Anya clear away used tubing and empty blood bags.

The door to the lab opened, and Jean-Paul walked in, pushing an empty wheelchair. He was followed by Greg, who was pushing another wheelchair. This one was occupied by a teenage boy. Calla sat up a little to get a better look at him.

He was tall and nearly skeletal. A few patches of dark hair sprouted from his otherwise bald head. His eyes were sunken and ringed by dark circles. His skin had a gray-green cast and a dry, papery look, as though it might slough off at the slightest touch. His head bobbed in tiny, almost imperceptible beats. Calla couldn't tell if the movement was intentional or not. It seemed like he was just clinging to consciousness. She had never seen someone who looked closer to death.

Greg parked the boy's wheelchair near the recliner next to Calla. Jean-Paul joined him, and together they gently transferred the boy onto the cushioned seat. His head lolled to the side, so his face was turned toward Calla. Now that he was closer, she could see his lips were laced with cracks and yellowy flakes. His chest heaved slightly as he fought for every intake of air. Calla's heart sank as she watched him. It seemed impossible that he could be saved.

The door to the lab opened once more, and Dr. Kraft's partner strode into the room.

"Why is she still here?" her captor demanded, jutting his chin in Calla's direction.

"We only just finished, *mein Herr*," Anya said softly. She stared at the floor while she spoke. "I was not expecting Luca so soon."

At the sound of his name, the boy stirred slightly. The man rushed to his side and placed his hand on his son's head. His face was a mask of wretchedness. It was the first truly human emotion Calla had seen him exhibit.

Luca's lips parted, and he moaned softly.

The man glanced at Calla, then turned to Jean-Paul. "Get her out of here," he ordered, keeping his voice low. "Now."

"Yes, Sir."

Calla was perplexed. Why was he so anxious for her to leave? She looked over at Luca again and was surprised to find him looking back at her with his eyes wide open. She saw his lips move, forming words without sound. But before she had a chance to respond, Jean-Paul and Greg yanked her from her seat and plunked her into the empty wheelchair, affording her none of the tenderness they had shown to Luca.

Greg spun the wheelchair around and began pushing it toward the door to the lab.

"Wait!" Dr. Kraft emerged from a small side room near the front of the lab, where he had ensconced himself for the past two hours. He looked surprised to see so many people in the room. "Where are you taking her?"

"The boss wants her gone," Greg said, pausing only slightly before resuming his march across the lab.

"Stop." Dr. Kraft stepped in front of the wheelchair. "I'm not done with her yet."

Luca's father suddenly appeared by his side. "What is going on?" he hissed.

"I need to take some blood samples," Dr. Kraft replied. "It will only take a few minutes."

Luca's father shook his head. "Not now."

"Why not?"

"We agreed there would be no procedures until we are sure my son is cured."

"All I'm asking for is a few milliliters of blood. That hardly qualifies as a procedure, and it won't affect Luca's transfusions," Dr. Kraft argued.

"I'm afraid you will have to wait. I do not want her in the lab right now."

"But—"

"*Nein!*" Luca's father growled. "I have my reasons. You can take your samples later. For now, go tend to my son."

The look on his face made it clear he would tolerate no further argument.

With a huff, Dr. Kraft left them and stomped across the lab to hover over Anya as she prepared Luca for his transfusion.

Luca's father took one last look at Calla before pointing to the door. "Go."

In silence, Greg wheeled her out of the lab. Jean-Paul trailed behind them as they made their way back down the hall to her bedroom.

Once inside, Jean-Paul explained the ground rules to her.

"Your meals will be brought to you. You will eat in this room. If you need anything, pick up the phone. There is no need to dial a number. It will ring directly to one of our cell phones. Your door will be locked, and you will be monitored by cameras at all times. Even in the bathroom. There is no such thing as privacy here."

"Got it," Calla said wryly. "You're a bunch of peeping toms."

Jean-Paul looked indignant. "That is not the purpose of the cameras."

"Whatever gets you off." Calla enjoyed watching him squirm.

"I don't—"

Greg cut him off. "Drop it. She's just jerking your chain."

"Jerking my what?"

"Your chain, dude." Greg laughed unkindly. "It means she's fucking with you."

Jean-Paul shook his head irritably. "You Americans and your idioms."

"What about exercise?" Calla asked. "Am I allowed to go outside?"

"Once a day, supervised, for thirty minutes. If you aren't . . . jerking my chain." Jean-Paul glowered at her. "Cooperate, and you will be treated well. Break the rules, and there will be consequences. Do you understand?"

Calla nodded.

"Good. Someone will be by soon with your dinner."

Greg waggled his fingers at her. "Nighty-night, princess."

"Screw you, Greg."

The door clicked shut behind them. Though she knew it was pointless, Calla tried the handle. Locked. Jean-Paul was unlikely to do something so careless.

Calla walked over to the bed and flopped down on the mattress. The cumulative effects of the day were catching up with her, draining her last reserves of energy. It seemed impossible that she'd been talking with Reuben just that morning. The hospital felt like a different lifetime.

She curled into a ball, trying to hide from the feeling of despair that threatened to crush her. Her situation was bleak, potentially hopeless. So far, the people who had kidnapped her had proven relentless in their attention to the details of her imprisonment and totally devoid of any morality.

Only one person had shown her a shred of human decency, and she feared he wouldn't make it through the night.

She thought back to the moment Luca's eyes had locked onto hers in the lab.

I'm sorry, he'd mouthed.

No words of comfort. Only an acknowledgment that what was being done to her was wrong.

That was the tiny light Calla clung to as the dark folds of sleep closed over her.

FORTY-THREE

"RISE AND SHINE," Greg grunted. "You've got thirty minutes to eat and get dressed. Then Dr. K wants you in the lab."

Calla opened her eyes just in time to see him drop a tray on the nightstand beside her bed, then stalk out of the room. For a moment, she thought about rolling over and going back to sleep, but a sudden wave of nausea made that impossible. She bolted into the bathroom and knelt in front of the toilet, dry heaving until her abdomen ached. Nothing came up. There was nothing to come up. The graham crackers she'd eaten after the transfusion yesterday had long been digested, and she hadn't touched the dinner they had brought her.

She struggled to her feet and went over to the sink to wash away the sweat slicking her face. A basket of toiletries sat on the counter. She dug through it and found a new toothbrush and a tube of toothpaste, along with soap, dental floss, deodorant, and lotion.

There was something sinister about these touches of civility. Like she was somehow acquiescing to her imprisonment by accepting her captors' hospitality. She couldn't stand the grimy feeling in her mouth a moment longer, though. She decided to stop worrying about the implications and just brush her teeth.

After she cleaned up a little, Calla went back into the bedroom to inspect her breakfast. Yogurt, granola, fresh fruit, water, and coffee. She gulped down the water and left the rest. Her stomach was still too upset to contemplate eating. She picked up the coffee cup and held it between her hands, warming them as she stood near the window. It was a dreary morning, icy and overcast. Calla stared at the bleak landscape until the coffee went cold and Greg returned to escort her to the lab.

That first morning set the pattern for the following days. Wake up. Eat (or not eat). Get dressed. Go to the lab. Endure some combination of blood draws, transfusions, biopsies, and scans. It was a lot like the routine at the hospital, but worse. Here, there were no days off. No joking with Reuben. No Dr. Pemmaraju running interference for her.

Dr. Kraft finally got what he had always wanted—unrestricted access to Calla's body. Freedom to do whatever he wanted to her, without oversight or interference from hospital executives or government regulators. He took full advantage of the opportunity. Calla ached constantly from his daily expeditions for more blood, more tissue, more bone marrow.

When she wasn't in the lab, she was locked in her bedroom, cut off from the outside world. There was a television, but it wasn't hooked up to cable or the Internet, just an old DVD player. It took some rummaging around, but she finally located a stack of random DVDs that hadn't been updated since the early 2000s. Sometimes, she thumbed through a book, but mostly she slept or looked out the window, watching until the sun set on another day, grieving the life they had taken from her, and wondering desperately how the people she'd left behind would ever be able to find her in this vast wilderness that felt so very far from everything she'd ever known.

As promised, she was taken outside once a day for fresh air, usually in the late afternoon when Dr. Kraft retired to his microscopes and other equipment to run tests on his daily haul of blood and tissue. Either Greg or Jean-Paul would escort her on a well-worn path around the perimeter of the house, then take her straight back to her room. Their route never varied, but at least she was outside with the sun on her face and snow crunching under her feet.

Calla didn't see Luca again, but she spent part of nearly every day hooked up to the apheresis machine, so she assumed he had survived long enough to receive a second and, possibly, a third transfusion. As time wore on, though, she began to suspect that Dr. Kraft had found new recipients for her white blood cells.

On her sixth night in captivity (she'd taken to scratching the wall inside her closet with the sharp edge of a coat hanger to mark the passage of each day), she heard the sound of voices echo down the hall outside her bedroom. It was a significant departure from the near silence that usually blanketed the house.

Not long after that, Jean-Paul delivered her dinner.

"Sounds like a party's going on out there." Calla kept her tone purposely casual. Jean-Paul got cagey whenever she brought up anything related to security.

"The boss is entertaining clients tonight." He set her food down on a table near the window. She'd taken to eating her meals in that part of the room.

"Clients?"

He ignored the question. "I'll collect your tray in an hour."

As soon as he was gone, Calla pressed her ear against the door. The faint sounds of laughter and conversation trickled through the wood. Her stomach clenched into an angry knot. These had to be the clients Dr. Kraft had told her about—the rich, corrupt people who could afford illicit white blood cell transfusions. She wondered if they knew or even cared that the source of their salvation was locked in a bedroom just down the hall from their twisted cocktail party.

Seized by blinding rage, she started to scream and pound her fists against the door.

"Help me! Please! I've been kidnapped! You have to help me!"

It didn't take long to elicit a response. Footsteps pounded down the hall. The door burst open, knocking Calla to the floor. She looked up. Jean-Paul and Greg loomed above her, their expressions menacing. Anya stood behind them.

"HELP!" Calla screamed toward the open door.

Wordlessly, Jean-Paul leaned down and looped an arm around her back. He pressed his free hand against her mouth, muffling her protests. Greg grabbed her feet. Calla thrashed against them, but multiple days of procedures and transfusions had left her too weak to put up much of a fight.

The two men carried her across the room and dumped her on the bed. They held her down while Anya swabbed her upper arm and injected her with something. Moments later, the last of the fight drained out of her. A heaviness settled over her limbs, forcing her eyelids closed as she slipped into a drug-induced stupor.

FORTY-FOUR

AFTER THAT NIGHT, Calla was sedated whenever there was company in the house. And judging by the frequency of Anya's injections, business was booming.

It was a miserable existence. Calla begged for a reprieve, promising to keep quiet, pleading for just one night of lucidity, but there were no exceptions to the new rule. In this world, it was one strike and you're out.

Her days weren't much better. Dr. Kraft's procedures grew more invasive, the transfusions more frequent. Fatigue, body aches, bruises, even trouble breathing plagued Calla. Her mouth became full of sores, making it hard to eat. Her weight plummeted. When she could muster the energy for a shower, she had to sit on a plastic bench. She no longer took walks outside. Jean-Paul or Greg would push her onto the patio in a wheelchair for a few minutes of fresh air, then return her to her bedroom, where she only had energy to stare at the wall, clinging to memories from the time before all of this happened.

Hugs from Rae.

Laughing with Reuben.

Brandon.

Calla spent an inordinate amount of time replaying their first kiss in her mind, spinning it forward, imagining what might have happened if she hadn't stopped him that night. Would he have wrapped her in his arms and taken her to the bedroom? Would they have kissed and talked for hours? Gone further? She imagined a thousand sweet scenarios. But each one inevitably soured when she remembered what he had said to her on Thanksgiving night.

There's something you need to know about me. Something I should've told you a long time ago.

Could she bear it if he'd had something to do with her abduction?

She didn't think she wanted to live in a world where that was possible.

. . .

The days passed agonizingly slow, punctuated by pain and exhaustion and a growing sense of hopelessness. Calla was starting to imagine ways to end her torment when hope arrived in the form of an unexpected visitor.

It was a rare night off from sedation. The house was quiet. Calla lay on the bed, trying to ignore the stinging in her abdomen from a new set of stitches. Dr. Kraft had biopsied an ovary earlier in the day. He'd used a laparoscope to keep the incision small, but it still hurt.

Her dinner tray had already been cleared away, so she was surprised and a little concerned when the bedroom door opened again.

"Who's there?"

A tall, impossibly thin figure crept into the room. At first, Calla thought it was *him*, Dr. Kraft's partner, whom she hadn't laid eyes on since her arrival. But it wasn't. This person shared his silhouette but nothing else.

"Who are—"

"I'm Luca."

Calla was stunned. Her captor's son was transformed. The gray was gone from his skin, which now had a healthy, olive glow. His hair was growing in, thick and black. He was still rail-thin, but there were hints of muscle growth. He stared back at her, taking in her equally changed appearance.

"My god," he breathed. "What have they done to you?"

"Never mind that." Calla ignored his horrified look. "You can't be here. They'll see you. We'll get in trouble!"

He took a step forward. "Don't worry," he tried to reassure her. "No one saw me."

"You don't understand!" Her voice rose as her panic increased. She had no interest in discovering what fresh new punishment they would devise for this infraction. "They have cameras everywhere. Even in the bathroom."

Luca shook his head. "There aren't any cameras in here."

"How do you know that?"

"I snuck into the room where they keep the computers that run the security system." When Calla still looked skeptical, he added, "Trust me. The only cameras are outside the house."

She relaxed a little. He seemed pretty confident. And someone probably would have rushed into the room by now if they could be seen. "Guess I shouldn't be surprised that they lied to me."

"Lies and manipulation. My father's stock-in-trade." Luca gestured toward a straight-backed chair that stood next to the closet. "May I?"

"Sure." Calla watched as he pulled the chair over to her bedside and took a seat. "I can't believe you're alive."

Luca made a show of looking down at his body. "Thanks to you."

She stared at him in amazement. "It really worked? My blood . . . it saved you?" Despite everything that had happened to her, Calla realized she had never fully believed it was possible that her blood could actually cure cancer. Now the proof was sitting right in front of her.

"Officially cancer-free as of yesterday," he said grimly. "My oncologist declared me a medical miracle."

"You don't sound too happy about it."

"This isn't what I wanted. At least, not this way. My father tried to hide it from me, but I knew he'd kidnapped you. I told him I'd rather die than take your blood."

"So, that's why he didn't want us in the lab together."

Luca nodded. "He thought if I saw you, I would struggle, and they wouldn't be able to do the transfusion. But I was too weak." His gaze dropped to the floor in shame. "I'm sorry."

"I'm not," Calla said. "I saw how sick you were. I wouldn't wish that on my worst enemy."

"You may change your mind once you've been here a little longer. My father is an evil man."

Groaning softly, Calla pushed herself into a sitting position. Maybe she could finally get some answers about who had taken her. "Tell me about him. I don't even know his name. I just think of him as . . . him."

Luca grunted. "He's funny about names. Anonymity is very important to him." His eyes flickered nervously toward the door. "Ah, screw it. You deserve to know. His name is Oscar Kuhn. He calls himself a business-man, but he's just a thug in a suit."

"Oscar Kuhn," Calla repeated, trying the name out for herself. "Is that German?"

"Swiss. Which reminds me." He pulled something from the front pocket of his hoodie. "I brought you something. A little contraband."

Calla's eyes lit up. "Chocolate!" It was a bar of Cailler milk chocolate with almonds and honey.

Luca smiled at her reaction. "It's one of my favorites from home."

She peeled back the wrapper and broke off a square. She held the bar out to Luca, but he declined to take any. She popped the candy in her mouth and made a happy sound as it began to melt on her tongue. She had never tasted anything more delicious in her life.

"You're from Switzerland?" she asked as she broke off a second piece.

"Yes. I grew up in Zürich."

"It must be beautiful there. I've always wanted to go to Europe."

"It is. I miss it very much. Especially my mother and my little sister." A shadow fell across his face.

"They must be happy that you're better."

"They don't know. I haven't seen or spoken to either of them in six months."

"What? Why?"

"It's my father's way of punishing us." He rubbed a hand over his head. He seemed to be gathering his thoughts. "He wasn't always a crim-inal, you know. He started out in banking. But crime was more lucrative.

As he got sucked deeper into that world, he changed. He became cruel and abusive. My mother put up with it for years because I was sick, and we needed his resources.

"Then, I went into remission. Six months turned into a year, then a year and a half. We thought it was safe to leave. We made a plan to go to Italy, where my mother's family is from. But my father found out. He was furious. He said he would never let us leave him. He kept us locked in our house, always under guard. No school. No friends. Nothing. And then my cancer came back. The doctors said it was terminal, but my father wouldn't accept that. It wasn't about love, though. He just hates to lose." Luca gave Calla a tortured smile.

"So, he got me enrolled in a clinical trial and brought me to the States. And then he found out about you and started all of this." He waved a hand around, indicating the room, the house, the whole compound. "He's kept us separated the whole time."

Calla's heart went out to him. Luca was as much of a prisoner as she was. "What about now?" she asked. "Won't he let you go home now that you're better?"

"I doubt it. Keeping me away from Mamma and Paola is part of the punishment."

"There's no way for you to get in touch with them?"

He shook his head. "We're completely cut off in this house. No land-lines. No Internet. Nothing. Even the security system is a closed loop. I was hoping I'd find some way to call for help. But my father thought of everything, it seems."

Calla sagged against her pillow. Yet another disappointment.

"And anyway," Luca continued, "it turns out I'm good advertising."

"Good advertising?"

"For the clients. I'm proof the treatment works." His voice turned bitter. "Seeing me makes it much easier to convince people to part with their money."

"Well, it's working," Calla said. "I just can't believe there are so many people with cancer who can afford to come here."

"You know that most of them don't actually have cancer, right?" Luca asked.

Calla's mouth dropped open. "What? That's—that's crazy! Why are they coming if they aren't sick?"

"To stop themselves from ever getting sick. My father is selling it as a preventative treatment."

"Will that even work?"

"Who knows? I suppose it can't hurt. Most of these people are so rich that they're willing to spend money on anything."

"Do they know where the blood is coming from?"

"They know not to ask."

A grim realization washed over Calla. "And even if they did, they'd never say anything, would they?" She looked at Luca and finally said out loud the words that had been running through her mind for days. "I'm going to die here, aren't I?"

"I won't let that happen."

He spoke fiercely, but coming from someone who was still so frail, the words sounded more like a little boy's boast than an actual promise.

"Luca, you can't protect me. If your father knew you were even talking to me—"

A sound somewhere nearby made them both jump.

Luca held a finger to his lips.

They listened for a full minute, both barely breathing. Nothing. The house was silent again.

"I should go." He stood up.

Calla held out a hand to slow his departure. "Luca, thank you. Seeing you, talking to you, it—"

She choked up, unable to finish.

"I know," Luca said. "I'll be back soon. I won't forget about you."

FORTY-FIVE

TIME DRAGGED AFTER LUCA'S VISIT.

Dr. Kraft increased his demands again, doubling the number of blood draws and biopsies each day. He grew frenzied, perpetually muttering about antigens and adjuvants. He was even starting to look troubled, with dark circles under his eyes and his salt-and-pepper hair sticking up in oily bunches. When Anya, in a rare display of solicitude toward Calla, questioned the escalated pace of testing, he nearly bit her head off.

"Do what I say, or you'll be replaced!"

Anya kept her concerns to herself after that.

The only positive development was a halt in the transfusions. From snippets of overheard conversations, Calla gathered that Dr. Kraft couldn't afford any distractions—even lucrative ones.

Something was definitely up. She was starting to get the sense that, one way or another, she wouldn't be here much longer. She could feel it deep in her bones. Her body couldn't withstand much more depletion. And since it was unlikely she'd manage to escape on her own, she was forced to confront the very real possibility that Dr. Kraft's research ambitions might kill her.

Calla didn't want to die (and she'd do everything she could to avoid it), but the idea was no longer as frightening as it once had been. She had very little energy left for big emotions. Fear, grief, rage, denial . . . They were too exhausting. There was only a weary acceptance that time was running out—and, for all its finality, at least death offered a reprieve from exhaustion and pain.

One thing that stopped her from giving up completely was Luca's promise to visit again. Calla hoped he'd keep it. She had a favor to ask.

She was dozing when he tapped on her door.

"Calla?" he called out softly as he entered the room. "It's me. Luca."

She blinked him into focus.

"Wow. You look like shit," he said.

"And you look amazing." She groaned as she rolled over and tried to sit up. "I think you're stealing my life force."

Luca was the picture of good health. His eyes gleamed, and he had put on more weight.

"Easy there." He rushed to steady her and recoiled slightly when he touched her arm. "Jesus, you're skin and bones."

"Kind of ironic, isn't it?" Calla wheezed. Even the slightest physical effort winded her. "Finding the cure for cancer might be the thing that kills me."

"Don't talk like that."

"Just being honest."

"No. You've given up." Luca crossed his arms and glared down at her. "I've seen that look before. I've seen it in my own eyes."

"Yeah, well."

"I won't let you do that." He strode over to the closet and yanked the door open.

"What are you doing?"

He pulled out a heavy coat. "Bundling you up. We're going outside."

Calla noticed he'd brought a wheelchair with him this time.

"Are you crazy? We'll get caught."

"No, we won't." He helped her slide her arms into the sleeves of the coat. "My father and Dr. Kraft flew to New York today. We've got the house to ourselves."

"What about Anya? And the guards?"

"Anya is asleep on the other side of the house. And my father took the meathead with him."

Calla laughed. "The meathead? You mean Greg?"

Luca looked flustered. "Is that not the right word?"

"That's exactly the right word for Greg," Calla assured him. "But what about Jean-Paul? Is he here?"

"Yes, but he's my friend."

Calla stopped zipping up the coat. "He's not *my* friend."

"He looks out for you more than you know."

"Bullshit."

Luca rolled the wheelchair next to the bed. "Come with me. I'll explain." He kept a close eye as she transferred to the chair, then pulled a wool cap from his own coat pocket and placed it on her head. "There. Nice and warm."

"Thanks, Dad."

"Off we go." Luca spun the wheelchair around and pushed her out of the room.

"Are you sure about this?" Calla asked as they made their way down the hall.

"Quite sure." They entered a large formal living room at the back of the house. "I just need to grab a few things." He pushed her over to a sideboard. The top was covered with a glittering array of bottles. Luca was looking through them when someone said, "Raiding the bar?"

Calla froze. It was Jean-Paul.

Luca was unperturbed. He plucked a bottle from the bar and handed it to Jean-Paul along with two glasses. "Take these outside for us?"

Calla was shocked when Jean-Paul complied. He even held the door as Luca pushed her onto the back patio and parked her next to a low table.

"Be right back," Luca said as he set the brakes on the wheelchair.

Jean-Paul placed the bottle and glasses on the table. "Have fun."

Calla looked at him in surprise. "Uh, thanks?"

He dipped his head, then turned and left.

A minute later, Luca was back, carrying a wool blanket. "Can't have you catching cold," he said as he tucked it around Calla's legs.

"You know, you're a very kind person. It's hard to believe your father is . . ."

"A monster?"

"Well, yeah." She looked down. "Sorry."

"I like to think," he said lightly, "that all I inherited from him was his height. The rest came from my mother."

He picked up the bottle and poured healthy measures into the two glasses. He handed one to Calla and picked up the other. "Cheers." They clinked.

Calla took a sip and made a face. "That burns!"

Luca chuckled. "Good whiskey usually does."

"It tastes like wood and gasoline."

Luca sniffed his own glass appreciatively. "That's one good thing I can say about my father. He buys quality stuff."

"This is considered good?"

"Fairly good. It's a five-hundred-dollar bottle."

"Five hundred dollars?" Calla squeaked. "Better not waste it then."

Luca laughed again. "Don't worry. My father won't notice."

"You've done this before."

"Once or twice."

"How old are you exactly?"

"Nineteen."

Calla took another tiny sip. It burned a little less this time. And she had to admit that she was starting to pick up other, more pleasant flavors—caramel and woodsmoke.

"Can I ask you a question?" she said.

"Of course."

"Where the hell are we?"

"Montana. About an hour and a half north of Helena."

"Montana. Damn."

So far from home. But at least she finally knew where she was. That was something.

They lapsed into silence. The night felt immense. The sky was inky black, twinkling with numberless stars. The frigid air stung her lungs. Calla suddenly felt more awake, more alive than she had in weeks.

"Tell me why you trust Jean-Paul so much."

"Jean-Paul," Luca said slowly, "is not a bad man. He is a man who has found himself in a bad situation."

"He's a criminal, Luca."

"He's protecting his son."

"His son?"

"My father took the boy from him and sent him to school in Germany. He controls everything about his life. If Jean-Paul does not do as my father asks, he knows he will never see him again."

"That's awful."

"Anya, too. My father is the only thing keeping her brother safe in prison. One word to the wrong person, and he gets attacked. Or worse. He's done it before. They both know it, so they do what he tells them to do."

"What about Greg? What does your father have on him?"

"Nothing. Greg's a psychopath. My father doesn't need to persuade him to do his dirty work."

"Why does that not surprise me?"

She took another sip of whiskey. Luca was right. It really wasn't so bad.

"Luca, I need you to do something for me."

"Anything."

"I need you to get a message to someone. If I don't make it—"

"Don't say that!"

"Luca," Calla said gently, "I'm just being realistic. At some point, there won't be anything keeping your father here. You'll be able to go home. I know it might be hard with him watching over you, but I need you to find someone for me. A woman in Houston named Rae Wiley." She reached across the table and placed her hand on his arm. "Rae Wiley. Say her name for me. Please."

"Rae Wiley," Luca repeated, his reluctance obvious. "But—"

"Tell her I thought of her every day while I was here. That she was my real mother. That I'll always love her. And that I want her to tell the world what happened to me." She paused. "Can you do that for me?"

He crossed his arms stubbornly. "You're going to be able to tell her yourself."

"Luca." There was a warning note in her voice. "I need to know you'll do this."

"Okay, fine. I'll find this Rae Wiley for you. *If* you don't . . . make it." His face twisted as he said the words. "But that's not going to happen. I have a plan."

"A plan?"

"One that might get both of us out of here. If we can pull it off."

"We?" Calla shook her head. "There's no way. I can barely walk. I'd just slow you down."

"I know. That's why I'm not taking you with me. I'm going to bring help back to you."

"Absolutely not! You need to leave this place and never come back. You have your whole life ahead of you. I won't let you risk that for me." She glanced around, checking to make sure Jean-Paul was out of earshot. "You should go now," she hissed. "Tonight. While your father is gone."

"No."

"Why not?"

"Lots of reasons. First, my father would blame Jean-Paul for letting me escape, and I won't let that happen. Second, I'm not abandoning you. You say I have a future to protect? Well, the only reason I have that future is because of you. You saved my life. Now it's my turn to save yours. Besides, I'll never be free if I don't find a way to hold my father accountable for what he's done here. I'll always be looking over my shoulder, wondering when he'll find me."

"I don't know, Luca. Waiting could be dangerous. I think you should go now."

"There's something else you need to know."

"What?"

"Do you know why my father and Dr. Kraft went to New York?"

"I don't know. To catch a few shows? Do a little male bonding?"

"To meet with investors." Luca's tone was dead serious. "My father says he's ready to launch the next phase of the project, manufacturing a vaccine. That's going to take a lot of capital. More than even he has. But there's a problem."

"There's no vaccine yet."

"Right on the first try."

"That's why Dr. Kraft was so frantic this week."

"My father has given him two weeks. Dr. Kraft swore he could finish the research, but he said he'll need to carve you up to do it."

Calla wasn't surprised. "He's been doing that to me since day one."

"You don't understand!" Luca cried. "He mentioned causing cognitive deficits. Brain damage. Father said he doesn't care what Dr. Kraft does to you, as long as he keeps your body alive." He took a shaky breath. "You may be ready to die, but what if Dr. Kraft won't let you?"

That gave Calla pause. How long could Dr. Kraft keep her stuck in limbo, not quite dead, but not alive either? Knowing him—indefinitely.

"Fuck me."

"Now, are you willing to listen to my idea?"

Calla gave in. "What exactly do you have in mind?"

Luca picked up the bottle to refill their drinks. A few flakes of snow floated down from the sky. The moon was rising, bright as a star, above the mountains.

"Here's what we're going to do."

FORTY-SIX

THREE NIGHTS LATER, they set Luca's plan in motion.

At 11:30 p.m., as agreed, he knocked three times on Calla's bedroom door.

She was sitting in one of the armchairs, waiting for him. Her heartbeat quickened when he let himself into the room. He was dressed in ski clothes and snow boots. A backpack was slung across his back, and he was holding a pair of snowshoes.

"Were you able to get everything you need?" she asked.

"Yeah." Luca set down the snowshoes and patted the straps of his backpack. "I got into my father's safe the night he was gone. Grabbed some cash and my passport. I've got enough food and water for two days and some other supplies. I'm all set."

"You're sure you want to do this?" Calla was harboring serious doubts about the wisdom of their endeavor.

"Calla, we went over this last night. I'm sure." Luca sounded a little exasperated. He'd snuck into her room the night before for a final planning session.

"Just double-checking."

"More like triple-checking," he muttered.

"This is a big deal," Calla insisted. "If something goes wrong, you can't come back. Ever. Are you prepared for that? To never see your father again?"

"Never again wouldn't be long enough." Luca's expression was determined. "We're doing this. Tonight."

"Okay." Calla glanced at the clock on her bedside table. It was almost time.

Luca peered out at the dark, overcast night. "Looks like it's going to snow," he said.

"Will you be okay if it does?"

"Yes. The snow will cover my tracks. Make me harder to follow."

That was the part of the plan Calla had the most confidence in— Luca's hike out. He'd spent his childhood winters hiking and skiing in the Alps with his maternal grandfather. If the stories he'd told her about their many misadventures were true, the journey he was about to take would be comparatively easy.

"You want to go over everything one last time?" he asked.

"No. I know what I need to do."

"Just remember, keep them talking as long as you can."

"I will."

He placed his hand on her shoulder. "I'll be back with the cavalry before you know it, okay?"

She grabbed his hand and squeezed it. "Be careful," she pleaded. "And don't come back if it's not safe. Please. It's not worth the risk."

"Yes," he said. "You are."

"Luca." She clung to his hand a second longer. "Thank you."

He leaned down and kissed the top of her head. "Time for me to go."

"Don't forget my message."

"Rae Wiley in Houston. I won't forget. But you'll see her again. I promise."

He picked up the snowshoes and walked to the bedroom door. Opening it a crack, he shoved something into the strike plate. "This will stop the lock from engaging. Just pull the door open when it's time," he said. "Give me five minutes. Then it's your turn."

She lifted her hand to wave him farewell.

He gave her a wink in return. "See you soon."

Then he was gone.

She looked at the clock again to mark the time. 11:34 p.m. She pushed herself up from the chair and walked to the closet. If she was going to do this, she needed to look the part. She pulled on her winter coat and the wool cap Luca had given her. She didn't have boots, so the running shoes would have to do.

She checked the time. 11:36 p.m. Three minutes to go.

She unwrapped the chocolate bar Luca had given her the night before and nibbled on a square. A little sugar boost to get her through the next half hour or so.

One minute.

She hid the remains of the candy on a high shelf in the closet, then crossed the room to the door. Listened. No sound in the hallway.

The dots between the numbers on the digital clock blinked away the final seconds of waiting.

11:39 p.m. *It's time.*

Calla held her breath as she pushed down on the handle, trying not to think about all of the things that could go wrong. She pulled the door open and stepped into the hallway. It was quiet, dark. The house was asleep.

She crept down the hall to the high-ceilinged living room. Her eyes flickered over to the liquor cabinet they had pilfered from a few nights earlier. Maybe she should take a shot of courage. No. Luca was waiting for her. It was now or never.

She stepped up to the patio door and pressed her palm against the window. Cold radiated through the glass. Beyond the deck, the snow lay silver and undisturbed. She went over her instructions one last time. *Cross the deck, down the steps, turn left, around the house, find the driveway. Run. Run as fast as you can.* She knew she wouldn't make it far, but she would do her best to give Luca as much time as she could.

Calla flipped the lock and slid the door open. An icy blast of air enveloped her as she stepped onto the deck. A thin crust of snow crunched under her feet as the house alarm began shrieking.

Go.

Her first few steps were stumbles, but she quickly gained her footing and made it across the expanse of snow-covered wood without falling. The railing on the far side of the deck was ice-cold to the touch. Calla leaned heavily on it and scrambled down the wide stairs, gritting her teeth as each step sent a jolt of pain through her battered body. Once she was on the ground, she hazarded a glance over her shoulder. No one pursuing her yet. She lurched to her left and began wading through the snow, trying to leave as much of a trail as possible. Hopefully, somewhere on the other side of the house, Luca was making his way into the woods just north of the property.

The alarm screamed as she made her way through the yard, panting from the exertion of more physical activity than she'd done in weeks. Suddenly, the exterior floodlights blazed to life. Calla picked up her pace as much as she could. Surely it wouldn't be long now before Jean-Paul or Greg caught up to her.

"Come on, guys," she wheezed. "Come and get me."

She rounded the southwest corner of the house. She could see the carport leading to the side entrance two hundred yards away. She loped toward it, pushing past a sharp pain in her flank.

The ground beneath her feet shifted from snow to gravel. She'd made it to the driveway. The effort had exhausted her more than anticipated. But she couldn't stop. Not now. She had to draw the guards as far away from Luca as possible.

She made it to the front of the house. The side driveway merged with a larger one that curved off to her right, fading into the darkness. She'd made it further than expected. Luca had warned her there was a chance this would happen. He had disabled the exterior cameras, which he hoped would slow down Jean-Paul and Greg as they tried to determine if there was a glitch in the security system or an actual breach. It seemed he was right.

Shouts erupted from somewhere behind her.

Their grace period had run out.

Run, Luca, she thought. *Run.*

She slowed as she walked down the main driveway. The pain in her side was increasing, and it was getting harder to breathe. She wasn't going to make it much further. She laughed a little to herself as she realized that for the first time since she'd met them, she was looking forward to seeing Jean-Paul and Greg.

She didn't have to wait long.

"Stop!"

She kept going. *Just a little further*. It was all part of the show.

"Calla, stop!" There was a pleading note in Jean-Paul's voice. "There is nowhere to go. You're only going to hurt yourself!"

She stopped and turned around. He was about a hundred yards away and closing fast. With a sickening jolt, she realized he was alone.

"Where's Greg?" she asked.

Jean-Paul narrowed his eyes. "Why—"

"North side's clear!" Greg's voice boomed out from the front of the house.

Relief coursed through Calla. Luca had made it.

Jean-Paul yelled back, "I have Calla!" He advanced toward her. "Don't move."

She didn't intend to. She was struggling to stay on her feet as it was, totally spent from her mad dash around the house.

Jean-Paul stepped closer. "What were you thinking?"

Her knees buckled. He ran forward and caught her before she fell to the ground.

"I had to try."

He didn't respond as he hoisted her into his arms and began walking back toward the house.

"What are you doing?" Greg demanded as he met up with them, gun drawn.

"Put that away!" Jean-Paul remonstrated. "Look at her. She's not going anywhere."

"At least make her walk. Fucking troublemaker."

"I think that would do her more harm than good," Jean-Paul said coolly. "Remember, we were told to bring her back in one piece."

Before Greg could reply, his cell phone buzzed. He whipped it out of his pocket. "Yes, Sir?"

A long pause.

Then another crisp, "Yes, Sir."

He stowed the phone back in his pocket. "The boss wants to see her. Now."

. . .

They took her to a wing of the house she'd never seen before, up a flight of stairs and down a long hallway to a spacious room with floor-to-ceiling windows that offered a spectacular view of the valley and the distant mountain range.

Oscar Kuhn was seated behind a large desk, fully dressed despite the late hour. He was as imposing as a schoolmaster waiting to scold an errant student.

"Put her there." He pointed to a chair in front of the desk. "Wait outside until I call you."

Jean-Paul did as he was told, then left the room. Greg skulked behind him in silence.

Calla suppressed a quiver of revulsion as Oscar's eyes swept over her. "Did you really think you would be able to walk out of here?"

Calla raised her chin. "It was worth a shot."

"With no supplies? No proper gear?"

"I was trying to get to the main road to flag down a car. I'm not stupid. I knew I wasn't going to get very far."

Oscar folded his hands on the desk in front of him. "So, you just suddenly decided that you'd had enough of my hospitality?"

"You and I have very different definitions of hospitality."

"Then perhaps it's time for me to explain what you can expect during the remainder of your stay here." His expression hardened. "There will be no more midnight wanderings. I need you alive, but that is all. If you misbehave again, I will not hesitate to deprive you of things like hot food and the comforts of your bedroom. You most certainly have lost the privilege of stepping foot outside. Do you understand?"

"I understand that you have some very fucked up ideas about how to treat guests."

"Do not test my patience," he warned. "You have proven very valuable to me. More valuable than I anticipated. But I will not tolerate incivility, even from *una piccola oca d'oro*."

"What the hell is that?"

"My little golden goose."

"Cute. I guess that makes you the evil giant, doesn't it?"

He let out a short bark of a laugh. "I'm afraid this is not a fairytale. There is no Jack coming to your resc—" He stopped suddenly. "Jean-Paul!"

Damn. That was fast. Luca had warned Calla that this might happen. "It won't take him long to figure out what we've done," he had told her. "Just do your best to keep him distracted."

She wondered how long it had been since she'd tripped the alarm. Ten minutes? Fifteen? Was that long enough to give Luca the head start he needed? She had to stall for more time.

"What's wrong?" she asked.

"Quiet!" Oscar held up a warning finger as Jean-Paul entered the room and stood at attention next to Calla's chair.

"Sir?"

"Where is my son?"

"Luca?" Jean-Paul looked confused.

"Yes, Luca, you idiot!"

Jean-Paul flinched slightly. "I—I assume he is in his room, Sir."

"Go and check. Now!" Oscar's voice was acid.

"Right away, Sir." Jean-Paul spun on his heel and marched out of the room.

Alone again, Calla and Oscar sat in silence. Calla racked her brain for something to say, something to slow the inevitable discovery of Luca's disappearance, but the situation was bleak. It was only a matter of time before Jean-Paul returned and confirmed what Oscar already suspected.

"I should have sent him home to his mother," he muttered.

"So, he, uh, got better?" It was a lame attempt at misdirection, but she had to try.

"Don't insult my intelligence!" Oscar snarled. "You know he's better."

She didn't bother denying it.

"This is all making more sense now." He cocked his head to the side and studied her. "You weren't trying to escape, were you? You were a decoy. A distraction." His eyes narrowed. "What did you two have planned? Where did Luca go?"

Calla kept silent.

"Answer me!" He stood and leaned over the desk, menacing her with his incredible height.

"I don't know!" she cried. "I swear it!"

Oscar sat back down. "Oh, I see. He didn't tell you, did he?" He didn't wait for an answer. "Smart boy." The hint of a proud smile crept across his face.

"Listen, why don't you just let me go? You got what you wanted. Your son is healthy. Isn't that enough?"

The smile disappeared. "Don't mistake my admiration for sentimentality. I am grateful for Luca's improved health, but that was not why I brought you here. It was a side benefit, that's all. One he has squandered by his actions tonight."

"A side benefit?"

"I'm a businessman," Oscar said simply. "My business is money. And power." He didn't show even a hint of shame. "With your blood, I will control the most powerful vaccine known to man. Governments, banks, industry leaders will all come crawling to me on their knees, begging for the miracle I have to offer them."

"Excuse me, Sir." Jean-Paul was back.

"Yes?" Oscar seemed irritated by the interruption.

"Luca is gone."

"Then you must find him, Jean-Paul. Find him, or you know what will happen."

A look of barely concealed dread flickered across Jean-Paul's face. "Yes, Sir."

Somewhere in the house, a clock began to strike midnight.

The chase was on.

. . .

A little under thirty minutes.

In the end, that's how much time Calla estimated she had bought for Luca. She prayed it was enough.

Oscar had guessed correctly. Luca hadn't shared his destination with her.

"You can't tell him what you don't know," Luca had insisted.

She'd conceded the point reluctantly. "Can you at least tell me how long you think it will take to get wherever you're going?"

"One day. Maybe two. I have to get far enough away before I make contact with the police. He'll have people looking for me everywhere."

Luca knew his father well. The search had begun immediately, hampered somewhat by damage Luca had done to the two snowmobiles on the property.

"Fucking kid cut the damn fuel lines!" Greg raged as he and Jean-Paul rushed Calla back to her bedroom.

"We'll hike out," Jean-Paul replied. "It'll be easier to pick up his trail on foot, anyway."

"And where are we going to start, genius? The camera system's gone haywire. We've got no footage from the last two hours."

Calla suppressed a smile. Luca had covered all the bases.

"We'll just have to do our best," Jean-Paul said. There was a tinge of growing impatience in his voice.

"I'm gonna wring Luca's neck when we find him," Greg growled. "I hate snow."

"Take one of the trucks and check the highway, then."

"Surprised he didn't take one of those. He knew where the keys were."

"And that they all have trackers," Jean-Paul pointed out.

The two men deposited Calla on her bed.

"Search the room," Jean-Paul ordered. "Quickly."

"Why?" Calla asked. "You know I don't have anything."

"Then you don't have anything to hide," Greg said as he began pulling open drawers and throwing their meager contents onto the floor.

"There's no need to make a mess!"

Greg dumped a stack of t-shirts. "You'll have plenty of time to clean things up."

"Closet is clear," Jean-Paul announced. He caught Calla's eye and gave her an almost imperceptible nod. She felt a rush of gratitude. He'd found the candy and was covering for her. "Finish up," he said briskly. "We need to get a move on."

Within minutes, they were done tossing the room. As a final touch, Greg knocked some books off the shelf near the door while he waited for Jean-Paul to clear the strike plate.

"No more late-night visits from your boyfriend, huh?" he sneered. "Not surprised he ran off, though, with a face like yours."

"That's enough!" Jean-Paul yelled.

"Oh-ho!" Greg laughed. "Sounds like JP here might like to take Luca's place!"

This time, Jean-Paul grabbed the front of Greg's shirt. "One more word, and you're gone," he hissed.

Greg straightened his shirt and glared. "You're the one who needs to watch his back. The old man's pretty pissed you let this happen."

"Take the Suburban. Go into town and check things out. Luca might be closer than we think. He's still pretty weak."

"Whatever." Greg left the room in a huff.

Jean-Paul stepped into the hall. Before he pulled the door closed, he caught Calla's eye. "I hope you two know what you've gotten yourselves into tonight because Oscar Kuhn will stop at nothing to protect his investment in this place. Nothing."

She felt a chill run through her body as the door clicked shut. All she could think about was Luca, her last chance for rescue, out there in the cold darkness. Her fate was in his hands now. There was nothing more she could do for him.

"Be safe, Luca," she whispered. "Be strong."

FORTY-SEVEN

ONE DAY PASSED. THEN TWO.

Calla waited. And worried. Where was Luca? Had he made it to wherever he was going? Or was he out in the wilderness somewhere, wounded, maybe dead?

She should never have let him go.

Oscar flew in five additional guards to aid with the search and beef up security around the house. Calla watched them tromp through the snow outside her window—huge, burly men bristling with weapons. Anyone attempting to enter the property now would have to contend with a small, highly trained army. A rescue attempt was guaranteed to turn bloody.

Meanwhile, Dr. Kraft continued his research at a frenetic pace. Procedures followed one upon the other, stretching from early in the morning until late in the evening. Calla could sense Anya's growing concern for her well-being—demonstrated by a cool cloth pressed to her forehead or an extra dose of pain medication—but nothing fully dulled the agony that now constantly racked her body.

· · ·

On the third day after Luca left, Calla was woken at dawn by Anya.

"Eat this," the nurse said, peeling the foil off a small container of applesauce. "You need strength for today."

Calla struggled to sit up. "Why?" she asked groggily. "What's he going to do to me?"

Anya handed her the applesauce and a spoon. "Eat."

Without another word, she left the room.

Calla choked down a few mouthfuls of the pureed fruit, then sipped on some water that had been left for her. The cook no longer bothered to send hot food—likely the result of Oscar's orders and the fact that Calla hadn't touched anything solid in over a week.

As light from the rising sun crept across the landscape outside her bedroom window, a sense of foreboding filled her. A thick layer of fresh snow blanketed the ground, more menacing than beautiful. Something had gone wrong. Luca had been gone too long. Calla's stomach twisted at the thought of his eager face and bright eyes, frozen forever, destined never to see his beloved mother or sister again. She murmured a prayer, beseeching whatever higher power might be out there listening that if the end had come for Luca, it had been as swift and painless as possible.

She was dozing when Jean-Paul came to collect her for her daily trip to the lab. They did not converse as he lifted her from the bed and set her in the wheelchair.

He was pushing her toward the lab when Oscar's voice echoed down the hallway. Her heart beat a little faster when she realized he was talking about Luca.

"What do you mean you lost his trail?" he raged. "Tear this damn state apart if you have to! My son didn't vanish into thin air. Find him!"

Calla slumped in her seat. Oscar's outburst didn't give her any information one way or another. Uncertainty was the only thing she could truly count on at this point.

They arrived at the lab.

Dr. Kraft was waiting for them. His scrubs were wrinkled and stained, the skin under his eyes smudged with purple shadows. "Put her on the table in the procedure room."

"What are you doing today?" Calla asked nervously. Dr. Kraft seemed particularly edgy.

"Brain biopsy."

That got her attention. "What? Here?"

"Yes, here. Where the hell else would we do it?

"Are you sure this is necessary? You seem . . ."

"What?" he snapped.

"Tired."

"I'm fine."

"But—"

"Get her on the table!" he bellowed. "And you." He pointed at Anya, who was huddled on a stool in a far corner of the room. "Start her IV."

Jean-Paul rolled her into the small room used for surgical procedures. Calla shot him a baleful look as he helped her onto the table.

"I'm sure it will be fine," he said.

"Would you let him operate on you?" Calla asked. "Or your son?"

That hit close to home. "I—I don't know."

Calla turned away. "Never mind. Just go."

She was tired. Tired of hurting. Tired of hoping.

Anya approached with a stainless-steel tray.

"Can you give me something that will knock me out for the rest of the day?"

The older woman pursed her lips and set to work connecting the cannula in Calla's hand to a fresh IV bag. She uncapped a syringe and plunged it into the injection port. "This should help."

"Thank you."

Calla closed her eyes and waited for the drugs to take effect. Within seconds, she felt her body relax. Her mind wandered as she awaited the painless oblivion of general anesthesia. Maybe, this time, she wouldn't wake up.

"Is she ready?" Calla heard Dr. Kraft's voice as though from a great distance.

"Yes, Doctor." Anya's voice was equally muted.

"Good. Start the Propofol."

Boom. A muted explosion. The operating table shuddered beneath her.

"What was that?" There was fear in Anya's voice.

"I don't know." Irritation from Dr. Kraft. Another boom. Another shudder. "Stay here. I'll see what's going on."

Calla fought to open her eyes. "Unnnhhh."

"Shhh," Anya hushed her. "Lay still."

Calla fell into a light sleep, and then *Bang!* The door burst open. A familiar voice called out: "Anya! You have to wake her up!"

Someone shook her shoulder. "Calla. Wake up. It's me. It's Luca."

Calla forced her eyes open. "Lu-ca?"

He smiled down at her. "Yes, it's me. I made it!"

Such a beautiful face. Such bright eyes.

"I'm sorry it took so long." Luca knit his brow. "American bureaucracy. Even in a kidnapping."

"Is this . . . a dream?"

He took her hand and squeezed it. "It's not a dream. I'm right here. It's going to be okay—"

But then something was wrong. Terribly wrong. The smile slipped from Luca's face. He made an odd, grunting sound. He dropped her hand and raised his own to touch the back of his neck. His head turned slightly, and Calla saw a scalpel buried deep in the soft spot near the base of his skull. Behind him, Dr. Kraft's face loomed—a snarl curling his upper lip.

"She's *mine*."

Calla watched in horror as Luca collapsed to the floor.

"NO!"

"Luca!"

Through a flood of tears, Calla saw Oscar barrel across the lab and tackle Dr. Kraft. Anya got caught in the wave of movement and flew across the small space, landing in a limp pile against the back wall. The operating table lurched sickeningly but remained upright. Calla heard a series of grunts and cries. She managed to turn on her side just in time to see Dr. Kraft stomp viciously on Oscar's knee. The man screamed, but the pain seemed to spur him to greater action. He climbed on top of Dr. Kraft, wrapped his hands around his neck, and began to squeeze.

"You. Killed. My. Son." His grip seemed to tighten with every word.

Dr. Kraft's eyes bulged. A strange, garbled sound escaped from his throat. His hands scrabbled uselessly against Oscar's iron fists.

Calla watched in horror as Oscar pressed closer to Dr. Kraft, his grip unrelenting as the doctor's movements grew weaker and weaker. It was several long minutes before, panting with exertion, Oscar finally released him. Dr. Kraft's head flopped to the side, his eyes wide and mouth agape, as though in disbelief that his life had come to such an ignominious end.

With a low moan, Oscar scooted across the floor and gathered Luca into his arms. He pulled the scalpel from the boy's neck, then began rocking his body and muttering to him in a low, unintelligible language. Somewhere in the background, Calla thought she heard faint yells and strange pop-popping sounds, but nothing pressing enough to distract her attention from the tragedy unfolding in front of her.

She finally turned away, too heartbroken to watch any longer.

The movement caught Oscar's attention.

"You." He laid Luca gently on the floor, then struggled to his feet. "This is your fault," he rasped. "He never would have left here if it wasn't for you." He limped over to the operating table and grabbed Calla's arm. With a rough yank, he pulled the IV catheter from the back of her hand. She yelped as blood spurted from the gash left behind. Oscar ignored it and dragged her off the table and into a standing position. He leaned in close, his breath hot and stinking on her cheek.

"We're leaving."

Calla gasped in pain as he dragged her toward the door.

"You're not going anywhere."

Both Calla and Oscar looked up.

"Jean-Paul!" Oscar's relief was apparent. He shoved Calla toward him. "Take her for me. I've hurt my leg."

She stumbled and nearly fell. Jean-Paul reached out a hand to steady her, then placed her behind him.

"Let's go." Oscar's voice was suddenly brisk, businesslike. He took one last look at Luca's body, then limped past them.

Jean-Paul didn't move. "I don't think you heard me."

Oscar turned around, an irritated look on his face. "What did you say?"

"You're not going anywhere." Jean-Paul lifted his right hand. "Ever again."

Two shots rang out. Two neat, red holes appeared in Oscar's shirt. He looked down at them in surprise. "But I—"

His heart stopped beating before he had a chance to finish the thought.

At the same moment, the door to the lab burst open. Three men dressed in camouflage fatigues, tactical vests, and helmets rushed into the room and fanned out. They were all carrying assault rifles. One of them yelled, "Gun!"

Jean-Paul held up his free hand and slowly crouched down. "Don't shoot. I'm putting my weapon on the ground." His voice was loud but calm.

"Hands where I can see them!"

"I'm sliding it across the floor," Jean-Paul continued. He placed his gun on the ground and pushed it toward one of the men. Then he knelt completely and placed both of his hands on his head.

"Jean-Paul?" Calla asked uncertainly.

He turned to look at her. "It's going to be okay now." He gave her a sad smile. "I'm sorry."

The yelling continued. One of the men in fatigues grabbed Jean-Paul and threw him flat on the ground. Calla started shaking uncontrollably. The room started spinning around her.

Another man approached her. Put his hand on her shoulder. "Calla Hammond?" he yelled, trying to make himself heard above the din. "Are you Calla Hammond?"

She attempted to answer, but it was too overwhelming—the noise, the guns, the blood, the dead bodies. Luca. Luca was dead. It was all so wrong. So very wrong.

She sank to the floor. The man reached out to cushion her fall.

"She's going into shock," he called over his shoulder. "Get him in here."

The edges of her vision were turning black. Everything around her zoomed away like she was falling down a dark hole. But then a face leaned in—a face she knew, a face full of concern and relief—and pulled her back from the brink.

"Calla?"

It was Brandon.

FORTY-EIGHT

"IT WASN'T YOU."

"Wasn't me?" Brandon looked confused. He leaned closer to Calla, shielding her from the sight of Jean-Paul being handcuffed and hauled out of the lab.

"Dr. Kraft said it was someone on the team who helped them take me."

"And you thought it was . . ." Brandon's voice trembled. "Oh, Calla. I would never—"

A new man, dressed in the same fatigues as the others, stepped into the room. "House is secure," he announced. He pointed at Brandon. "Medevac in ten."

"Understood." He looked back down at Calla. She shifted her position slightly and winced.

"Let's get you out of this room," he said.

He slid his hands under her and began to pick her up.

"I've got a heartbeat!" someone shouted.

Calla's head jerked toward the operating room. "Luca?"

"Get a medic in here," the voice commanded. "NOW!"

"Is it Luca?"

Brandon flagged down an officer who was rushing past him. "Who's the heartbeat?"

"The boy." The answer was terse, given on the fly as the man ran to find medical assistance, but it filled Calla with hope.

"They have to save him." She gave Brandon a pleading look. "Please."

He stood up with Calla cradled in his arms. His expression was resolute. "If they can, they will."

Slowly and carefully, Brandon carried her out of the lab and down the hall toward the living room. The room was bustling with activity. Brandon set her down on the couch. "Medic!"

A fresh-faced man who didn't look much older than Luca double-timed over to them.

"Yes, Sir?"

"Can you bandage her hand and do a quick assessment?" Brandon glanced at his watch. "Medevac's in seven minutes."

"Right away, Sir."

As the medic got to work, Brandon stood nearby. His eyes never left hers.

"I can't believe you're really here," Calla said.

Brandon placed his hand on her forehead. "You're a hard woman to find. It was smart of you to tell Luca about Rae."

"I hoped that would work." Calla inhaled sharply as the medic pressed a stethoscope to her chest. "Sorry. Everything hurts right now."

The medic listened to her heart for a moment, then gave her a tight smile. "No problem. I'll give you a little something to help with the pain, okay?"

"Sounds good."

The medic stood up and addressed Brandon. "Sir, can I speak to you for a moment?"

"Sure." Brandon touched Calla's head again. "Be right back."

The two men disappeared from view.

Alone for the first time since the tumult began, Calla closed her eyes and tried to soak in the fact that she had been saved, that the long nightmare was finally over. But at what cost?

"Calla?" Brandon's voice was gentle. "I'm back."

"Hey." She sniffled.

He knelt next to her. "God, you've been through so much."

The medic returned with a cotton swab and a syringe. "Ready for a little pain relief?"

Calla nodded gratefully.

"You're going to feel a little prick and a burn."

Someone reached over the back of the couch and handed Brandon a blanket. "Chopper's two minutes out."

Calla felt her body start to relax and some of the sadness beginning to dull.

Brandon leaned close. "Ready to go home?"

She smiled. "Home."

He helped her sit up and draped the blanket around her shoulders.

"Hey, Amit?" a voice called out.

The medic looked up. "Yes?"

"The whiner won't stop bitching about his ass wound. Will you come check it out?"

Amit rolled his eyes. "Sure."

Calla wondered if the medicine was making her punchy. "Did he say ass wound?"

"Yeah. One of the men we took into custody got himself shot in the ass." Amit shook his head. "Idiot."

"Big guy? Stupid looking?"

"That's the one."

"His name is Greg. He deserved it."

Amit gave her a salute. "Good to know."

"Up we go." Brandon gathered her into his arms again. "Our ride is here."

He nestled her snugly against his chest as he carried her across the living room and out onto the deck. She could hear a helicopter thumping in the distance, but for a moment, everything was tranquil. Light from the late morning sun trickled through a thick layer of clouds. Snow fell lightly all around them.

"Brandon?" she murmured sleepily.

"Yes?"

"Thank you."

"For what?"

"For finding me."

He looked down at her, his expression fiercely protective. "I'll never let anyone hurt you again."

The roar of a rotor suddenly filled the air, and the snow whipped into a frenzy. Brandon pulled a corner of the blanket over Calla's face to protect her from the icy maelstrom. The sound increased. He tightened his grip on her, then surged forward. She heard a metal door slide open and a voice shout out. Her body was lifted; transferred to another pair of arms. Someone laid her on a litter and strapped her down.

Brandon climbed into the helicopter and sat down next to her. It was too loud for any further conversation.

She wriggled her hand out from under the blanket and the straps and held it out to him.

He took it. Pressed a kiss to her palm.

Safe for the first time in weeks, she slept.

FORTY-NINE

BRANDON HELD HER HAND the whole way home.

Calla slept for most of the trip, waking periodically when she was moved from the helicopter to a plane and then back to another helicopter.

The sun was beginning to set when they landed on the roof of St. Peregrine's in Houston. Calla gritted her teeth as the paramedics unloaded her from the helicopter, the last round of pain medication beginning to wear off.

"Calla?"

Dr. Pemmaraju's voice cut through the whirlwind. Her white coat danced crazily in the downwash from the still-spinning rotor. She held her hair back with one hand. With the other, she touched Calla's cheek.

"You're safe now." She turned her attention to the paramedics. "Let's get her inside."

Calla was taken down a series of hallways and on and off multiple elevators. The voices of Dr. Pemmaraju and the paramedics passed back and forth above her, discussing vital signs and other medical issues in language that was too cryptic for her tired mind to grasp.

Finally, they reached their destination. Some sort of examination room. White walls, bright lights. Machines beeping and squawking. A flood of people in scrubs appeared out of nowhere, asking her to open her mouth, blink her eyes, and hold out her arm. She was stripped down, dressed in a gown, taken to another room for a scan, brought back to the first room, and given an IV. Somewhere along the way, Brandon got lost in the shuffle. All around Calla, the lights and the voices and the beeping and the squawking swirled together in a dizzying kaleidoscope of color and sound. She closed her eyes to shut everything out. Just before she gave in to the dark comfort of a dreamless sleep, she heard two voices murmuring.

"Do you think she knows?"

"I don't know." A pause. "Let her sleep."

. . .

Someone was humming a lullaby.

Calla lay still, letting the sound wash over her. It was low and sweet. Familiar.

Finally, she opened her eyes.

"Rae?"

"Hello, angel." Tears were streaming down Rae's face.

"I missed you so much."

"I missed you, too, baby."

"Is—is Reuben . . ."

"I'm right here."

Calla turned her head. "Reuben? Thank god." It was her turn to start crying. "I was so worried about you."

"They did a number on me." He pointed to his head. "But I'm better now."

"He coordinated the search for you," Rae said fondly. "This young man's a wizard with the Twitter."

Calla chortled. "The Twitter?"

"Yes. What do you call those pound sign things?"

"Hashtags?" Reuben looked amused.

"Hashtags," Rae said. "He's very clever with those. Hashtag find Calla. Hashtag where is Calla. You name it, he tried it."

"That's me." Reuben took a little half-bow. "The king of hashtags."

Calla looked from one to the other. "Wait, so, me being kidnapped is a thing? On Twitter?"

"Oh, honey," Rae said. "It's not just a thing on Twitter. It's a thing everywhere. The Internet. Television. Newspapers. Magazines. You've had thousands of people praying for you, Calla. Hundreds of thousands. Maybe millions. Every single day. They held a candlelight vigil outside the hospital the first week you were gone. And so many people sent in tips. I don't know how the FBI waded through all of them. Reuben and Brandon helped as much as they could."

"Brandon." Calla thought about the look on his face when he'd found her.

"He started looking for you the second he heard you were gone," Reuben said, his tone serious. "I don't think he's slept more than a few hours a night for the past few weeks."

"I can't believe I thought he did this to me." Calla hesitated. "Do the police have any idea who it was?"

Reuben and Rae exchanged a look across the bed.

"Come on, guys. Just tell me."

When Rae hesitated, Reuben jumped in. "It was Kendra."

"Kendra?"

Rae frowned. "She disappeared the day they took you. The police tracked her down last week, holed up somewhere in Michigan. She swears she had no idea you were the target. She thought they wanted access to the security plans so they could rob the lab. She texted Jimmy to lure him into the hall so she'd have an alibi. When she realized what really happened, she bolted."

"Do you believe her?"

Rae shrugged. "I don't know. I'd like to. Makes her a little less of a monster, if it's true."

"I suppose." Calla fell silent for a few moments, thinking. "God, I can't believe she'd do something like that to me."

"Money does strange things to people."

"That's why she did this? For money?"

"From what we've heard," Reuben said, "she was neck-deep in some pretty serious gambling debts."

"You've got to be kidding me."

Rae laid a protective hand on top of Calla's. "You're home now. That's all that matters."

Reuben placed his hand on top of Rae's. "Amen to that."

. . .

"Knock, knock."

The voice was soft, but it startled Calla.

"Sorry." She blinked a few times. "I guess I fell asleep."

Dr. Pemmaraju smiled down at her. "Don't apologize. You've been to hell and back. Of course you're exhausted."

"I don't know. This feels different than tired." Calla placed her hand on her chest. "I feel . . . heavier. Slower."

Dr. Pemmaraju sank into the chair next to the bed. "Oh, Calla," she said sadly. "How could he do this to you? What was he thinking?"

"He wasn't thinking. Not at the end. All he cared about was his stupid legacy. But he—" She stopped to catch her breath. "He couldn't figure it out. And now he's gone." She closed her eyes as a surge of fatigue swept over her. "Maybe it's better this way."

"Why do you say that?"

"He said the world wouldn't accept a vaccine. That the hospitals and the drug companies would fight it. To protect their turf."

Dr. Pemmaraju narrowed her eyes. "Dr. Kraft said that?"

"Yeah. And it kind of makes sense, doesn't it? Hasn't the hospital been pushing treatments over a vaccine?"

"Only because treatments have been easier to develop and test." Dr. Pemmaraju locked eyes with her. "Calla, Dr. Kraft was wrong. Of course people want a vaccine. But vaccines can take time to bring to market. And they should. When we give them to people, we need to be damn sure they'll help and not hurt. And keep in mind that even after we have one, it won't be a magic bullet."

"Why not?"

"Lots of reasons. Not everyone will take it—there are a ton of vaccine skeptics. Others will never be given the opportunity. There are almost eight billion people on this planet. Inoculating every one of them is a worthy goal, but it's not something that will happen overnight. Or maybe ever."

"Then why do it?"

"Because it's the right thing to do. Vaccines save lives."

"And you really think this one is possible?"

"I know it is."

Calla studied her friend. "You figured it out, didn't you? The vaccine."

A pause. "I did. I just need some time to be sure."

"Good for you." Calla smiled. "I always knew you were smarter than him."

"Don't get too excited," Dr. Pemmaraju warned. "There's a problem."

"What? You need my blood?"

"Yes, but—"

"No buts. Take whatever you need. If you think you can do this, let's finish what we started."

"Calla, it's not that simple."

"What do you mean?"

"There's something I need to tell you."

. . .

Three hours later, Calla asked her nurse to page Dr. Pemmaraju.

"I've made up my mind," she said as soon as the doctor walked into her room. "Call Mary Ann."

Dr. Pemmaraju held up a hand. "Calla, I think you should take the night to think about this."

"I've had plenty of time to think about it over the past few weeks. I don't need any more."

Dr. Pemmaraju pursed her lips. "Are you absolutely sure?"

"I'm sure. I mean, one way or another, this is happening, right? That's what you told me."

"Yes," Dr. Pemmaraju admitted. "It's only a matter of time."

"Well, then, I want it to mean something. For Luca. For Lizzie. For me." She stopped to take a breath. "There's just one thing I need to do before we start."

"Anything."

"I want to see Brandon."

FIFTY

"ANY CHANCE YOU CAN GIVE ME something to pep me up?"

Dr. Pemmaraju thought for a moment. "Actually, yes."

"Great. Do it."

A few minutes later, Dr. Pemmaraju returned to the room and stuck a needle in Calla's arm.

"Ow."

"Ready?" Reuben asked. He parked a wheelchair next to the bed where Calla was sitting.

"I'm never going to escape that thing, am I?"

"Just trying to help you conserve energy."

"Fine." Calla let him help her into her coat. Very carefully, she shifted from her bed to the seat of the chair.

"He's right. You need to take it easy," Dr. Pemmaraju cautioned. "That injection will only last so long."

"Don't worry," Calla said. "I'll behave."

Dr. Pemmaraju put a hand on her shoulder. "Take your time, okay? Mary Ann and her people won't be here until tomorrow morning."

"I seriously doubt I'll be there that long."

Both Reuben and Dr. Pemmaraju exchanged dubious looks.

"Yeah, right," Reuben quipped.

Calla blushed.

"Go on. Get out of here," Dr. Pemmaraju shooed them away. "And Calla?" Her voice caught a little. "Have a nice time."

Reuben grabbed the handles of the wheelchair and steered Calla out of the room. He greeted the police officer standing guard outside her door.

"Walk us down to the service entrance?" he asked. "Private security has a car waiting for us."

The officer nodded. "Sure thing." He walked a little ahead of them to push the call button for the elevator.

Calla tilted her head to look up at Reuben. "Private security?"

"Jimmy."

"Really?"

"He insisted."

They took a service elevator to the first floor. The back corridors of the hospital were quiet. Calla was grateful for the lack of prying eyes. It didn't take long to make their way to a loading ramp that was usually used for deliveries. Jimmy was standing by the passenger door of a silver Chevy Tahoe.

"Hey." His face was a picture of guilt as Calla and Reuben approached him. "I hope it's okay that I'm here."

She stood up and wrapped her arms around him. "It's good to see you."

"I'm so sorry, Calla." He trembled in her embrace. "I should've known something was off that day."

Calla took a step back and looked him in the eye. "It's okay. They were going to get me one way or another. I'm just glad you weren't hurt. We're good. Really."

"You sure?"

"I'm sure."

"Okay." He didn't sound convinced. "Should we get going?"

"Yeah." Reuben looked around nervously. "Let's get in the car before someone sees us." He gave the police officer a wave. "Thanks for the escort."

Jimmy settled Calla in the front passenger seat, then ambled around the car to the driver's side. As soon as everyone was buckled in, he made his way down the narrow driveway to the side road that ran around the back of the building.

Calla sucked in a breath as they turned onto the main drive that passed the hospital's entrance. A low brick wall was covered with hand-lettered signs. Heaped on the ground were mounds of flowers, stuffed animals, and votive candles.

"What the . . . ?"

"That's all for you," Jimmy explained. "People have been coming every day since you were taken. Lucia and the girls, too. Claire insisted on bringing you a unicorn."

Calla's eyes were suddenly wet with tears. "Tell her thank you for me."

"All hell's gonna break loose when the media finds out you're back," Jimmy continued. "This may be the last time you're able to just walk out the door."

"Yeah." Calla tried to force a laugh.

"So," Reuben swooped in to cover the awkward moment, "where are we headed?"

"The Heights. Shouldn't take too long this time of night. Fifteen minutes or so."

Calla's stomach fluttered as they got on the highway. What would Brandon say when he saw her?

They exited the interstate and turned onto a residential street.

Her heart was racing as the car slowed down.

They pulled up to a small bungalow. The exterior looked freshly painted. The yard was neat and trimmed—Brandon's house.

Reuben seemed to sense Calla's anxiety. "You can do this," he said gently. "We'll wait here for you until you're ready to leave. Even if it takes all night."

"Reuben." She gave him an incredulous look. "Don't be ridiculous."

"I'm just saying, it's not outside the realm of possibility." He inclined his head toward her door. "Now go."

"Want me to walk you up?" Jimmy asked.

"No, thanks. I need to do this alone."

Calla opened the car door and stepped onto the sidewalk.

FIFTY-ONE

A WROUGHT IRON GATE surrounded Brandon's front yard. Pieces of chalk littered the walkway, which was adorned with hearts, stars, rainbows, and other scribbles. Calla smiled at the thought of Brandon's military precision butting heads with the artistic whims of a young girl.

She opened the gate, crossed the small yard, and climbed the steps onto Brandon's porch, leaning heavily on the rail as she went. It wasn't just exhaustion slowing her down. An insidious nervousness knifed through her gut. She glanced over her shoulder at the car where Reuben and Jimmy were waiting, undoubtedly watching her.

The passenger window slid open. Reuben stuck his head out. The expression on his face was determined. "I'm not letting you back in this car until you ring that bell!"

"Okay, okay," Calla hissed, gesturing for him to keep his voice down.

She squared her shoulders and crossed the porch. Her hand shook as she knocked on the front door.

No answer. She waited ten seconds. Knocked again. Still no answer.

Calla turned around to face the car and shrugged her shoulders. *No one's home*, she mouthed. She was just about to leave when the door opened behind her.

"Can I help you?" a little voice asked.

Calla whipped around. "Uh, yes—"

The words caught in her throat. Standing before her was a wisp of a girl, completely bald, fragile as a baby bird, with bright, inquisitive eyes. She cocked her head to the side, waiting for Calla to continue.

"I, uh," Calla stammered, "I'm looking for Brandon? Brandon Foster?"

The little girl smiled. "That's my daddy."

"Oh. Are you—are you Sydney?"

The girl's smile broadened. "That's me!"

"Sydney?" Brandon's voice rang out from inside the house. "Where are you?"

"At the front door!" she yelled back. "With . . ." She gave Calla a questioning look. "What's your name?"

"Calla." Her answer was drowned out by the pounding of footsteps.

"Sydney!" Brandon barked. "You know better than to answer the door when we're not expecting—"

He caught sight of Calla.

"She doesn't look like a bad person, Daddy."

Brandon stepped in front of his daughter. "Go to your room, honey."

Sydney poked her head around his waist and peered at Calla. "Why?"

Brandon looked down and cupped her little chin. "Because the grownups need to talk."

"Who is she?"

"A friend," he said, giving Calla a sad look. "I hope."

Sydney narrowed her eyes at him. "Well then, don't screw it up."

"Bedroom," Brandon growled. "Now!"

They both watched the little girl scamper away.

"She's sick, isn't she? Is that what you wanted to tell me on Thanksgiving?"

Brandon ran a hand over his close-cropped hair. "Will you come in? We need to talk."

He held the door open a little wider. Calla hesitated, then stepped over the threshold. She had come too far not to get some answers.

Brandon led the way down a short hall into his living room. A Christmas tree stood in the corner. Calla noted it with a pang. She'd forgotten about the holiday.

Brandon invited Calla to take a seat on a small couch, then sat down on another one across from her. She watched as he fiddled nervously with a loose thread poking out from the upholstery.

When it seemed as though he might never speak, she gently prompted him. "Brandon, what's wrong with Sydney?"

"Cancer. She has cancer."

"What kind?"

"Ewing's sarcoma."

"That's a type of bone cancer, right?"

"Yes. It's more common in teenagers, but Syd's was diagnosed when she was seven. She'd been limping around for two months before we finally got a diagnosis. Cancer was the last thing we were expecting to hear." Brandon drew a calming breath. "By the time the doctors figured out what was going on, it had metastasized. Poor kid's been through the wringer these past three years. Surgery, chemo, radiation. We had about six progression-free months and thought we might be out of the woods, but it came back in November."

"Is that why you said you had to leave the team?"

Brandon stood up and started pacing around the room. "She had a regular PET scan right after the gala. The cancer was starting to spread again. I tried to get her enrolled in a clinical trial up in Boston, but she was rejected. Her disease was too advanced. We came home and got her back on chemo. It seems to be slowing things down a bit. And her doctor is applying for a compassionate use drug. We were hoping I'd be a match for a bone marrow transplant, but it didn't work out."

"What about her mother?"

"Christy?" Brandon let out a low, bitter laugh. "I haven't heard from her in three years. It's why I left the SEALs."

"My god."

He squeezed the bridge of his nose. "We were so young when we had Syd. And Christy was never the most stable person. It was hard on her when I deployed. She just couldn't deal when Syd got sick. Took off a few days after I got back. No one knows where she is. Not even her parents. She could be a match, and we'd never know."

"I'm so sorry."

He sat back down. "When Syd's cancer recurred last month, I realized I need to be home full-time. And that I couldn't lie to you anymore."

"It wasn't a lie," Calla said stiffly. "It was your personal business. You weren't obligated to tell me about it." Though it hurt—deeply—that he hadn't.

"But I did lie," he said. "I lied about why Bruce gave me the job in the first place."

Calla's heart was suddenly in her throat. "I don't understand," she said slowly, her brain refusing to connect the dots he'd laid out for her.

Brandon's eyes were fixed on the floor. "He thought . . . he hoped . . ."

Oh. "That I would save Sydney."

"Yes." His voice was barely audible.

A painful silence stretched between them.

"I didn't like the idea," he said, "but I didn't turn him down, either. I guess part of me also hoped you would help." His voice took on an anguished tone. "There's no thinking straight when your child's life is on the line. You're willing to try anything. Justify anything. I was actually jealous of you at first. I thought you couldn't possibly appreciate the gift you'd been given. But then I saw what you were putting yourself through every day. The tests, the scans, the procedures, the crazy people wanting to touch you. You could've walked away from all of that, and you didn't. And then Dr. Kraft got caught selling your blood, and I realized . . ."

"What?"

"That I was just as bad as him. So many people were taking advantage of you. I couldn't be another one. I cared about you too much." A long pause. "I knew I had to leave. I was going to come clean and tell you everything at Thanksgiving. But Syd got sick that night. I had to drive to the hospital in Austin to be with her. She was in the ICU that whole weekend. That's where I was when you were taken." His eyes filled with tears. "I failed you. I failed you both. I'm so sorry."

Calla's mind was spinning as she watched him, trying to reconcile what he'd told her with everything she'd experienced since she'd met him.

It all made sense. Perfect, horrible sense. He'd wanted to use her, just like everyone else. But could she really blame him? His daughter was dying. The sweet, vibrant little girl who'd answered the door was dying. Just like Lizzie. Calla had barely known Lizzie, and she'd fought for her life. How much fiercer must Brandon's will to save Sydney be? But he'd resisted it. In the end, he'd valued Calla's autonomy above his daughter's life. That had to mean something.

She crossed the space between them and sat next to him. Hesitated, then mustered the courage to place her hand on his knee.

"You haven't failed. I'm here."

"But I—"

She touched a finger to his lips. "Whatever you did, you've more than made up for it. You saved my life." She suddenly felt shaky. "Brandon, I need to tell you something. I'm—" She stopped, reaching for the courage to tell him exactly why she had come to see him. "I came to tell you that I'm . . ."

The words just wouldn't come out.

He took her face in his hands. "I know." He said it so gently.

"You do?"

He nodded.

"How?"

"Amit told me."

"Amit?"

"The FBI medic. Back at the house in Montana." He stroked her cheek with his thumb. "Are you in a lot of pain?"

Calla closed her eyes and let herself enjoy the feel of his touch. "Not much. Dr. Pemmaraju gave me something before I came over here."

"And there's nothing . . ." He didn't finish the question. He didn't have to.

"No."

He dropped his hand from her face. When she opened her eyes to look at him, his expression was unreadable. Her stomach twisted. Had she said the wrong thing?

"I should go," she mumbled. "I just wanted to say thank you. And . . . goodbye."

He helped her to her feet and made sure she was steady. But when she turned toward the front door, he stopped her. "Don't go. I mean, if you need to, if you want to, then of course you should." He paused. "But I don't want you to go."

Calla's heart leaped. "Are you—are you sure?"

He wrapped his arms around her. Pulled her closer. "I am. But the more important question is, are you?"

She felt simultaneously elated and foolish. "I told you before. I don't know what I'm doing," she admitted. "I mean, look at me. No one's ever . . . wanted to, you know, be with me."

"I *am* looking at you, Calla. I've always looked at you. You're beautiful."

She shook her head. "That's not a word people use to describe me."

He dipped his head down. "Then people are idiots," he whispered. His lips hovered over hers, waiting for her permission, showing her the way, but letting her make the decision. She tipped her head up and invited him in.

For the first time. And the last.

FIFTY-TWO

IT WAS JUST AFTER DAWN when Calla woke up in Brandon's bed.

"Jimmy and Reuben!" she gasped. "I forgot about them."

"It's okay." Brandon slipped an arm around her waist, gently inviting her to nestle back into the warm, solid curve of his body. "I texted them hours ago to go home. They're coming back to get you at eight."

She glanced at the clock on the bedside table. They had a little over an hour. She settled back into their cocoon of sheets and blankets but angled her body toward Brandon so she could study the planes of his face while listening to the rhythm of his breathing. She tried to commit each detail to memory.

His lovemaking had been so gentle, so patient, acutely aware of both her lack of experience and her physical fragility. Afterward, they had talked for hours. Mostly about the future, about things that would never come to pass. The idle dreams of two people in love. How bitter was the fact that the remainder of their time together could be counted in minutes?

"I wish we had longer," he murmured, reading her mind.

"Me too."

His arm tightened around her. "Maybe they're wrong. Doctors *are* wrong sometimes."

"Not about this."

"Do you want me to go with you?"

She stayed silent for a long time, thinking. "No," she said finally. "I don't want you to see me like that. I'd rather you think of me like this. Here. Right now."

He twined a finger around a curl of her hair. "Are you sure you can't wait another day?"

Calla's throat constricted with emotion. "I'd give anything for that," she said. "But if I took another day, I'd just want another after that and another after that. Eventually, I'd run out of days. And then, this chance I have to make a difference would be gone, too."

"Oh, Calla." His voice was full of sadness and wonder. "People don't make this kind of sacrifice. Not really. They might talk about it, but they don't do it."

"Yes, they do." She touched his cheek. "You did when you joined the Navy."

"That's different."

"How? You put your life on the line every day when you were deployed."

"Yeah, but at least I had a chance of surviving."

Calla didn't say anything. Whatever Dr. Pemmaraju had given her the night before had worn off long ago. The bone-deep pain and exhaustion were back, leeching her final stores of energy. How could she make him understand that this was less of a choice and more a matter of timing? She didn't think she was being brave. She simply wanted to be in control of her fate rather than a victim of it.

"Are you scared?"

She tried to smile. She wanted to reassure him. To reassure herself. "Not really."

Brandon's cell phone buzzed with an incoming call. He rolled over to grab it.

"Yeah?" He was quiet for a minute, making listening sounds. "Okay," he said. "I'll let her know."

"What is it?"

He looked at her for a long moment before answering. When he did, his voice was heavy. "The FBI held a press conference announcing the rescue operation last night. The hospital's getting mobbed with media. Reuben and Jimmy are outside with the car. They want to take you back now before it gets any worse."

Calla took a deep breath and tried to ignore the sudden pounding in her chest. "I guess that's my cue."

"Not yet. They can wait a few—"

"Daddy?" Sydney's voice wafted across the hall. "I don't feel so good."

"Go to her," Calla said gently. "She needs you."

"Calla." His eyes seem to bore a hole into her soul. "I—"

"No. No goodbyes." She pressed a kiss to his lips. Long, lingering. "Thank you. For Montana. And for last night. For giving me something to dream of."

FIFTY-THREE

"NOT THE BACK."

"What?"

"Take me in the front door," Calla said.

Reuben and Jimmy had picked her up from Brandon's house twenty minutes earlier. They were less than a block away from the hospital.

"Are you crazy?" Reuben asked. "It's mobbed with reporters."

"Don't worry about it," Calla replied. "This is part of the plan."

"You *want* to talk to them?"

"I'd like for them to know I'm here."

"What if they get aggressive?" Reuben worried.

"Just keep moving," Jimmy said, pivoting immediately to accommodate Calla's stated desire. "If anyone gets too close, I'll make them regret it. We'll go in the main doors and head for the blue elevators."

He pulled up to the main entrance of the hospital and shifted the SUV into park. "Wait here while I get the wheelchair," he instructed. A few moments later, he opened the passenger door. "Ready?"

"Ready."

It took only a few seconds for the first reporter to identify them after they cleared the entryway. After that, it was chaos. Shouting, cameras clicking, devices thrust forward, movement. Jimmy cut a path through the bodies. Reuben followed as closely as he could. Calla kept her head up and her expression neutral. She didn't respond to any questions, but she didn't look away from anyone either. She wanted them to see her. To record this moment.

Reuben was completely flustered when they finally made it onto the elevator.

"That was insane!"

"That should be the worst of it," Jimmy said. "The cops have cleared the fifth floor."

"Is that where we're going?" Calla asked.

"Yeah. Dr. P has a room set up for you there."

Calla fell silent as she contemplated the enormity of what she was about to do. She was grateful that no one spoke as the elevator rose slowly upward. She needed to save her words—and her energy—for one final hurdle.

Two familiar faces were waiting for her when the doors slid open.

"Rae." Calla grabbed her friend's outstretched hand. Rae looked shaken. "Did Dr. Pemmaraju talk to you?"

"She did, but honey," there was a hitch in her voice, "you don't have to do this."

"Yes," Calla said gently, "I do."

Dr. Pemmaraju stepped forward. "Would you like to see your room?"

"Okay." Calla kept a tight grip on Rae's hand and looked up at her oldest friend. "Stay with me?"

"Always."

Rae walked next to Calla's wheelchair as Dr. Pemmaraju led them into a large room. Calla couldn't believe her eyes. It had been transformed into a spa-like sanctuary. The walls were draped with swaths of a soft, neutral fabric. Someone had brought in potted plants and vases of cut flowers. A pair of lamps cast the room in a pleasant, yellow glow. The bed was heaped with comfy-looking pillows. Soothing music played in the background.

"Is it okay?" Dr. Pemmaraju asked. She sounded a little nervous. "We wanted to make it nice for you."

"Only you would be so thoughtful," Calla said. "Thank you."

"I can't take all the credit." Dr. Pemmaraju gestured toward the door. "I had some help."

Calla turned in her seat as two more people entered the room.

"Hi, Valerie." She waved at the communications director, then greeted the petite redhead behind her. "Thanks for coming, Mary Ann."

The ABC producer gave her a sober nod. "Thanks for calling me."

"I hope this doesn't weird you out."

"No. I'm honored you trust me to do this. But you're sure you don't want David? He'd probably figure out a way to teleport down here if you change your mind."

"I'm sure. I feel like this requires . . ." Calla searched for the right words. "A woman's touch."

"Well then." Mary Ann smiled. "I'm happy to provide that." She leaned into the hallway and invited a few more people inside. "You remember Toni, right? She did your hair and makeup in New York." The stylist gave Calla a smile. Two young men followed her into the room. "This is Max and Jai. Camera and sound."

"Nice to meet you," Calla said.

"We'll start setting up." Mary Ann turned and began issuing directions to her team in a low voice.

"Calla?" Valerie took a step forward. "I have the documents you asked for ready to sign." She held up a manila folder. "I prepared them myself."

"You did?"

"Believe it or not, once upon a time, I was a lawyer. Who knows? I might go back to it. I've resigned as communications director."

"Why? I thought you liked it here."

"Let's just say that I've become a little disenchanted with all the politics. I've been offered a position at a non-profit that focuses on patients' rights. They thought I had some relevant experience."

Calla eyed Valerie with newfound respect. "Good for you."

"Thank you." Valerie opened the folder and handed Calla a pen and a stapled document. "This is a durable medical power of attorney," she explained. "Per your request, it names Dr. Pemmaraju as your agent. She'll be able to make medical decisions on your behalf after you're . . ." Her voice trailed off, a momentary betrayal of uncertainty.

"Not able to," Calla helped her out. "I understand. I have something I'd like to add, though. Can I do that?"

"Sure. There's a spot on the second page for you to write any special instructions."

"Okay, thanks."

"The second document sets up your trust. Take your time. Read it through and let me know if you have any questions. When you're ready to sign, I'll have my assistant notarize everything. She's already arranged delivery of the other item." Valerie placed her hand on top of Calla's. "And Calla? Thank you. What you're doing is . . . well, thank you."

She walked away before Calla could answer, which was good because she wasn't sure what to say. Everything today felt unprecedented.

Calla read through the documents carefully. When she got to the section in the power of attorney for special instructions, she thought for a moment, then wrote out her last request.

"Juhi?" she called across the room.

Dr. Pemmaraju looked surprised. "Did you just call me Juhi?"

Calla laughed. "Yeah. Why?"

"Just that it's about time." She walked over to where Calla was sitting. "What's up?"

Calla held up the power of attorney. "Are you okay doing this?"

Dr. Pemmaraju scanned the section Calla was pointing to. Her expression softened. "Of course I'm okay doing that."

"As soon as possible?"

"As early as this evening."

"Good." Calla took a deep breath and caught Mary Ann's attention. "Let's get started."

. . .

"Calla, why are you doing this?"

Mary Ann was seated across from Calla in one of the faux leather chairs found in every in-patient room at the hospital. Calla was sitting in another one. A camera was set up perpendicular to them. Pursuant to a special agreement with Mary Ann, Reuben stood nearby, recording everything on his cellphone. If, for any reason, the network stopped airing the footage they were broadcasting, he would post it on every social media platform available.

They had already gone over the particulars of Calla's story. The brain tumor, the study, the instant fame, the kidnappings. Now they'd arrived at the why.

"After everything I've been through," Calla said, "I'm sure of two things. The first is that my body *can* cure cancer. It might even be able to prevent it. The second is that I'm dying. All of the surgeries and blood draws weakened my body past the point where it can heal. My doctors say I'm suffering from multiple organ failure. And that's the problem. If there's going to be any chance of figuring out for sure how my immune system can do what it does, my doctor, Juhi Pemmaraju, needs as much of my blood and tissue as I can give her. And I'm running out of time to do that."

The room was silent.

Calla continued. "That's why I've asked her to put me in a medically induced coma so that she can keep my body on life support for as long as possible while she harvests what she needs to complete her research." She looked directly at Mary Ann. "And it's why I asked for this interview. I hate to say this, but I've kind of lost my faith in the system."

"What system?" Mary Ann asked.

"The system that's supposed to treat and cure and prevent diseases, regardless of the effect on the bottom line." Calla sat up a little straighter in her chair. "I'm well aware that a cure for cancer will change the world in ways I can't begin to imagine. A vaccine could be even more disruptive. A lot of really smart people, doctors, scientists, engineers, and investors might find themselves out of work. But here's the thing. The world is full of problems. And I know those people will find the next big one and apply their considerable intellect and ingenuity to solving it. Would it really be so bad to take cancer off the table? I don't think so. And I'm willing to bet my life on it."

She turned and looked straight into the camera.

"But just in case someone tries to stop or delay Dr. Pemmaraju from sharing her work with the world, I'm counting on you, all of the people watching this, to hold the system accountable. Expect progress. Demand explanations. I can't stop what's going to happen to me. None of us can, in the end. But I can control how it happens. I'm about to go to sleep for the last time in my life. Please, don't let it be in vain."

FIFTY-FOUR

AFTER THE INTERVIEW, Calla allowed the camera crew to stay in the room, filming as she said goodbye to her closest friends. She thought it was important for people to see her final moments. To shock them, perhaps, but also to put a human face on a story that was so much bigger than her.

Dr. Pemmaraju and Rae sat at the foot of the bed while Reuben started her last IV.

"I still say you're the best at those," Calla told him.

Reuben blinked hard. "Thanks," he whispered.

When he was done, Calla sank back into the pile of pillows propping her up. Her final task completed, she felt utterly drained—a kind of exhaustion that she knew not even sleep could undo. Time was gushing by like a river current. She felt herself beginning to separate from it, lift into some different dimension where seconds, minutes, hours, days—they all had less meaning.

She wasn't scared. She had left fear behind in Montana. But there was sadness.

A hospital worker pushing a cart entered the room. A sweet aroma wafted through the air.

"Cookies?" Calla was surprised.

"Chocolate chip," Rae said. "Should be fresh out of the oven. I gave them your recipe."

Dr. Pemmaraju took the cart from the worker, who shot Calla a curious look, then hightailed it out of the room.

Calla accepted a cookie from Dr. Pemmaraju. "Is this allowed? Eating before anesthesia?"

"Not even a little bit," Dr. Pemmaraju said. "But these aren't exactly normal circumstances, so I'm making an exception."

Calla took a bite and sighed. "Thank you. This is perfect. I just wish . . ."

"What, honey?" Rae asked. When Calla didn't answer right away, she added, "Please tell me."

"There were just . . . so many things I wanted to do."

Calla's voice broke, and suddenly they were all crying. Calla, Rae, Reuben, Dr. Pemmaraju, Mary Ann. Even Max and Jai.

Another wave of exhaustion washed over Calla. Her heart lurched oddly in her chest. She set the cookie down. She didn't want to dwell on regrets.

"I'm ready."

Dr. Pemmaraju stood up and walked around the bed to the IV pole.

Calla turned her head to look at her doctor one last time. "You promise I won't feel anything? No pain?"

"No pain. I promise."

Calla closed her eyes for a moment. Took a breath. Opened them. "Okay."

Dr. Pemmaraju uncapped a syringe. Her hands shook slightly. "Thank you, Calla."

Calla held out her hands to Reuben and Rae. They each grabbed one. "I love you both," she said. "So much."

"Love you, too," Reuben sniffled.

Dr. Pemmaraju drove the needle into the port and depressed the plunger.

"Tell Charlie I said goodbye?" Calla asked Rae. She looked at Reuben. "And Michael, too?"

Reuben whimpered, then gave her a nod.

"Of course we will." Rae stroked Calla's cheek with her free hand. "My sweet, brave girl. Did I ever tell you what your name means?"

"No." Calla shook her head slowly. The drugs were already taking effect.

"It means beautiful." A soft sob escaped from Rae's throat. "And it's perfect for you. Because you're beautiful inside and out. I always knew you were special."

The darkness beckoned, full of rest and contentment. But Calla kept her eyes open as long as she could, watching her family, until, at last, it was time for her to go.

FIFTY-FIVE

THEY WERE BREAKING DOWN THE ROOM when Brandon arrived. Maintenance workers were carrying out the flowers and plants, taking the fabric down from the walls, and unplugging the lamps.

Dr. Pemmaraju was standing guard by the bed, watching as Calla slept.

"Is it over?" he asked from the doorway.

"Yes."

"Is she comfortable?"

"She is."

"Can I sit with her?"

"Of course." Dr. Pemmaraju pointed to a chair on the other side of the bed.

Brandon sat down, picked up Calla's hand, and rubbed gently over the soft spot next to her thumb. "I was going to ask her not to do this," he said softly. "I thought there was a chance she could get better."

"I'm afraid not. Life support is the only thing that will keep her body going now."

Silence fell between them.

"Brandon?" Dr. Pemmaraju's voice was gentle. "Calla asked me to do something for you. For your daughter."

He looked up with his eyes full of tears. "My daughter? What do you mean?"

"One of her conditions for doing this was that we give your daughter a blood transfusion. Her name is Sydney, right?"

"Yes." He breathed the word.

"She has cancer?"

"Yes."

Dr. Pemmaraju smiled sadly. "When you're done saying goodbye, why don't you go home and get your little girl? We'll be waiting for her."

"Oh, Calla." Brandon began crying in earnest as Dr. Pemmaraju left the room.

FIFTY-SIX

Calla Hammond, the "Cure for Cancer," Dies at 23

January 29, 2026

C alla Hammond, whose blood could cure cancer, died on Wednesday in Houston. She was 23. Her death was announced by her oncologist, Dr. Juhi Pemmaraju. Despite her short life, she changed the world.

Calla Grace Hammond was born on September 28, 2002, in Cleveland, Texas. Her mother died when she was four years old. Her father remains unknown. She was subsequently raised by foster parents and in group homes. In August 2025, she was diagnosed with a malignant brain tumor. During surgery to remove the growth, doctors discovered that it had disappeared. After ruling out the possibility of error, her recovery was categorized as a case of "spontaneous regression," commonly defined as the disappearance of a malignancy in the absence of treatment.

Ms. Hammond was enrolled in a medical research study focused on identifying immune responses to cancer. Within weeks, scientists verified the ability of her blood and bone marrow to cure cancer in lab animals. The study's progress was marred, however, by in-fighting and corruption. A lab technician leaked an early draft of a paper summarizing the capabilities of Ms. Hammond's immune system to the press.

Dr. Carson Kraft, the lead researcher on the study, was caught selling Ms. Hammond's blood to well-heeled cancer patients to fund his research pursuits. He was fired from his job and stripped of his medical license.

The revelations about the ability of Ms. Hammond's immune system to cure cancer made her an object of intense interest to the national media and the general public. She also became the target of people with more malign intentions. In October of last year, she was abducted by a couple determined to use her blood to cure their son's cancer. Ms. Hammond escaped by jumping out of the couple's vehicle onto a busy city street. Two months later, she was abducted again, this time by the Swiss billionaire Oscar Kuhn. She was held captive in a secluded compound in northern Montana for 16 days. Working with the disgraced Dr. Kraft, Mr. Kuhn collected Ms. Hammond's white blood cells for sale to a select clientele. Meanwhile Dr. Kraft continued his research for both a cure and a vaccine for cancer, subjecting Ms. Hammond to invasive procedures daily.

Responding to a tip from a local informant, an FBI hostage rescue team recovered Ms. Hammond on December 15. Upon her return to St. Peregrine's Cancer Center in Houston, doctors discovered that injuries she had sustained during her confinement had caused multiple organ system failure. Ms. Hammond was given days to live. Aware of the possibility that the key to understanding her immune system's ability to cure cancer might die with her, Ms. Hammond elected to be put into a medically induced coma and placed on life support so that doctors could harvest as much of her living tissue and blood as possible.

To ensure continuing public interest in her story, Ms. Hammond televised the procedure that put her into a coma. When it aired on December 17, it became the most-watched event in television history, eclipsing the 2012 Summer Olympic Games in London. Over 5 billion people worldwide tuned in to watch Ms. Hammond's final conscious moments.

Exceeding even the most optimistic expectations, doctors kept her body alive for an additional six weeks. The time enabled researchers to finalize work on a drug that cures cancer, which was granted emergency use authorization by the Food and Drug Administration on January 25. Additionally, a vaccine is now being tested in a small number of human patients as part of a Phase I trial.

Dr. Pemmaraju, who was recently promoted to lead research physician of the study, praised Ms. Hammond's decision to donate her living body to science: "Calla sacrificed her final days so that humanity could be freed from the tyranny of a disease that claims millions of lives every year. Our research has the potential to unlock the mysteries of the human immune system, which will allow us to treat and cure not only cancer but countless other diseases. Her contribution to scientific understanding is unparalleled in this millennium."

Ms. Hammond was also a savvy businesswoman who negotiated a fractional ownership share in any drugs or vaccines generated by research using her blood and tissue. Had she lived to witness the authorization of the first drug derived from her blood cells, she would have been one of the wealthiest individuals in the world. One of her final acts was to set up a foundation in her name, to be funded by her estate, dedicated to the treatment of autoimmune diseases.

Across the world, cities and nations are planning memorials in Ms. Hammond's honor. Streets, schools, and parks are being renamed after her. She will be awarded the Presidential Medal of Freedom in a ceremony that will take place in mid-February, and a campaign was recently launched to co-award her the Nobel Prize in Physiology or Medicine with Dr. Pemmaraju, despite the long-standing prohibition against posthumous awards of the prize.

FIFTY-SEVEN

THE TELEVISION WAS ON with the sound low. The screen showed a hearse driving slowly down an access road next to a six-lane highway, followed by a long train of cars. People lined the grassy strip on the other side of the road, some holding up signs, many with their heads bowed as the hearse passed them, bearing its occupant to her final resting place.

As the procession slowed and entered the cemetery, a commentator described the scene, detailing the scientists and politicians and celebrities in attendance, reviewing the order of events for the graveside service. But the young man lying in the bed across from the television had fallen into a light sleep and wasn't listening.

A woman entered the room. She had olive skin and thick, black hair. With a sigh, she sat down on the edge of the bed and ran her fingers gently along her son's forehead, hesitant to wake him. He was still so weak.

His eyes fluttered open.

"Mamma?" he whispered. There was a note of surprise in his voice, one that had been there ever since they'd been reunited at the hospital in Montana, as though he couldn't quite believe she was sitting next to him.

"I'm here, Luca." She touched his forehead again. "I have something for you."

She pulled an envelope out of her pocket. It had been delivered weeks earlier while Luca had been clinging to life in the intensive care unit. She'd kept it safe until she felt he was ready—physically and emotionally—to read its contents.

By some miracle, Dr. Kraft's scalpel had only nicked Luca's spinal cord. He would survive, and his mother prayed every day that he would enjoy a full or nearly full recovery, but her boy had a long road ahead. A few days earlier, he'd finally been cleared to travel. Now they were at her parents' home in Italy, where Luca could continue to heal in peace, surrounded by family, safe for the first time in years.

"It's a letter from Calla," she told him. "Would you like for me to read it to you?"

He nodded.

She slid a finger under the back flap of the envelope to break the seal and pulled out a single sheet of paper.

Dear Luca,

By now, you know that we won't get a chance to see each other again. There just isn't time. But I couldn't leave without saying goodbye.

You saved my life when you hiked into those snowy woods that night. I know that might seem like cold comfort given what I've decided to do with what's left of it, but you made it possible for me to go out on my own terms. To tell my story. To maybe make a difference in the world. I can never thank you enough for that.

Your doctors tell me they are hopeful about your recovery. I know you will recover. You are smart and strong and so incredibly brave. It makes me happy to think that a part of me will live on in you.

Give my best to your mother and sister. They're on their way to see you. Everything is going to be okay now. You're all finally safe. And free.

Think of me when you get home to Europe. I always did want to visit there. And go easy on the whiskey, okay?

With love,
Calla

FIFTY-EIGHT

THE CAMERAS AND CROWDS were gone. The pomp and circumstance of the funeral service had been replaced by the rustling of leaves and the warbling of a lonely bird. The cemetery was quiet and calm. The only evidence that something of note had happened earlier in the day was the mound of flowers heaped on the freshly dug grave.

In years to come, it would become a destination for survivors, for those who never had to survive, for the merely curious. But today, it was just another gravesite.

A man and a girl wandered through the park, reading the headstones. The man stood ramrod straight. He held a bouquet of yellow calla lilies in one hand. In the other, he gripped the little girl's hand. She bounced as they walked—full of life and energy. Her head was covered with thick, dark fuzz.

They came to a stop in front of the newest grave marker.

The man handed the flowers to the girl.

She knelt to the ground and laid them down carefully. She gazed at the words etched into the marble stone in front of her.

CALLA HAMMOND
September 28, 2002–January 26, 2026
She gave her life so others could live

"She was a hero," the little girl said.

"The bravest person I've ever known," the man agreed. He watched as the girl rearranged a few errant flower buds. "Are you looking forward to going back to school next week?"

The girl threw a look over her shoulder. "Daddy, is the sky blue?"

He threw his head back and laughed. "Sydney, please don't ever change."

"Oh, I won't." She stood up. "Should we go?"

"In a minute."

Brandon stepped around the flowers and placed his hand on Calla's stone. He closed his eyes and bowed his head. "Thank you, my love."

Sydney slipped her hand back into her father's.

"Is it okay to feel sad and happy at the same time?" she asked.

Brandon dashed away a tear. "Honey, I think that's exactly what she would want."

"Can we come back to see her?"

"Anytime you want."

They turned to leave, weaving their way back through the cemetery.

The sun was setting.

The future awaited them.

Just as Calla had hoped.

END

ACKNOWLEDGMENTS

TWELVE YEARS AGO, my husband brought home a catalog of continuing education classes offered at a nearby university. He'd marked a day-long seminar for aspiring novelists. "You should sign up for this," he said. Apparently, I had been talking about writing a book. A lot. I decided it was time to stop talking and start writing. I attended the seminar and the experience set me on a path that led—oh so slowly—to the publication of this book. Along the way, I leaned on an extraordinary community of people for their love, guidance, and support. It is an honor to take this opportunity to thank them:

My incredible team at Greenleaf Book Group: Brian Welch, Morgan Robinson, Cameron Stein, Laurie MacQueen, Valerie Howard, Amanda Marquette, Corrin Foster, and Daniel Sandoval.

Deborah Brosseau, publicist and social media coach/therapist extraordinaire.

My fellow writers and editors, for sharing their knowledge about writing (and publishing): Sulay Hernandez, Kay Kendall, Chip Rice, Aditi Pemmaraju, Merritt Pulliam, Vicky Wight, Shannon Wiley, and Jeanette the Writer.

Emily Wolf Schaffer, a writer and dear friend who has been my companion on this journey from the very beginning. I am eternally grateful for her wit, wisdom, and unwavering conviction that we can and should get our stories out into the world.

Alyssa Foley and Jasara Peskie, for their unconditional love, late-night texts, and willingness to eat absurd amounts of Cotswold cheese with me when the occasion calls for it.

My dream team of friends, who have read my work, provided encouragement, helped with kids, kept me sane, and drank loads of coffee, wine, and other beverages with me over the years: Laura Bartolotta, Melissa Becker, Constantina Boudouvas, Sara Edwards, Laura Florence, Karien Goodwin, Denise and Salim Khoury, Sharalyn Lehman and Adam Summers, Elaine Loiselle, Toni Lundin, Simone Maher, Erin and Toby McMillin, Sunita Moonat, Whitney Neighbors, Lisa Palmer, Aditi and Naveen Pemmaraju, Shannon Petrick, Kaitlyn Scheurich, Bettina Siegel, Victoria Skinner, Anna Strickland, and Alicia Valentini.

My extended family, for their love and support.

Marly Driskell, our honorary third parent, for helping to raise my children with wisdom, kindness, and creativity. Your presence in our family afforded me the time and space I needed to balance being a mom and a writer.

Wenda Swenson, my mother and the strongest person I know, who raised me to believe I could do anything I set my mind to. I love you bunches and bunches.

Ethan and Lila, my most important creations and the jewels of my heart. Since I embarked on my writing journey, you've grown from toddlers to teenagers. I've cherished every moment and am so incredibly proud of you both.

And finally, Matthew, my husband, my champion, and the love of my life. Thank you for encouraging me to write and for never letting me give up on my dream of publishing an actual book one day. We did it!

ABOUT THE AUTHOR

CATHERINE DEVORE JOHNSON was born in Chicago and raised in Texas, with a short sojourn on the East Coast for college. A former attorney, she now works as a writer and editor for a children's hospital. When she isn't writing or haunting one of her favorite Houston coffee houses (or, even better, writing *in* one of her favorite Houston coffee houses), Catherine loves spending time with her husband and two children (one of whom is about to start driving, so please send your best wishes and any advice for sanity maintenance). You can connect with her on Twitter at @cdjohnsonauthor, Instagram at @catherinedjohnsonauthor, or her website at www.cdjohnsonauthor.com.